I0618886

THE
CASE OF THE
VANISHING
CONMAN

An absolutely gripping, escapist murder mystery

MITHRAN
SOMASUNDRUM

Joffe Books, London
www.joffebooks.com

First published in Great Britain in 2022

© Mithran Somasundrum

Cover art by Nick Castle

ISBN: 978-1-80405-607-3

PROLOGUE

Now

There's always a moment when you can cut and run. The trick is to not think too much.

Vijay took Khun Pleum's phone call sitting alone in his office, and it occurred to him he could quit being a private detective. Just pile everything he owned into his pickup and drive south until he hit the Malaysian border. But hard on the heels of that impulse was the worry of what would happen to his assistant, Doi. Because if he slipped out of Khun Pleum's grasp, there was always a chance the man would void his anger on her. And Vijay knew he couldn't let that happen.

Besides, he wanted to know why he was being summoned. At that point there were so many different things that could have gone wrong with Khun Pleum's case and Vijay's life. He had an odd, morbid desire to know which thread had caused the whole tapestry to unravel.

And so, late at night, with no weapon in hand, and very many forebodings, Vijay set out for the nearly empty mansion Khun Pleum called home, and his second meeting with his client.

CHAPTER 1

Sixteen days earlier

It all began in a hotel cigar bar in Bangkok's business quarter; studded leather armchairs, thick brass ashtrays and dim, discreet lighting. Vijay had worn his good jeans and a linen shirt he'd ironed that morning. Meanwhile, Khun Pleum in person matched the stolid respectability of his newspaper photos: an unsmiling, well-preserved sixty-something with greying sideburns. He'd arrived in a coral green silk shirt with heavy gold cufflinks and looked every inch the classic old-money patriarch — someone at the lofty heights of a government ministry, or benignly successful in the world of business.

He looked like he'd never killed anyone.

In one hand was a thick cigar. At the start of their meeting, he'd slid it out of a metal cylinder bearing the words *Cohiba Lancero*, and held it up. A young man in a button-down shirt had scurried across, snipped the tip, lit it for him and scuttled away again. Having established himself at the centre of his universe, Khun Pleum blew smoke in Vijay's direction.

"I suppose you know why my people called you," he said.

"Sure. That writer who got shot."

"Would you believe some individuals think I ordered it?"

Some individuals, thought Vijay. The whole country was convinced he'd ordered it. Every outraged letter writer to a national newspaper, every frowning-into-camera current affairs talking head, every sarcastic meme sharer on Twitter. They all thought it was him. And all assumed he was too powerful to ever be charged.

"As if my people would aim for the leg. Do I look like the kind of man who fires warning shots?" He raised an eyebrow.

"No, Khun Pleum," Vijay said. "But you must see why they think it's you. This book he wrote—"

"Have you read it?"

Vijay shook his head.

Khun Pleum frowned. "There you are, you see. I can't seem to find anyone who's read it."

Or is willing to admit the fact, Vijay thought, *and risk one of his nine mm "literary criticisms".*

"There's the subject matter, right?" he said. "I mean, they say it's about a guy who takes control of the organised crime in Samut Sakhon, becomes rich from it, and finally winds up running legitimate businesses, here in Bangkok. And, well . . . everyone thinks it's based on you."

"And if it is?" Khun Pleum asked. "Do you think I'm going to pay attention to a novel written by some nonentity? The deputy prime minister came to my son's wedding. The oldest son," he added, in an odd moment of pedantry.

"So basically, you didn't shoot the author? What we're saying is, someone got hold of this novel and thought it would be a great opportunity to make it appear as though you care about a . . . a nonentity?"

"I've often found people can be too clever for their own good."

The man took a long pull of the cigar and fumed the smoke out through his nostrils. It occurred to Vijay that if a dragon took human form, and smoked Cuban cigars, it would look like this.

"A friend of mine told me you did good work for one of his staff. A man called Adisorn. Some business about his wife," Khun Pleum said.

That, Vijay supposed, was how Khun Pleum had got his number. Khun Adisorn was a civil servant high up in the Department of Transport. Vijay wondered who Khun Pleum's friend was. The minister?

"He says you did it for some ridiculously small amount."

"I charge 4,000 baht a day," Vijay said, immediately doubling his rate.

The man waved his cigar at that detail. "No one would believe I'd hire someone as cheap as you. And that's important, of course. You will tell no one you are in my employ."

"So, you want to know who shot this guy? And why, I suppose? And you want me to make sure it doesn't happen again in any way that connects to you?"

Khun Pleum's face was expressionless. "I want the first one. You don't have to bother with the other two." Still looking at Vijay, he put his hand out and made a beckoning gesture. Cigar Flunky came over again and this time handed Vijay a paperback with the words *Jao Por* on the blood-red cover. It meant "godfather", but not the type that stands by the font at christenings. Under the title was the author's name, Montri Tongta. "This is the book. My people bought a copy on Amazon. I haven't read it, of course."

Vijay wondered if that was true. After all, he cared enough to hire a private detective. Who knew what vanities the man was prey to?

"Had you heard of this guy — before the shooting?"

Khun Pleum shook his head. "I told you, he's a nobody."

"Okay, well I'll be happy to look into this. And just so you know, I'm also going to charge for minor expenses, which I'll itemise for you, and provide receipts where possible. I'll query major expenses first. And I'm going to want the first week's money in advance. I'll give you my bank account details."

Khun Pleum pointed to Cigar Flunky, who'd gone back to his seat and was crouching forwards like a sprinter at the starting blocks.

"Him," said Khun Pleum. "You'll give them to him."

* * *

"So that's the story," Vijay said to Doi. She'd been his assistant for the last six years, and was probably in her late twenties by now. It was impossible for Vijay to be sure, as she never let him catch a glimpse of her ID card. Even when he stopped at the 7-Eleven for a cake and a candle every thirteenth of March, she refused to tell him which birthday they were celebrating. She did, occasionally, use the honorific *pii* when speaking to him, though. So he knew she was younger than his thirty-five, at any rate.

Vijay was back in their "agency", which consisted of a single room with two desks set back against the walls at right angles to each other, with the door at the join. Opposite Vijay was a teal-coloured refrigerator, a dark green, slightly dented, filing cabinet he'd bought in a fire sale, and in the corner of the room, diagonally opposite the door, a standing fan.

Whenever Vijay was asked about the location of his agency, he would describe it as convenient, even though he couldn't actually tell you what it was convenient *for*. Nonetheless, it sat on the boundary between the Chinese and Indian sections of Bangkok, and had all the surface energy you found at an interface. If he went west from the building, there were shops crammed with towering bolts of cloth and saris in the windows, and if the wind blew the right way, there'd sometimes be a light waft of incense from the Brahmin temple. In the jostling crowd, Vijay would be surrounded by people who looked just like him: the *khaek*. If he went east, there'd be the soft gleam of the gold shops, marble-floored jewellery stores and bannered Chinese signs running down the sides of the buildings.

Vijay's own blue-on-white sign, jutting sideways from below the third-floor window, read: *Translations — Detective.* Originally it was just *Translations.* That had been the plan after he quit the English Success language school. He'd spent just over five years tutoring the offspring of wealthy parents in preparation for their university entrance exams. The eye-watering tuition package came with the tutor's email address, which, Vijay discovered, was provided so that the tutors could do their students' coursework. It was a deal that could continue right the way through university if their parents were willing to stump up for it.

During the whole five years he had spent writing essays about the ethical and patriotic duties of Thai citizens, Vijay had sensed another kind of life eluding him. He knew he was cut out for the world of business, even if he couldn't think what business it ought to be. He knew, though, that he was meant to employ other people rather than *be* employed. He was meant to seize opportunities and be daring. He wanted to be defined by the sentence: I saw my chance and made a go of things.

All the while Vijay was teaching English, he was learning Thai, in the belief he would tutor better if he could think in his student's language. His ear gradually — though imperfectly — became tuned to Thai's five different tones. Eventually, as Vijay's vocabulary increased, it became possible to read a script that had no punctuation and no spaces between the words. The most difficult part was writing, and knowing how to pick the right consonant and tone mark from a seventy-two-letter alphabet. Even here, after a large amount of repetition, Vijay found he could express himself on the page, to a certain degree of confidence. At that point it seemed obvious that "freelance translator" was the business opportunity he'd carved out for himself. So he had rented the office and employed Doi. However, as he wrote home to his father, it had taken him time to "land and expand".

One evening, Vijay had found himself in a small, dark cubbyhole of a karaoke place off the Rama II Road, listening to his friend Petch reinterpret the Eagles ("You ca-an *high* your lyin' eye"). Coming back from the toilet, he had stumbled over what turned out to be the feet of a man called Edwin and they had got talking. He had one of those Welsh accents that always sounds morose, and he certainly had something to be morose about. Having been laid off from his job as a forklift truck operator, he'd decided to spend his severance pay on the holiday of his dreams in Southeast Asia — Edwin, who'd only been out of Gwent once and thought London was "bigger than it needed to be". Two days in, he'd got talking to a friendly tuk-tuk driver who'd let him in on a once-in-a-lifetime opportunity to go with his once-in-a-lifetime holiday. It had all the standard elements: high-quality rubies; a man desperately selling low for cash in hand; a money lender's goons already on the way. It was the kind of thing that would get deleted as spam if it turned up in your inbox, but Edwin had bought it in the flesh. He had cashed in his traveller's cheques, even the ones he was keeping for Malaysia. And of course, three days later, when he had tried to start making a return on his investment, it had turned out they weren't rubies at all. The receipt, written in Thai, only said "red stones" and the cops weren't interested.

Vijay had explained he had a friend called Mana, who was in the Thai police. After a chat, Mana had agreed to have a couple of his officers visit the scammers and tell them that bad things would start happening to them, and that calling the police wouldn't help.

The scammers had paid up. When Vijay returned Edwin's cash, the man had extracted ten per cent and pushed it across the table. Vijay had tried laughing him out of it, but Edwin had insisted.

He'd expected that to be the end of the matter, and sure enough he had never seen the man again. But almost three weeks later, a tubby guy in a retro Arsenal top had stomped up the three flights of stairs to his office. "You the bloke who gets money back from jewellery scammers?" he'd asked. "Helped out a Welshie with some rubies?"

"Is this Edwin we're talking about?"

"Spatterface, I call him. Anyway, there's this mate of mine. Well, I say 'mate', more of a pain in the arse, to be honest. Anyway, he goes and chats up this fit Thai bird who's kite-flying in Sanam Luang and she tells him her uncle is in the gem trade. Guess what happens next?"

"Wild stab in the dark — same thing that happened to Edwin?"

"He says you charge ten per cent, is that right?"

Why Edwin had told him this, Vijay couldn't imagine. Perhaps it made for a cleverer, more resourceful story. Or perhaps Edwin really remembered it that way. Vijay had been about to put him right when, behind him, Doi had begun violently nodding her head while mouthing the words, "Say yes." Their only work at the time had been translating the menu of a seafood restaurant. It wasn't even a long menu. And so Vijay had swallowed and said, "Yup, that's the going rate."

Mana didn't have any objection to sending the boys round again and Andy the Arsenal Bloke became client number two. After that, Doi and Vijay had taken stock. What with so many gem shops — and hence gem-seeking tourists — in the vicinity, they realised they were at the centre of a niche market. It wasn't a job to make a living from, but as a temporary measure, just until the translation business achieved lift-off, it couldn't hurt. So Vijay had taken down the sign, whitened it out and repainted it as *Translations — Detective*, which seemed general enough to attract the right clients and still provide a certain amount of plausible deniability from angry out-of-pocket scammers.

Even with the sign up, Vijay didn't expect to get any clients other than those affected by the fake gem trade. But one afternoon in the rainy season, a middle-aged Thai woman in a high-collared silk blouse came in, trailing a dripping umbrella across their floor. She had fixed Vijay with a steely look and said, "My husband is having an affair and I want the name."

Over the woman's shoulder, Doi had mouthed her usual silent career advice, and Vijay had thought, *How difficult can it be?*

It wasn't, in the end, although the job had required a huge amount of patience, and by the time it was over, Vijay had developed the kind of jumpy, obsessive relationship to Khun Parichard's husband and his lover that he imagined big game hunters had for their prey. Ideally, he'd have had them both stuffed and mounted over a fireplace, but he settled for a business card and photos of the pair exiting a love hotel.

So that was the beginning of Vijay's second line of work. Although, even after five years, there was still no doubt in his mind that the latter part of his job title was temporary.

He now said to Doi, "Basically, the country's got it wrong. Not only did he not shoot this guy, it's bugging him that everyone thinks he cares enough to have wanted to."

"So, one of his friends?"

"I suggested that before I left, but he didn't seem to think so. 'My friends aren't fools,' he said. How much of that have you got left?"

Doi was translating the text for a website selling Thai silk. "Just two more pages. Two and a bit."

"You might as well leave, before it starts bucketing." It was the rainy season and a vast black cloud was looming over Chinatown like a spaceship of evil intent. Even though it was barely half past four, they had the lights on.

After she left, Vijay phoned Mana and told him the situation.

"Khun Pleum? Khun *Pleum* hired you?"

"Right. So what I wanted to know is—"

"What would he hire you for?"

"Obviously because I meet his needs vis à vis my core competency."

"I know what it is! He doesn't want anyone to think he cares enough to have this investigated. Why else would he get someone as cheap as you?"

"Right, plus we're a culture fit. Look, anyway, I noticed yesterday the police chief at Pak Kret came out and said he'd put his best officers on this case. Do you know if that's actually true, or just a line for the press? And if it is true, can you find out what they've got so far? Just don't say it's Khun Pleum who wants to know."

"Yeah, I can ask." He paused. "Vijay, are you sure you want to take this job?"

"I don't see any reason not to."

"Well for one thing, whoever shot this writer made Khun Pleum look bad, probably by intention. Not that I've got any sympathy for people shooting other people, but in this case, if you hand their name over to Pleum, you're putting them in his cross hairs."

"Right, but I've tabled an exit plan. If I find this guy, sure, I'll tell Khun Pleum. But I'll tell the police beforehand and make sure they get to him first. That's believable with Pak Kret's best officers on the case. And the police will want to take the credit anyway."

There was an even longer pause. "Do you think any part of that sounds like a good idea?" Mana said quietly.

Vijay didn't. He'd certainly had better ones. However, there was a large, impending reason for wanting to work for Khun Pleum. He just didn't feel like telling Mana what it was. "Trust me, it's a game changer."

After Mana rang off, Vijay thumbed the Wi-Fi connection on his phone and found the travel agent downstairs was still using the date his wife had left him as his password. Vijay would know the man had finally moved on when he became locked out.

He went on Facebook. Although he didn't have a page of his own, Vijay had set one up for the translations side of the business. Every so often, he posted pictures of misspellings in English, like the menu listing "pizza with herpes" and "circumcision fish". In the year since Vijay had created it, he'd made thirty-seven friends, which he considered a promising start in the world of e-marketing. It now occurred to him that if he couldn't approach *Jao Por*'s author as an investigator, then he could do it as a translator.

Vijay searched for the writer, Montri Tongta, and sure enough, he had a page. The book cover was his profile picture. Vijay fired off a message introducing his professional self and assuring Montri his novel was ideal for the foreign market, just the kind of thing they'd want to stock in the bookshop at Suvarnabhumi Airport. Quoting a seriously reduced version of his translation rates, Vijay typed in his mobile number and urged Montri to get in touch.

He then did a Google search for the book's publisher, S & K Books Ltd. Vijay had stopped off at four different Thai language bookshops after meeting Khun Pleum at the cigar bar. None of them had stocked *Jao Por*, nor anything else by the same press. At each place he had asked the staff about ordering a novel and whether they had dealt with S & K Books before? They never had.

However, it now turned out the company did have a website, and it was a surprisingly good one. Only in Thai, but slickly laid out. To enter, you clicked on a picture of a bookcase and it slid back like the secret panel in a country house library. Inside were enthusiastic descriptions of their authors, their forthcoming titles, their mission statement and a profile of their CEO, one Somsak Kriengsakul.

Khun Somsak was devoted to the written word, apparently. His greatest pleasure in life was to discover previously overlooked Thai voices and bring them to the country's notice. He supported the SEA Write Award and was a passionate advocate of adult education. "Everyone's life is a work in progress."

The accompanying photo showed a man with a beaming oval of a face. He looked to be in his mid-fifties and was sitting at a desk strewn with papers, fountain pen in hand, lit by the soft yellow glow of a brass table lamp. The impression was of someone busy but genial, interrupted from his work but showing kindness to the photographer. Behind him, slightly out of focus, was a packed bookshelf.

The *Contact Us* page gave a phone number and address, and said they invited prospective authors to discuss their projects at an early stage.

Khun Somsak answered Vijay's call on the third ring.

"I was thinking about writing a sort of fictionalised version of one of my more interesting private detective cases," Vijay explained after introducing himself. "I thought people might be interested in—"

"Yes, yes, yes. Very interested," the man interrupted. "People always want to read about this kind of thing."

"Basically, I once had this case, the daughter of a very rich man—"

"Yes, yes. The daughter of a rich man is always good."

"Her father used to collect Indian bronzes—"

"Excellent. You should make an appointment. Come and see me."

"One day she found someone had replaced them with fakes—"

"Of course they had. People like this kind of story. You come and see me and we can talk about marketing. We can discuss the packages available."

"And what's a good time to come and see you, Khun Somsak?"

"Why don't you come tomorrow? Take a look at our website. There's a map, directions."

They agreed on ten a.m. and Vijay rang off. He then leaned back in his chair and examined the book. A stiff, glossy cover with the words *Jao Por* set against a red background, below them the silhouette of a man with something black pooling at his feet. It was smaller than a regular paperback and was printed on such thin paper the type showed through the pages. He began reading, got to the end of the first page and decided he needed a beer. It wasn't exactly Nabokov.

As he passed the shuttered-up gun shops, a cool breeze lifted the veil of the evening's humidity. At the Ban Mor intersection, he went right onto Tanon Phahurat. The fabric stores were switching off their lights and a woman was stacking plastic chairs upside-down on top of her noodle cart. There was an Indian corner shop here that stayed open all hours. He carried back a large bottle of Leo beer and a packet of salted peanuts.

Fat drops of rain began to fall. By the time Vijay was in the office, it was slamming down, and the flash of the lightning was flinging sudden, instant shadows of the venetian blinds onto the wall. He poured the beer into a glass, tore open the peanuts and put his feet up on the bottom drawer of his desk. And like that, he began working through what the country believed were Khun Pleum's life and times.

It wasn't easy.

Montri seemed determined to make the *jao por* look as bad as possible. He added his opinion about any event, flung exaggerations at every fact. The main character was described as "Khun L" and in Montri's deathless prose, Khun L didn't think, he "schemed". He didn't eat, he "gorged". When a plan worked, it was an "evil fruition". No wonder, Vijay thought, people believed Khun Pleum had wanted him shot. It wasn't so much a novel as a 200-page sneer.

He phoned Mana again.

"I've just got started on this book. Mana, how much do you know about Khun Pleum's actual life?"

"A certain amount. I know his construction company is a real business. I don't suppose they pay more or fewer bribes than anybody else."

"I was thinking more of his early days. For instance, this guy in the novel starts out working for a man called Sia Heng."

"Oh, Sia Heng was real, all right. He was a scary guy, from what I've heard. Basically, he ran Samut Sakhon's port. Ships would go through there running guns, smuggling gems. The story is, he even levied his own personal tax on every fishing boat that anchored."

Vijay flipped through some more pages. "It's got him killed here by a rival gang. In 1982, it says here. A Claymore landmine—"

"Detonated by remote control. Yeah, that's true as well. I think his people took out the guy who ordered it, and then

13

Sia Heng's empire split into a civil war. His two sons against each other, something like that."

Vijay skipped ahead some more and read out, "'Khun L slithered in a viper-like way, until he was in-between the two brothers — whose previous relationship had only ever been fraternal.'"

"Good grief."

"The whole book's like that. I'm starting to think Montri was shot by whoever taught him Thai in high school. Which reminds me, it's got the *jao por* leaving school at twelve, after his father dies. He goes to help his mother run a stall fixing bicycles. Was that also Khun Pleum?"

"No idea. Could have been. A lot of those men come from that kind of background. People with street smarts. Poor but ruthless."

"You should see him now. It looks like he's ended up richer than this Sia Heng ever was."

"Well don't kid yourself he's become any less ruthless because of it."

After Mana rang off, Vijay picked up the book again, finished the peanuts, and washed them down with the last of the beer. Outside, the rain had slowed to a light patter. When he craned his head, he could see Chinatown's neon glisten on the roads. An after-the-rain coolness wafted in through the mosquito screens. Nudged out of his reading by the comfort of the weather, Vijay sat back and let his mind drift over the restless city. Out across the shuffle of lights at the Ban Mor intersection, above Chinatown's shuttered shopfronts, the street cleaners and the children selling garlands at traffic lights, over the dark windows and chipped brownstone of the Old Siam Plaza . . . to where?

He pictured Khun Pleum in a penthouse in the city centre, or some high-ceilinged, marble-floored mansion in the suburbs, sipping a brandy or clipping a cigar. It was strange, Vijay thought, how the country's opinion had affected the man so much. He should have been above all of this, but somehow Montri Tongta's writing had got to him.

14

His phone rang.

"Hello, is this Mr Vijay? Vijay Mistry? My name is Montri. You sent me a message on Facebook."

"Khun Montri, of course. I was just thinking about you, and reading your novel, funnily enough. I mean, reading it again, obviously."

"You think it's a good story for foreigners?"

"Definitely. I mean, what's not to like? You've got everything here, the rise from rags to riches, the crime angle, the family feud. I can see tourists buying this at the airport and reading it on the beach."

"That's good, yeah. And your rates are . . . they're good rates. Just to be clear, you're not asking for a share of the royalties?"

"No, no, no. Nothing like that. Khun Montri, I'm just a translator looking for work. A one-time payment is all I'm after, the copyright stays with you. And I'd be happy to provide you with samples of my work and the contact numbers of some clients. You can ask them about my reliability. I admit I haven't done fiction before — it's been mostly legal documents, articles for bilingual magazines, the results of marketing surveys, that kind of thing. But I've wanted to get into translating fiction for a long time now. I'm an avid reader."

"Well, that sounds good. We were actually thinking about the foreign market. More visibility."

"We?"

"My girlfriend and me. She's the one who designed the cover."

"It's a great cover, very striking. I'm sure we can find a publisher who lets us keep it."

"She'd like that."

"Khun Montri, I've got to say, I read about your shooting in the news. It's a bit worrying."

"Yeah. It hurt like hell, I can tell you. Like hell. I'm suffering for my art."

"Who do you think is responsible?"

"That's obvious, isn't it? Someone whose name begins with P didn't like what I wrote."

"And the book is actually about him?"

"Of course not. The book is art, but sometimes art holds up a mirror to life."

"Perhaps we could meet and discuss this project? Like I said, I think this book will sell, but I still want to find out a bit more about what I'd be getting into."

"Sure, sure. Come over. We're on Ko Kret."

It was a carless island sitting in the Chao Phraya at a spot where the river curled through Bangkok's northern suburbs. Meanwhile, Montri's publisher was in Makkasan Junction in the centre of the city.

"I've got some errands to run in the morning. How about late afternoon?"

"No problem, we'll be here all day."

CHAPTER 2

The next morning, Vijay headed out to Makkasan Junction in the back of a taxi. He knew there would be no parking space for his pickup, and anyway, he was now travelling on Khun Pleum's fat wallet.

The day was blisteringly hot — the kind of weather that promised an evening of heavy rain. In the heat, Vijay searched out building number 138 and found it was a shop selling TVs and music systems. To demonstrate the quality of their products, they'd propped a giant speaker up on the pavement and it was pumping *mor lam* music into the roar of Makkasan Road. The baseline vibrated through the soles of Vijay's shoes. Inside the shop, he shouted into the ear of one of the assistants and the man turned and pointed to the side of the building, where there was a steel door with an intercom and CCTV camera. Vijay rang and yelled his name over the wail of pipes.

The door clicked open onto the smell of melting solder and a narrow, wooden staircase, warped with age. Vijay left behind the muffled boom of the music to a landing cluttered with tubs of capacitors, bristling circuit boards, and a man sitting at a table. He had a soldering iron in one hand, and a strap around his forehead keeping a thick magnifying glass in place. One giant eye gazed at Vijay and then blinked. Before he could say anything, a voice called, "In here, in here."

Vijay stepped over a stack of amplifiers and made his way across the landing to a tiny, cramped office at the far end. Behind the desk was the beaming oval face from the website photo, though this wasn't the picture's location. No polished rosewood worktop, no brass table lamp, no bookshelves. Somsak was sitting at a coffee-stained trestle table with a computer on one side.

"So you're the detective, yes? Take a seat, take a seat." He waved a hand at the door. "Don't worry about Oot. He didn't say anything to you, I suppose? Four years. I've been here four years and still not a word."

Vijay sat. "You've got good security, Khun Somsak."

"Not me, them. The shop. They think someone's going to come up and steal Oot's soldering iron." He leaned across the desk and said in the kind of stage whisper you could hear at the very back of the stalls, "Most of their stuff's fake, you know. They get Sony cases and put in their own boards. Oot has no conscience, he only knows about circuits." He sat back and cupped his chin between his thumb and forefinger. "So this idea for a book. Let's hear what you've got."

"As I was telling you on the phone, I had this one client whose dad collected Indian bronzes from the seventeenth century and earlier. One day, a friend who worked in an auction house told her they were fake. Now the thing is," Vijay said, "her dad had bought them in reputable shops, so that meant someone must have swapped out the real ones at some point. And only her family had the key code for the room. She was convinced it was her stepbrother who'd done it, and she wanted me to find out what kind of trouble he'd got himself into that he was so desperate for money. Anyway, it was actually her stepmum who was responsible. She needed the cash because she was being blackmailed over an affair."

Somsak was still cupping his chin and had a frown that was both weighty and serious.

"I'm probably not explaining this very well, but I just thought it was interesting because the explanation wasn't the obvious one. And that's actually very rare in my line of work."

Somsak nodded. "Okay. I would say you've got something here. In my experience of publishing novels, this is something. But it's not just about the writing, you see. The thing is to look at the business side. And this is what I know about." He opened his palms. "It's my life. Ask yourself this. First of all, how long have you spent writing this book?"

"I haven't. I mean, I haven't started it yet."

He waved that away. "Okay, no problem. The point is, you've got a vision, haven't you? And as a writer, an artist, you're going to put a lot of work into this vision. You're dedicated, you're driven to write, am I correct?"

"Sure. That's me."

"And I respect that. I respect the artist's vision. That's why, at S & K Books, we give our authors fifty per cent of the royalties."

The way he said it — sitting back in his chair, leaving space for Vijay's reaction — suggested this was higher than the normal amount.

"That's very generous, Khun Somsak."

He nodded. "It surprises people. They ask me, 'Khun Somsak, what kind of publisher pays fifty per cent royalties?' And do you know what I tell them? 'One who cares about his writers.'"

"And the fact that it's going to be in English—"

"Not a problem. I have years of experience." He leaned in. "You're going to put your soul into this book, aren't you, Vijay?"

"Right."

"You don't have to be embarrassed telling me that. I know what you writers are like. But the point is, your soul is no good without marketing. You don't have marketing and the book is a lump of wood. It's sitting there. No one knows it exists. You don't want that."

"Of course not."

"We have different marketing packages. There's the Exclusive, the Royal and the Celestial."

"And which one would I get?"

Somsak opened his hands again. "Up to you. It only depends on your ambition. On how much you care about having your work in front of the public."

"Hang on a minute. I have to pay for these packages, is that what you're telling me? This doesn't sound normal, Khun Somsak."

The man gestured to the world beyond his small window, the traffic thundering past the exhaust-blackened buildings of Makkasan Road. "Out there, it's not normal. But for me, someone who wants to give his writers more—"

"You've got to get that money from somewhere."

He beamed. "You've got it."

"So, these packages, what are we talking about?"

"Exclusive is 200,000 baht, Royal is 500,000. Celestial is one million."

"Khun Somsak, that's a lot of money."

He took on the self-deprecating expression of someone modest who'd received a compliment. "It is. So you can just imagine what we're going to do for you. This is not about me. It's all about you and your ambition."

"Well, I'd have to think about that. But in the meantime—" Vijay unbuttoned the cargo pocket of his trousers and brought out Montri's novel — "I wonder if I could ask you about this?"

Somsak's face took on the beaming joy of someone being shown a picture of their favourite grandchild. "Ah, now here we are." He pawed the book out of Vijay's hand. "You see, this is what we provide. This is the product." He lovingly stroked the glossy front. "This is the kind of cover we make. Your name could be here, just like this." He opened the book. "And this would be your story, out there where the world can read it."

"That's great, Khun Somsak. But I can't help worrying about what happened to this guy. You know, he got shot and everything."

"In the leg, the papers said. I'm sure he's still alive."

"Right, but what if whoever did this decides to extend the campaign to his publisher or to his publisher's other authors?"

"Not to worry. Not a problem. I think the book was about Khun Pleum. I would say the shooting was more of a personal thing."

"You *think*? Khun Somsak, haven't you read it?"

"Of course, of course. But one reads so many books. It's my life's work, you know."

"Which package did he opt for, can I ask?"

"The Royal."

"He must be rich then, this guy. Half a million baht."

Somsak shook his head. "Not as I remember. No, he didn't seem to be."

Vijay was prepared to take that as gospel. Somsak's antennae being what they were, he imagined the man could spot a rich client as quickly as he could spot an easy mark. "There isn't by any chance some kind of Celestial package upgrade, is there? Where you shoot the author in the leg to get his name in the papers?"

That set the man giggling — the high-pitched giggle of a delighted child. "*He he he.* At S & K Books, we don't shoot our writers."

"Okay, well I'm going to go away and have a think about this. A minimum of 200,000 baht, fifty per cent royalties and you promise not to send a hitman after me."

"*He he he.* Your vision, Vijay." Somsak handed back the copy of *Jao Por.* "You just work on your vision and leave the rest to us."

When Vijay went back out across the landing, Oot blinked at him again with his giant cyclops eye. Sure enough, the metal box on his desk had *Sony* printed on the side. Even so, Vijay wondered which of them needed the building's security more.

It was now close to noon. He made his way down the heat and noise of Makkasan Road and then stepped out of the sun's fierce glare into a noodle shop. Taking a free spot at one of the metal tables, he ordered a bowl and then phoned Mana. "How's it going? Are they actually investigating anything?"

"They are. I talked to the boss at Pak Kret. He's a good guy, but they don't have much to go on. The slug in the victim's leg is a .38. But there's no match to any previous shooting."

"I hadn't realised before, but Montri's actually on Ko Kret. Haven't they talked to the locals? I'm pretty sure there's only one way on and off that island."

"There's two — two piers. Also, they've talked but it's not simple. The shooter isn't going to get onto the ferry wearing his balaclava. And people from the mainland go to Ko Kret all the time. They want to escape the traffic to an island of calm. That's what the boss said. Those actual words. Thought he was going to start selling me real estate."

"I'm pretty sure the shooting happened on a weekday. There couldn't have been that many tourists. Not Thai ones, anyway."

"I told him this, but he says it's still a lot. Anyway, no one noticed anything. His men asked."

"Mana, do you think it's possible the cops are going intentionally slow on this? Because they don't want to find out Khun Pleum is responsible?" *Which*, Vijay thought, *would be ironic.*

"I don't think so. I told you, he's a good guy."

After Mana rang off, Vijay considered that. A good guy in the Thai police force was someone who wasn't involved in the big scams, who didn't know where the bodies were buried (literally on occasion). It was, most of the time, the good guys who got hung out to dry. Plus, if all this attention was really embarrassing to Khun Pleum, then it was most likely to be coming from one of his enemies. So, in other words, someone almost as powerful as him, and almost as well connected.

Vijay finished off his noodles and was about to pay when his phone rang.

"Am I speaking to Khun Vijay?"

"You are."

"My name is Supaporn, I'm Pleum's wife. You're doing this 'work' for my husband, aren't you?" she asked.

"Correct."

"I think you should come and talk to me about it. I'm in a coffee shop on Sukhumvit Road at the moment, Tonglor. How long is that going to be?"

"I'm sorry?"

"How long will it take you to get here? It's called China House, you can't miss it. They've got red Chinese lanterns outside. Where are you now, Khun Vijay?"

"I'm at Makkasan Junction."

"So twenty minutes then." She rang off.

In what, a helicopter? Vijay rang back. "Hi, I'm afraid that won't be possible. I've got a meeting at Ko Kret to go to."

"And you're not postponing it because . . . ?"

"This is actually your husband's problem I'm looking into." It seemed a prime opportunity to show they were getting value for money. "I've made contact with the writer of the book. I offered my services as a translator, for an English edition. I'm going to go and see him now. Obviously, I'll try and get everything I can about the shooting out of him. Also, a policeman friend of mine has got in touch with the cop at Pak Kret who's dealing with this case. I know everything they know. Which is that the same gun was used on the house and the writer. A .38 that hasn't turned up in ballistic records before."

"That's so interesting," she said in a drawl. "I'm going to have a foot massage tomorrow. The Aiyala Spa, it's down Sukhumvit 53. I should be finished at eleven. They have a café." With that, she rang off again.

Vijay was tempted to call back and tell her he couldn't make that appointment either, just to see what her reaction would be. But she was his client's wife, after all.

* * *

He didn't want to trek all the way back to Chinatown for his pickup, so he hailed a taxi and added the ruinous fare to Khun Pleum's mounting expenses. The driver headed north on the expressway, away from the sun-struck glass of the city centre, away from the city's future and back into its past — boxy apartments, a sprawl of corrugated metal roofs, and later, a sudden patch of green bisected by a dark canal. Having peeled off the fast traffic, they came back down to ground level, fetching up at the Sanam Nuea temple. It was a blaze of gold and blinding white in the sunlight.

Vijay made his way along the worn red flagstones of the temple grounds to the pier at the far end. Here a cloudy green river was carrying water hyacinths downstream. The two-baht ferry took just a few minutes to tack across. Vijay could see what Mana meant about tourists still coming during the week. Standing shoulder to shoulder on the warped wooden boards, the ferry crowd had a day-tripper feel — sunglasses and cameras, a young family kitted out in matching yellow-and-blue "Bike for Dad" T-shirts (a celebration for the king's birthday). On the other side, he disembarked at another temple, which had cheerfully added to the midweek holiday vibe by setting up a loudspeaker in its forecourt, blasting out pop songs.

A concrete path led away from the temple grounds and traced the island's perimeter. Overhead, a metal awning ran its length and trapped the wet heat.

The path was lined all the way down with stalls: cloth shoulder bags, cheap plastic toys, traditional Thai desserts, framed pictures of the king, terrapins in a plastic tub and, of course, all the pottery the island was known for. Behind these stalls sat houses, because the people here were selling directly from their homes — sometimes selling out of their front rooms. Beyond the saleable clutter on a blue-tiled floor, you'd see an open door, a bed and a TV playing to no one.

Vijay phoned Montri and asked for directions, then made a point of saying he might be a while, as he wanted to shop. He bought some *khanom khrok* (small, sweet white discs made of flour and coconut milk), and then asked the woman selling them about the shooting. She'd heard about it, but only from the papers. Same thing for two other stall holders he spoke to. And no, the police hadn't been round to talk to any of them.

Montri had told Vijay to follow the walkway until it came to a place selling small ceramic figures. There would be a concrete path going off to the left and he should follow it to the end. Vijay had decided he first wanted to take a few other passages into the island's interior, just to see what happened. Each time, he found himself brushing past spiky bushes and broad green palm fronds to end up at someone's front yard. None of the paths interconnected.

Montri's was a similar deal. The narrow raised concrete ribbon cut through a cool green shade. Vijay passed banyan trees with their long vertical roots trailing down from the branches like string. Then an old-style wooden house, up on stilts. There was a white Bangkaew tied to one of those stilts with a rope leash. It was a Thai breed people kept for their reliability as guard dogs and, true to type, this one came out barking, spittle flying.

Vijay went on, following the path round, and the dog continued to bark until he was out of sight. A couple of minutes later the concrete ended at the red earth of Montri's compound. There was another house of old, dark wood, built on stilts. With all such places, during the day, life is lived outside and underneath it. A corrugated metal roof extended over the dusty ground. On a raised wooden platform was a fridge and some cushions, and further back a metal sink and table. A cooking gas cylinder with a metal saucepan on the hob sat on the gravel. Closer to Vijay, a hammock was slung between two of the wooden pillars supporting the roof. A young couple stood next to it, in an oddly formal pose. The man had his hand around the woman's shoulder, as though readying himself for a portrait. Obviously they'd heard the dog.

They were both in their early to mid-twenties. The man had shoulder-length hair and wore a northern-style collarless shirt. He had a soft, in some ways unformed face, and friendly brown eyes. The woman wore a figure-hugging sky-blue T-shirt and tight white capris. She was pretty but watchful.

Vijay *wai*ed, greeting them with his palms together. "Khun Montri? I'm Vijay, the translator."

"Come, come." The man squeezed his girlfriend's shoulder.

"Aim," she said. "My name's Aim."

The three of them sat on the wooden platform. Montri carried over a glass of water from the fridge and was noticeably limping.

Vijay put the bag of *khanom khrok* down between them. "Please, help yourself."

Montri took one. Aim pushed a strand of hair back behind her ear and said, "So, the book."

"It really is a great story," Vijay said. "Like I was saying on the phone, you've got it all here. I definitely think it's just the thing for a foreign readership."

"And you're not asking for royalties?"

"I told you he's not," Montri said to her. "You're not, are you?"

"No. Look, I'll be honest with you. The number I put in my Facebook message, that's much lower than my usual rate. The fact is, I've been trying to get into fiction translation for a long time now. I think it's something I'd be good at. So far most of my work has been documents for court cases, MOUs, magazine articles, firms that want English-language websites, that kind of thing. It's quite boring. Basically, I've been looking for the right Thai novel. Something with potential. Something you could see on a shelf at Kinokuniya or Asia Books." As Vijay spoke, Montri's expression said he was hungering after the same vision. "I've always imagined someone browsing, opening the front cover and inside it says, '*Translated by Vijay Mistry*.' That will be my beginning. A good book will bring in other work. But if you choose to hire me again, I'm going to give you my regular rate."

Aim reached over and took a *khanom khrok*. Montri said, "I'm working on something else now."

"It's not his best work," said Aim. "That book you've read."

Montri stroked her back. "What I'm doing now, it's a more literary style, different points of view. These people, they've all seen the same event. But then again, have they?"

"Great. I'd love to see it when it's done."

"The one you've read, that was a genre novel."

"Right." Vijay drank some water. "Look don't get me wrong, as I said, I want this project. But your shooting — that's a pretty worrying development. What can you tell me about it?"

Montri straightened his right leg and rolled his jeans up. "Just look at that." He had a bandage wrapped around his calf. He pointed to the outside of the leg. "Went in here and came out there. I'm going to have a scar for life." He sounded oddly proud of the fact. "You know, when most writers tell you they suffer for their art, it's a load of rubbish. Suffer what? A difficult morning because the coffee maker doesn't work?"

"Other people suffer for them," said Aim.

Montri nodded. "Exactly, but you look at me."

"And this attack came out of the blue?" Vijay said.

"Hardly," said Aim and wrapped her arms around her body.

"It's the third time," said Montri.

"Bloody hell. This is the third time you've been shot?"

"No, no. Sent a message."

"He decided to ignore the first two," said Aim, with a look of reproach. Montri rubbed her back again.

"So what were these messages?"

"The first was a bullet," said Montri. "This little box came, posted from the city. *Seiko* it said, which are actually nice watches. When I opened it, there was a bullet rolling around."

"They'd written his name on it in felt tip," Aim said.

"Can I have a look?"

"It's with the police now. I don't know what they did with it."

Montri said, "They told us there's a law against posting live bullets but not against writing on them."

"And message number two?"

He pointed to a small room constructed of concrete breeze blocks, beyond the metal sink. "I was in there, having a wash and someone fired three times, into the side of the house."

"So messages of increasing force," Vijay said.

"Exactly," said Aim. "That's exactly what I told him."

"And where were you when it happened?"

"I'd already left for work."

"Around here?"

She shook her head. "On the mainland. I'm a copywriter."

"I assume you called the police again?"

"Sure," said Montri. "A guy came on his motorbike, borrowed a knife from me and dug the slugs out. Then he took pictures with his phone and went off. We never heard from him again."

"The fact is," said Aim, "everyone knows Khun Pleum's behind this and so no one wants to do anything. It's the same with the press. Montri phoned all the papers and they weren't interested."

He nodded. "*Khaosod, Thai Rath, Matichon.* I said, 'I've written this book and now people are shooting at my house, posting me bullets.' It shows you the public's opinion of writers. If you're not some big shot who's won the SEA Write, absolutely no one cares."

"Well they do now," Vijay pointed out. "This is on the evening news, social media — it's everywhere."

"Because they all feel guilty," said Aim.

"Where were you standing when you were hit?"

Aim frowned. "You're asking a lot of questions, aren't you?"

"I just want to get the facts straight in my head. Especially, as you say, with the police maybe not investigating it properly."

Montri swung his legs off the platform and pushed his feet into his sandals. "I'd just got off that hammock and I was about to turn and walk back. See, like this." He limped over there and stood with his legs apart and his torso half-turned towards them.

"And the gunman?"

"He'd just stepped off the path."

"Wow. That's good shooting. I mean, if he was actually aiming for your calf muscle."

"Or he was a bit closer. As you can see, I couldn't spot him immediately." He was still holding the same pose.

"What did this guy look like?"

"Nothing special, I would say. Jeans and a black T-shirt, balaclava on his head."

"Any tattoos?"

"Not that I noticed."

Aim said, "You sound like you're going to investigate it yourself."

"It's the kind of mind I've got. I need to visualise. If I can picture a thing, it reassures me."

"That doesn't make any sense at all."

Montri had limped back. He did seem to have a tenderly tactile relationship with his girlfriend. "Aim was at work again," he said. "But then someone's got to have a real job."

She gave that a thin smile and brought a slim metal case out of her pocket. She handed Vijay a name card reading, *Deep Blue Advertising*. "We're just getting started. But we're good. If any of your clients, you know, the firms with websites, if you hear they're looking for someone, we do TV ads, viral marketing, social media platforms. We can give you the whole package."

"Definitely. I'll pass it along." He slipped the card into his wallet. "But you must have heard the dog, right? That Bangkaew up there, it must have been barking."

"Sure."

"And you didn't run, try and take cover? I mean, after him shooting the house?"

Aim shivered. "Look how exposed we are out here."

"It barks all the time," Montri said. "There's always people coming through. Dried squid, *pla salit*, mangoes, someone's always coming along selling something."

Aim said, "He doesn't bark at the *pla salit* woman."

"What about the dog's owner? Did they see the shooter going past? Because he must have come and gone the same way, right?"

Aim rolled her eyes. "Leung Tor, that drunk old fool?"

"He came over though. When I called for help," Montri said. "I couldn't say anything straight away, the pain was too much. It's nothing like you'd expect — you know, when the movie hero gets shot and he keeps on going and pulls himself up the side of the building or whatever. It was a sledgehammer. Took my breath away for a while. Then I called out, 'Leung Tor, Leung Tor.'" He said to Aim, "And he did come."

"*Then*," said Aim.

"Can I just ask, why did you set out to write about Khun Pleum?" Vijay asked.

"I wouldn't say it's *him*, exactly. As an artist, you use your imagination. Things in the real world inspire you, they set your creative process going in a certain direction." He frowned and said to Aim, "You'd think the police would have finished with the slug by now."

"He wants the bullet that shot him," she said to Vijay.

"It's my leg it went through."

Aim shuddered. Vijay changed the subject. "The other issue here is the publisher. You're only hiring me as a translator, so it's up to you what you do with the text. But having said that, the more people who read it, the better it is for me." He looked from one to the other. "And for you as well, right?"

"Definitely," said Montri. "That's it."

"So maybe we could look for a bigger outfit? White Lotus, Silkworm Books, somebody like that?"

"We tried the big places when we started," said Aim. "We tried everyone."

"They were scared of Khun Pleum," said Montri. "I mean, no one would admit to that. They all made up excuses, said things about the writing style. But basically, Khun Pleum's the reason."

Vijay found himself thinking of that writing style — the sour, curdled disdain dripping off every page — and tried to match it to this friendly young man living here so simply. "I can't help noticing, you wrote this book with a certain . . . a certain tone. It feels very personal. Did Khun Pleum do something to you or your family, by any chance?"

"Nothing at all," said Montri. "Writing, for me, it's a very instinctive thing. I use my instincts to uncover the story, the voice. I'm like an explorer trekking through the wilderness, drawing the map as I go."

"I understand," Vijay said, even though he didn't. "And I'm sure I can put that map into English for you. So, guys," he asked. "Do you want to hire me?"

Montri said, "Absolutely." Aim nodded.

He *wai*ed to them both. "I'll write down my account number. I'd appreciate a week's advance."

* * *

After squaring things with Montri and Aim, Vijay headed off down the walkway. From the path, all he could see were banyan trees and banana palms. He stepped down onto the damp earth and tried to push his way through the foliage. It was hard, sweaty, and impossible to tell which direction to head for. It seemed to Vijay that unless the shooter knew the area very well, he would have had to return using the path.

And that made him want to talk to Leung Tor.

The Bangkaew went for Vijay as soon as he was in sight. Skirting the circumference of its leash, he called out, "Hello, Leung Tor," and waited. He was about to assume there was no one home when a hammock at the back of the compound swayed up to deposit a skinny figure unsteadily onto his feet. He shuffled out to the front of the house, a gaunt unshaved man, possibly in his sixties. White hair, white stubble, a vest and sarong.

"Leung Tor, I'm a friend of Montri. Can I talk to you for a minute?"

Leung Tor waved him in while taking hold of the dog's leash. "E-yen, enough of that." Vijay followed him to the back of the house, and behind them the barking stopped. Vijay was now one element of E-yen's territory. Something else to be protected.

"It's about the shooting," Vijay said.

The man guided him towards a wooden armchair of varnished teak and sat up sideways on the hammock. He had some other nice pieces of furniture, Vijay noticed. A low, varnished table that also appeared to be teak, a thick carved wooden bench. They sat among the rest of his household clutter like treasure salvaged from a wreck. An ancient standing fan with a frayed electrical cord was beating through a half circle, riffling the curling pages of a commercial calendar three years out of date. His hammock was made of sacking, the ends bunched together with thick rope. Behind it, an empty paint can functioned as a bin.

"I'm a bit worried about Montri, Leung Tor. About what happened to him."

"I found him," said Leung Tor. "He called out for help and I went over there. He was lying on the floor. Really in pain, I would say." A light, sweet smell of rice whiskey wafted across with his words. Under the hammock was a bottle and a half-full tumbler. "I took the phone out of his pocket and called Nong Sai. She left her shop and came running. Then we phoned the hospital. They had to send people, he couldn't walk."

"It's scary stuff. Good job it was only in the leg. You didn't see the shooter, I suppose?"

The man shook his head, and then gave a watery smile that contained a certain degree of shrewdness. "You haven't come by here before, have you?"

Vijay held up his hands. "I'm not really a friend. 'Scared business associate' would be a better description. I'm actually supposed to be translating Khun Montri's book into English. I could do with the work but I just don't know what I'm getting into."

He nodded. "Khun Pleum, isn't it? That's what the papers are saying. I don't know why anyone would want to write about him."

"Leung Tor, where were you when the shooting happened?"

He patted the hammock. "I was here, just taking a rest."

"And this would have been when?"

"Middle of the afternoon, maybe. Something like . . . now."

Vijay looked out beyond the red earth and E-yen resting with his head in his paws. Out to the sunlit green of the path. Aim was right, he thought. Living like this, in the old style, it was all so open. Any gunman could come stalking into what was essentially your front room. He pictured Montri and Aim, waiting in the shadows like prey, and then imagined himself as the shooter, bringing his shock of lead and gunpowder, materialising out of the glare of the sun. The image didn't sit right with him.

"Did you hear the gunshot?" he asked.

"I heard, but it wasn't loud. I couldn't be sure." The foliage, Vijay presumed, had muffled the noise. "I called out but no reply, so then I went back to . . . to lying here. I thought I must have imagined it. Then I heard, 'Leung Tor, Leung Tor, help.' So I went round."

"How long was it, would you say, between the shot and Montri calling for help?"

"Maybe five minutes. Something like that."

"That's a long time, Leung Tor. You're sure you don't mean a couple of minutes?"

He thought about it. "No, I would say it was more like five. Because I remember thinking, you see. I was thinking, 'What did I just hear?'"

"And how long between the shot and E-yen barking?"

"He didn't bark."

"Really? But what about *before* the shooting? You must have heard him then?"

He shook his head. "No, I wouldn't say he barked then either." He gave a sad smile and Vijay realised the man had caught the downward sweep of his gaze to the bottle and tumbler. "I doze a bit, in the afternoons. But E-yen can always wake me, he's a good dog. I don't tie him up at night, you know. In the mornings, he comes up the stairs and licks my hand."

Vijay didn't want to say something patronising in reply. He looked away from the old man to the back of the compound, which was shaded by a corrugated metal roof set on concrete poles. The floor back there was concrete too. Sticks of firewood were tied together in bundles and behind them was a waist-high concrete chamber. "Is that a kiln, Leung Tor? You're a potter?"

"I used to be. I don't do so much these days. A few little things. My hands aren't as steady as they were." He levered himself up. "Look, I'll show you." He made his slow way to the kiln, and there on the far side, stacked against the wall, were red clay teacups and saucers, coated with dust like a glaze. "What do you think?"

Vijay squatted down, picked up a cup and wiped it clean. It really was a nice little thing. With thick sides and a chunky feel, it was comfortable in your hand. And it looked good. He'd filigreed a lotus pattern all the way around. Vijay could picture it on his desk at work, filled with black coffee.

"These are some of my older pieces," Leung Tor said.

"You're not selling them?"

"I like having them around to remind me of what I could do. And I don't need to sell these days. I'm a lucky man. I have a son who works on the mainland. He sends me money every month. He bought me the chair you were sitting in, had them deliver it."

"It's a nice chair."

Leung Tor gave Vijay a look that was clear-sighted, and Vijay had an idea of how much intelligence the alcohol hadn't yet dimmed. "He doesn't have the time to visit me anymore. Hasn't been home in more than two years, doesn't have time to phone. And if I phone him, I get that 'speak after the tone' message. But he sends me money every month. So that makes me a lucky man . . . wouldn't you say?"

"I suppose he's got to do the work to earn the money, right?"

Leung Tor looked past Vijay to his lifeless kiln. "Something like that."

CHAPTER 3

Come the next morning, Vijay had a strong suspicion he wasn't going to be able to stick the taxi ride to Khun Pleum's wife on Khun Pleum's expenses. So he drove down to the Aiyala Spa and, in the small, gravelled car park, backed his fifteen-year-old Toyota pickup into the space between a white Mercedes Coupé and a BMW 5 series so new it still had the red showroom plates on.

The ground sloped down to the spa below. Inside, a reception desk faced onto a red stone floor, black wicker armchairs and scented candles flickering in glass bowls. The receptionist wore a severe black turtleneck, and the general feel was of somewhere that took your wellness as seriously as you took your stock options. When Vijay asked for the café, the woman pointed left.

It was a high-ceilinged, glass-walled place with wrought iron pillars, giving it the look of an old-fashioned conservatory. There were thick white tablecloths, palms in ceramic pots, gleaming cutlery and air con turned up high enough to counter the bright sunlight. At eleven o'clock it was fairly empty, though there was more than one single woman in the room. Vijay was still wondering whom to approach when a lady at the back looked up, saw him, and made a palm-down beckoning gesture. Assuming he hadn't been mistaken for a waiter, Vijay went over.

She looked to be about Khun Pleum's age, a well-cared-for early sixties, with a royal blue silk scarf around her throat, diamond earrings and a shortish, youthful hairstyle. In front of her was a salad and a thick orange concoction in a glass.

"Khun Supaporn?" Vijay asked.

"Sit then, don't stand over me."

He did so and a waiter materialised at his shoulder.

"He's not having anything," she said. "So. My husband's case. You've read the book by now, I suppose?"

"Of course."

In fact, he hadn't picked it up again, but it seemed a good idea to sound conscientious. She gave him a long look at that, and Vijay had the strange feeling he was supposed to know why she'd wanted the meeting.

"Do you know how old I was when I met Pleum?"

He shook his head. Presumably it wasn't in the book, or she wouldn't be asking.

"I was twelve and he was fourteen."

"So you were childhood sweethearts."

Her eyes slid away from his and Vijay had an intimation of what was coming next. He'd seen that look so many times in his office. The thing to do, he'd come to realise, was just let people talk. Give them a listening space and they would tell you their own story in their own way.

After a pause, she said, "My bicycle had a puncture. That's how we met. I was cycling down the pavement with my *yai* walking next to me." From that description alone, Vijay could picture her childhood. "I told her my back tyre had gone flat and she said to me to get off. Then she wheeled the bike down a small *soi*. There was this boy sitting on a mat on the pavement. I remember him *wai*ing to my *yai* when she told him what we wanted. And then looking at me." She sipped some of her orange gloop. "I didn't like that. The word 'insolent' wasn't part of my vocabulary then, I don't suppose, but that's what it was. He just looked and weighed me up. My dress and my servant and everything else about me, I could feel him doing it. And then after he'd patched up the hole and my *yai* asked him how much, he said, 'It's a small job, there's no charge.' And I was furious. He's sitting there on the floor with his torn shirt and his dirty hands and his broken slippers, and he dares to offer us charity? Can you understand that?"

"I think so."

"I spent the whole evening thinking about him and then the next day I marched down there with my pocket money and told him I wanted to pay him what I owed."

"And then?"

"He just shrugged and I had another reminder of how unbothered he was." She gave a faint smile. "And handsome, I suppose. That was our beginning. Telling my *yai* I didn't need her with me when I went out on my bicycle. Then I'd stop at his stall and talk while he worked. I used to describe what I'd done that day. It couldn't have been a world he could even imagine, I don't suppose — the private girls' school I went to. But he never seemed impressed. Instead, he'd ask me these careful, precise questions." She wet her throat with some more of her health drink. "I had one of those new American bicycles, with the long handlebars and the front wheel lower than the back one. People would come up to get their chains fixed or whatever, and I'd see them looking from me to him." She raised her chin. "I liked that, I liked the picture we made."

He was sure they were going to get down to it at that point, but instead she played with her salad for a bit.

"He got his start because of me, did you know that?"

Vijay shook his head.

"The underground lottery he was running. In the book, the details are mostly correct. One-baht tickets, betting on the last four digits of the state lottery's winning number." She moved a square of feta cheese with her fork, like a croupier pushing a gambling chip. "A fifty-baht prize is nothing. Even in the seventies, it was nothing. And I told him that.

He needed to offer a bigger win. I was thirteen, fourteen by then, and without my parents knowing, I pawned some of my jewellery. Nice things my mother had bought me — a jade necklace, silver earrings. She would have been furious if she'd known. And he put up the ticket price, but not by much. It made his draw the best game in town." She put her fork back down. "And that was how he came to Sia Heng's attention. The man's goons turned up one day and dragged him off for a talking to. And at the end of it, he was offered a job."

"That's quite a turnaround, isn't it? Those are usually the kind of discussions that end in broken kneecaps."

"I think he probably reminded Sia Heng of himself. Another son of a Chinese immigrant. Another poor background, someone else who couldn't afford to stay in school very long. Plus, the kind of person he was. You can't see it now, can you?"

"I'm not sure. See what?"

"His *hunger*. So many plans, so much ambition burning him up. You know, he was thirteen years old when he started running that lottery." She placed her elbows on the table and rested her chin on her fists, then raised her head. "I had plenty of men after me. I was a *very* good catch."

"But your other suitors weren't hungry like Khun Pleum, right?"

She studied Vijay. He had the feeling something more had been required from him.

"You haven't even read it, have you? The book."

He said, "I have started . . . I mean, I'm getting there. The prose isn't exactly Kukrit Pramoj."

"There are things in that book that are very accurate. The description of our family compound in Samut Sakhon, the car I use, my driver's uniform, my sons' business careers." She gave him a flinty stare. "In the book, Khun L has a *mia noi*. I want the name of this woman."

A mistress? You just let them talk and they always spit it out in the end. "That, for me, would be problematic."

"I can't see why."

39

"Khun Supaporn, I'm working for your husband."

"Well of course you are, that's the whole point. You're ideally positioned to investigate him, aren't you?"

"He told me he doesn't fire warning shots."

"Oh, don't be such a baby. Nothing's going to happen to you if you're working for me."

"Even if we assume that's true — and I've got my doubts — there is still an ethical dimension to this."

"No there isn't. You're not a doctor, there isn't some Hippocratic oath for private detectives. You've probably done all kinds of grubby things in your career."

"If I have, they never looked grubby to me at the time."

"Didn't they? You're some monk-in-training, are you?" She pushed her plate to one side. "I'll pay you twice my husband's rate."

And that, Vijay thought, summed up so many of the rich. Lacking charm or grace or morality, they assumed no one else had them either. *You possess only money and so you think everyone can be bought.*

He took a deep breath. "I'll give you my account number. I'm going to want the first ten days in advance. Transferred within the next hour, if that's possible."

* * *

Half an hour later, having received the details of her husband's movements, Vijay was back in his pickup, considering his life. As he keyed the ignition, his phone went. Another number he didn't recognise. He switched on the cab's air conditioning and answered.

"Vijay, it's me. Montri's girlfriend."

"What can I do for you, Aim?"

"I'd like to have a chat about our . . . project. You said you were in Chinatown. On the Facebook message. Why don't I come and see you?"

Suddenly, Vijay thought, everyone's spouse wanted to talk to him. The problem was, he didn't want Aim seeing that *Translations — Detective* sign and getting the wrong idea. Or the right idea, depending on your viewpoint.

"I've got an important meeting to go to right now," he said, which was true. "I don't really know how long it's going to take. Tomorrow would be better. In fact, why don't I come to you?"

"All the way out to Pak Kret? Do you really want to do that?"

He told her it was no problem, lied that he had a friend in the area and received directions for where to meet. He then made a phone call and set up his next rendezvous.

Driving back to Chinatown, Vijay reflected on how he'd achieved a new career low of taking money to investigate his own client. The problem was, it seemed to be the only possible solution to his previous career low of having had someone threaten to turn his feet all the way round. A *nak leng* called Lek had promised Vijay it was possible, and only needed going at his ankles with a claw hammer, like the one he was carrying.

Lek worked for a money lender called Kritisak. Vijay had gone to the man when his debts had piled up. He'd been faced with the choice of either letting Doi go, giving up his apartment and sleeping in the office, or finding a loan from somewhere to tide him over. The banks were out of the question, due to Vijay's credit history, and firing Doi felt like an admission of complete failure.

I saw my chance and made a go of things.

Sleeping in his no-staff office, the "go of things" would have gone. And after a decade in the country, Vijay would have the stale, defeated sense of having returned to his beginning. So he turned to Kritisak. The man like the title "Sia" (the Chinese term for businessman). Sia Geng, you were supposed to call him.

Vijay's meeting was set for five, so he went back to the office to kill some time. Doi told him the website translation was finished and the money had been paid into the company account. He poured out some iced tea from the fridge and gave her Montri's book. "His girlfriend asked to see me, so I'm guessing she wants a progress update. If you start putting it into English, I'll edit. Don't worry about the grammar."

Doi flicked through the pages. "It's not the grammar that's going to be the problem." She looked up. "He really hates Khun Pleum, doesn't he?"

"I suppose a lot of people do. You should hear my journalist friend Petch when he gets onto organised crime and what it did to Thai politics."

Doi frowned. "But it's not only corruption, he hates . . . everything." She turned some more pages, stopped and read out, "'Khun L's twin sons went through their school life with fat complacency, while being obesely spoiled by their snob-like mother.' What is that supposed to mean?"

"Unless it's a typo and it should be obscenely?"

"And 'snob-like'?" She riffled again. "'Khun L's evil wiles were making him the worst of the worst, even in comparison to people as bad as himself.'"

"He does like going on about Khun L's wiles, I've noticed."

"Has he written anything else?"

"Good question." Vijay took out his phone and typed Montri's name into Google. "It just brings up newspaper articles about the shooting. He did say he was working on something else though. 'More literary' was how he put it."

Doi switched on her computer and rested her empty mug on the book to keep it open. She worked through the afternoon, and the sun dropped down to their side of the building. Vijay changed the angle of the venetian blinds. He then opened a drawer in his desk, put his feet up on it and did some more Googling of Montri. The man was a member of an alumni group of Silpakorn University. He'd written an article in a lifestyle magazine about the Bangkok barbers who could give you an old-style hot towel shave. Another article in the same magazine was about why he preferred using a manual typewriter to a computer. And that was it. If he had a personal hatred of Khun Pleum, the reason wasn't to be found online.

At four thirty, Vijay told Doi he was going to talk to Mana about the case, and then went off to see Kritisak. The walk took him down Ban Mor Road and its strict division of commerce. On one side of the street were electronics shops, with tables set out on the pavement, and people like Oot working with soldering irons under the shade of the acacia trees. On the other side was the gleam and sunshine sparkle of the gold and jewellery stores. Leading off Ban Mor were all the road's particular specialities. Vijay went past the *soi* with photocopy machines being constantly sated with paper like hungry gods, and then the *soi* of the seamstresses, where women sat in the heat, working the pedals of manual sewing machines.

The road came to a bridge spanning a wide *khlong*, where fat pigeons flapped across the cloudy, grey-green water. It continued on the far side, and then leading off was a *soi* so narrow it had no name or number. It was just an alley between peeling white walls. The angle of the sun had dropped it into a shadow that was made cooler, somehow, by a songbird cooing from a high window. This passage of old, three-storey houses curled left, past a red garlanded shrine to the area god, and opened onto the gravel courtyard of a tiny Chinese restaurant.

As far as Vijay had been able to tell, there were no signs to this place anywhere and only the locals knew it existed. Kritisak had, for some reason, chosen it as his unofficial office. He was always ensconced here at the same circular table (one of just three) under an awning. Even away from mealtimes, he'd be sipping Chinese tea with his goons, holding court.

There were three of them there when Vijay arrived, and now Kritisak had food in front of him. He was clutching a bowl under his chin and shovelling fried rice into his mouth with chopsticks. Vijay coughed into his hand and said, "Sia Geng."

Kritisak stopped with the chopsticks cantilevered half-way to his wet lips and looked up. He had the beginnings of a double chin and, despite being in his thirties (so Vijay had been told), still possessed the smooth, pink skin of a teenager. Being a moneylender obviously agreed with him.

"Vijay," he said, then continued eating. It was more like an observation — "cloudy" — than an invitation to sit down. Meanwhile, his two goons had paused along with him and then resumed in sync. It was all so practised, Vijay was sure they'd seen it in some Chinese gangster flick.

"Sia Geng," Vijay said, "I've got 20,000 baht here for you."

Kritisak used his chopsticks to point to the goon furthest away from him — a bald guy who was wearing dark glasses, despite sitting in the shade. The man came round from the table. Vijay gave him the wedge of thousand-baht notes, whereupon the goon licked his thumb and demonstrated he could indeed count to twenty.

Kritisak nodded his head and slurped up some more tea, still without looking at Vijay. The goon put the money on the table and sat down again.

Vijay cleared his throat. He didn't get a reaction. "Sia Geng, I just want you to know, I'm going to be on time with the rest."

Kritisak put his glass down and began rotating the central section of the table to bring a plate of roast duck towards him.

"I've got a job now and it's well paid," Vijay continued. "I'm actually getting twice my usual rate."

Kritisak took a piece of duck with his chopsticks and busied himself with the important task of dunking it into a saucer of soy sauce. It was impossible for Vijay to know if he'd been dismissed, since the man had barely acknowledged his presence to begin with. He decided to go, but then thought it would be good to offer some evidence this well-paying job existed. "Did you hear about that writer who got shot?" he said. "The one who wrote the book about Khun Pleum? Well, it's Khun Pleum who's hired me."

There was a sudden absence of table noise. The clink of tea glasses stopped, the movement of dishes was suspended.

The bald goon's cheeks were full. He'd stopped chewing. In the silence, Vijay heard him swallow.

"So Lek doesn't need to visit me again," Vijay finished.

Kritisak turned to Vijay and his eyes widened. He had the look of someone trying to force a vast thought out of his mind. "Ha, ha, ha," he laughed. "Khun Pleum." And then, turning to the goons, he did it again. "Ha, ha, ha." The laughter was literally that — a forced repetition of the word "ha".

"The point is, I can expect him to pay on time."

Kritisak came round from behind the table, firing like a machine gun. "Ha, ha, ha, ha, ha." He put an arm around Vijay's shoulder and attempted to squeeze him onto his shirt front. "We-jay," he said and "ha"ed some more. It gradually came to Vijay that this was Kritisak attempting reassurance. In its way, it was more terrifying than the claw hammer. "Lek came to see you? Really? I didn't even know this."

"He said you sent him."

"Vijay, do you think I'm that kind of a person? You and me, we have a relationship — don't we?" His smooth face was pink and beaming. Still with a hand on Vijay's shoulder, he turned him round to face the table. "Didn't I say that to the two of you?" he asked the goons, who were staring back at them with a look of tense readiness. "Didn't I say Vijay was a guy with big plans?"

The two men nodded cautiously.

Kritisak clapped Vijay on the back. "Sit down and have some food. You're too thin." He called out for another plate and, when it came, began rotating dishes to Vijay while announcing their content, as though they were heads of state arriving at a reception. "Asparagus tips fried in oyster sauce. Prawn fried in garlic. This is a piece of pork. You can eat pork?"

"Lek said he was going to turn my ankles around. He mentioned a hammer."

"Lek always mentions a hammer. Do you know what he did before he came to me? He was a carpenter. That's his problem, he can't leave his old life behind." He raised his glass in the attitude of someone making a toast. "Khun Pleum now. You're going up in the world. Isn't he going up in the world?"

"This is just a one-off case. It's not as though he's made me his personal private detective."

"No, no, no. You're being too modest. Isn't he being too modest?"

There didn't seem to be any way of escaping Kritisak's ferocious goodwill. Vijay had the feeling that if he left the table, the man would rugby tackle his legs while smothering him in compliments. At least it was nicer than his last meeting with Lek. So Vijay sat on in the wet heat and the evening's last light, letting Kritisak rotate more dishes in his direction, refill his glass with Chinese tea and drop lubricous hints about Khun Pleum happening to see the two of them together. And the funny thing was, by the end of it, sated on roast duck, fried rice and compliments, Vijay did feel successful. Here he was, working for a big shot, charging twice his normal rate, even if he was going to have to give most of that away. Later on, he would look back on dinner with Kritisak as the tail-end of his days of peace — those days when he'd still believed he was witnessing the start of better things.

CHAPTER 4

The next day, Vijay went out into mid-morning sunlight to search for a taxi. Another long journey to Pak Kret, another expensive taxi fare. Well, why not? It would look good on his expenses claim. All these trips out to see the wounded writer, busily investigating. And he'd have the toll booth receipts, assuming Khun Pleum's money men needed evidence.

The address Aim had given him was the Be Trendy building — what else for an advertising firm? It turned out to be a tall, imposing place with an information desk at the centre of a marble-floored lobby. In one corner was the Starbucks where they were supposed to meet. Before going in, Vijay went over to the lifts and scanned the names on the brass plate above them. He couldn't find Deep Blue Advertising. The woman behind the desk said that no, there was no such company on the premises.

Inside the Starbucks, Aim was already sitting over a cappuccino. Vijay got himself a mug of tea and joined her. She was wearing a tight black T-shirt and black leggings under a gauzy white miniskirt. She looked both chic and preoccupied.

He sat down. "This is impressive. Your firm must be doing well."

She met that with an eye-roll. "You don't think we're based *here*, do you? I just thought this place would be easy to find. Plus, it's got air conditioning."

"So, we've started work," Vijay said. "My Thai colleague has begun a literal translation of Montri's book and then I'm going to clean up the grammar. That's how we do it for Thai to English."

She nodded. "Good . . . It's kind of you to come all this way, Vijay. To see me. What does your colleague think? About the book?"

"She thinks it's a great story. An important story. In a way, it shows you how a certain type of corruption entered Thailand's political system. It shows you the soil that corruption grew from." Aim crossed her legs and placed both hands around her coffee cup. Vijay had the impression of a sleek, watchful pedigree cat who didn't much trust his intentions.

"Do you read much Thai fiction? Does your colleague?"

"Some. I think Uthis Haemamool's, *The Brotherhood of Kaeng Khoi* was the most recent," Vijay replied, leaving out the fact that he'd actually read the Montalbano translation. He took a guess at what Aim was after. "To be honest with you, we liked the story more than the writing style. And I don't mean to be in any way critical of Montri and his . . . his art, but it can be a little over the top in places."

"That's what I wanted to talk to you about. When you put this into English, it might need more . . . more of an editing, or let's say a rewriting type of process. Only I'm not sure we can find the money to pay you any extra for that."

"No problem. I want this book to be a success as much as you do. I want people to see it on bookshelves."

"It might be better not to tell Montri. Just redo it how you feel is best. You don't have to phone him and ask about your edits, for instance. In case you were thinking of doing that. Do you understand what I'm saying?"

Vijay did, and was touched by the way she was protecting her boyfriend's feelings. "He must really hate Khun Pleum."

Her gaze slid away from his. "He's got his opinions."

"And what are yours?"

"It could be a good start for us. He's going to do other things. More literary works. That's where his real strength is."

"So this was a commercial project, something to make money on?"

"If you like."

Vijay could feel her withdrawing from the conversation. He thought of Montri claiming most writers didn't suffer for their art and then Aim saying that other people suffered for them. "It must be difficult for you, being the only breadwinner in the relationship."

"It's not the money that worries me, it's Montri's safety."

"You know, I did get the feeling the shooting troubles you more than it troubles him. He seems almost proud of the whole experience."

She gave a deep, shuddering sigh. "The way he explained it to me was that it's easier to shoot someone in the centre of the body than to shoot them in the leg. So that proves the gunman didn't mean to kill him."

Vijay thought of his approach to their house again. Montri and Aim, waiting in the shade like prey. "Just to teach him a lesson?"

"From the way you speak Thai, I'm sure you've been here long enough. You must know how it works. Everyone wants to have a big hand behind them."

"So this was someone's route to getting Khun Pleum as a patron, you think? Going and telling him, 'That writer guy, I've taught him a lesson for you.'"

"Of course, if they'd actually killed Montri, the police would have to get off their butts and do something. But with a flesh wound, they can just sound busy for the press."

As a theory, Vijay reflected, it made sense in every aspect. Other than Khun Pleum hiring him. "And how did you get to be on Ko Kret? It's a family-owned house, is it?"

"No, no. We're paying rent. Montri says he needs peace to create. He needs to be out of the city. But then I got a job at Deep Blue, so Ko Kret fitted both of us."

Count off another financial burden then. She wasn't just paying their living costs, she was fronting up the rent money as well. On top of Somsak's Royal marketing package.

"He's a good writer, you know," Aim said defiantly. "He could even become great one day. At Silpakorn, my friend ran this short story magazine, that's how I met Montri. She published a story of his. It was about a mother whose son is away at university. The mother is washing and ironing his shirt and trousers so tenderly. And then at the end, you find out he's been killed in a car crash and she's preparing the clothes for his cremation. I told my friend, 'I want to meet the person who wrote this.'"

"Style-wise, Montri's gone in quite a different direction since then."

"*Jao Por* was a different kind of storytelling. He's very versatile."

"By the way, I forgot to check. When does the ferry to Ko Kret stop running?"

She made a face at that. "'Forgot to check.' You still sound as though you're investigating us."

"Just making sure I know what I'm getting into."

She gave him a long stare. "Seven."

"That must be a problem. What happens if you miss it?"

"I can phone someone. There's a guy with a long-tail boat who'll take me across for fifteen baht. A lot of people on the island have their own boats."

So that was another way the shooter could have come and gone. He hadn't even needed the ferry. Vijay was starting to understand why the police hadn't got anywhere. The big question was, for how long would *he* be allowed to go on getting nowhere while receiving Khun Pleum's marvellous cash injections?

"I had a chat with Leung Tor." He held his hands up. "I know, I know. Here I am investigating you again. Anyway, he told me his dog didn't bark, either before or after the shooting. Your place isn't easy to get to, other than by the path, so I wondered how that was possible." He sipped some tea. "He could have come across the land, I suppose, if he had military training. But even that wouldn't be simple. He'd have run the risk of crossing other properties on the way. It's all so open on Ko Kret. I bet almost everyone owns a guard dog, am I right?"

"Vijay, Leung Tor slept through the whole thing. He drinks practically all day, but he doesn't want people to know. He's trying to get pottery work again, I heard."

"He did have a bottle and glass under his hammock."

She looked away. "Sometimes when I come home, Montri's hammock has got a saucer under it and there's four or five cigarette butts. I say to him, 'What did you do today? Were you just lying here smoking?'" And then in quick defence, she added, "But he's a good writer. You should read his short stories."

* * *

Vijay made it back to Chinatown in time to have lunch with Doi at their usual noodle place. Away from the Starbucks air con, it was another day of wet heat and low, dark clouds. Sprinkling flakes of dried chilli into her bowl, Doi asked, "So what did she want?"

"She understands it's badly written. She wanted to find out whether we had the critical facilities to see that for ourselves, and to ask us to improve it, rather than just put it into English. And she was worried about the cost of that service."

"And you told her?"

"I said there'd be no extra charge. After all, we need to stay close to them. Also, she wanted me to be tactful with Montri. Not just tell him, 'It was so crap we've redone the whole thing.'"

Doi giggled. "She knows it's so bad but didn't say anything while he was writing it?"

"No, it's odd. Actually, everything about this book is odd. It came to the attention of a friend — or an enemy — of Khun Pleum, but I couldn't find it on a bookshelf anywhere.

It was written for commercial success, but is barely readable. Meanwhile, they've paid out all this marketing money to a publisher who is obviously a conman."

"But they didn't realise he was a conman when they hired him. And maybe Montri's just not a good writer."

"Aim says he's written better things, more literary stuff. He might just be good in a different way. I mean, if you think of the kind of people who win the SEA Write Award, I suppose they'd find it hard to knock out a commercial thriller."

Doi didn't look convinced. "Vijay, this book is not a normal kind of bad. It's . . . something else."

The clouds finally broke and rain rattled down like gunfire on the metal awning. The smell of the damp street drifted in. Doi sighed at the downpour. They'd be marooned in the noodle shop until it slowed. "What do you think of her?"

"Aim? I like her, actually. Although I don't think she trusts me all that much. She's basically working to support the two of them and it doesn't sound as though her job even pays that well." Vijay thought about it some more. "They've invested so much money in this non-selling book, you'd think they'd be more desperate."

"Maybe they are but don't want to show it?"

"The shooting seems to be what's most on their minds. In Aim's case, worrying about it happening again, and as for Montri, my guess is it's worked as a kind of validation for him. He thinks, 'One of Khun Pleum's people shot me, so I must have written a great novel.'"

"Perhaps somebody's got rich parents?"

"Maybe." It was always possible, in spite of Somsak's assessment.

After that, Vijay and Doi left the case and went on to other ways of killing time. Doi talked about the problems her sister was having with her husband. Doi's brother-in-law was a mechanic, but had a hobby trading Buddha amulets. The hobby had taken over his life and now he wasn't concentrating on the garage anymore. "Lieng says he sits at the computer trying to make deals on the internet. They swap stories in these chat groups about discovering rare amulets in street markets and turning huge profits. Lieng says they're really just dreaming about finding money."

The comment got Vijay thinking of Montri again, and what was essentially a fantasy of best-sellerdom. But then, he thought, didn't everyone have the same dream? Something magical that banishes the claw hammer from your life for ever?

Eventually the rain slowed and Doi and Vijay hurried back to work through a light drizzle, while trying to avoid the gushing spouts of the overhead drains.

Their office was on the third floor. A narrow staircase rose through the middle of the building, and then *Translations — Detective* was the first door on the right-hand side. A couple of *katoey* masseurs worked in the two rooms on the left. Between their two doors was a row of chairs for clients to wait. The other room on the right now sat unused. The accountant who'd occupied it had moved back to Chiang Mai to care for his ailing mother. When he left, Vijay had only been a translator. Edwin and the fake sapphires had still lain in his future, and when that future had arrived, Vijay had had mixed feelings about the change to his building sign. On the one hand, "Detective" seemed to soil the business purity of "Translations". And yet, returning to the office after lunch, he couldn't help looking up at the sign from the Ban Mor intersection and imagining exciting things happening to him. Not the mundane work of spousal surveillance, but a beautiful woman stalking into the room and asking for his help.

Of course, it never happened that way. Not that some of his clients couldn't have been attractive in other circumstances, but they never were when they turned up in the office. Hunched over by suspicion, riddled with sadness . . . You can't ask a stranger to follow your partner without feeling you've already failed at life. The repainted sign never had ushered any glamour into Vijay's office.

Until now.

She was sitting in one of *pii* Haan's chairs and looked unlike any client either of the masseurs had ever had. Probably in her mid-twenties, a tight canary-yellow skirt that finished just above her knees, a black silk sleeveless top, gold at her ears and around her wrist, high expensive-looking heels and a heart-shaped face full of the imperious knowledge of her own beauty. Her hands were on the crook of a white, rolled-up umbrella that was dripping onto the wooden floor. As Vijay came level with her, she said, "Translations — Detective? Is that you?" She looked amused at the thought of it.

He said it was and ushered her into the office.

She took a queenly survey of the room but didn't appear too disappointed. Swivelling on her heels, she said to Doi, "And you are?"

"My assistant," Vijay replied. "You can say anything you would to me in front of her." Doi was in her usual outfit of shorts with cargo pockets and baggy T-shirt. She met the woman's gaze with indifference while settling herself behind her computer. She wasn't going to pay this hundred-watt beauty the compliment of attention.

Vijay took a seat behind his own desk and gestured to the chair in front of it. She sat and crossed her legs.

"So are you looking for translation or detective work? My name's Vijay, by the way."

Something about the way she received that made him think it was information she already had.

"I'm Ploy. And I'm here for the second one."

Behind her, Vijay could see Doi waiting, chin in hand, for him to explain they were already busy with a case. "What can we help you with?" he said.

"I want someone found. It's a man. He'd be in his mid-sixties by now. The name is Bundit — Bundit Pacharachoen."

He pushed a pad of paper across the desk for her to write it in Thai. Doi mouthed the word, "What?"

"But he could be going under something else," Ploy said. "He changed it often, even went as Na Nakhon one time. The nickname was Gai though. He usually kept that."

"And why are you looking for this guy?"

"What are you doing?" Doi mouthed at Vijay. He ignored it and brought his attention back to Ploy.

"He cheated someone I know out of a lot of money."

"And who is this someone? Can I speak to them?" Now Doi seemed to be mouthing, "Chop."

"That won't be possible. She doesn't want him found herself. She doesn't even know I'm doing this."

Vijay realised it was "Stop" that Doi was saying. "So, what are the details of the con?"

"A fake land certificate. He cooked up the whole thing with someone in the land office at Rayong. They made her think she was getting a piece of beachfront real estate. She sunk all her savings into it, was going to build a small guest house, and then discovered she'd never owned the land to begin with. It was government property."

Doi had gone on to: "Me have a gate."

"When did this happen?" Vijay asked. "And what's the woman's name?"

"Sometime in 2003. And I can't tell you that, either."

"Look, I won't go and talk to her if you don't want me to, but it will help me to get the facts. I have friends in the police force. I can possibly go through their channels if I know who she is."

"But I've given you his name."

"Got it!" *We have a case.*

She leaned forwards. "Yes?"

"Sorry, I was thinking of something else." Vijay wondered if there was any way he could get Doi to either stop distracting him or mouth her words more clearly. "Would I be right in thinking this is not the only scam this man's ever been involved in?" he said. "I mean, Na Nakhon? He was passing himself off as being descended from royalty?"

She gave a thin, tight smile. "There's probably quite a lot in his past."

"In which case, he will probably have used a number of different aliases. People like this know how to make themselves hard to trace."

"There you are then. Knowing who she is won't help anyway." She swivelled in her seat to look at Doi. "Are you all right?" To Vijay: "Is she all right? That cough sounds quite bad."

Doi said, "I'm trying to do something about it."

"Well let's just accept it's not working," Vijay said.

She began rustling around in her desk at that and then started slamming each of the drawers.

"If this woman doesn't want him found, then what's it to you? And are we talking about your mother, by any chance?"

"We're not related. I just think it's wrong, that's all. For him to disappear from her life like that. The fact is, when the victim is small, no one gets called to account for their crimes."

And she's willing to hire me just on that point of principle? Vijay thought. The question was given dramatic impact by Doi slamming another drawer.

When it came to a fee for this act of apparent altruism, Vijay decided, *What the hell.* Kritisak might like the idea of being friends with an employee of Khun Pleum, but if Vijay missed his next payment, that novelty was going to wear off. And anyway, Ploy looked as though she could afford it. He gave her Khun Pleum's rate, asked for a week in advance, and she agreed without demur.

After she'd gone, Doi said, "Vijay, how are you going to do both of these jobs?"

"I'll multitask. That's how it is in business sometimes, you have to diversify your functionalities."

"*Hmph.* Just because she looks the way she does. It's the only reason."

And that, thought Vijay, was the perfect alibi. "Okay, so I may have noticed her looks. But I can assure you, they had nothing to do with it."

Doi gave a long, theatrical sigh. "Men. Only have space in their heads for one thing."

* * *

Doi's objection to his taking on two cases reminded Vijay he actually had three cases, and hadn't yet done anything on the second. So, come late afternoon he asked Doi if she wanted any iced dessert (no: still in a huff) and went out to make a phone call. He then decided he wanted some anyway. There was a drinks stall around the corner from their building with a couple of folding metal tables in front of it. Here, *pii* Mo made the traditional Thai iced sweet black coffee called *oleang*, along with tea, hot chocolate, and also bowls of shaved iced doused in syrup and condensed milk. Vijay paid for a bowl and took a seat at one of the tables.

Before he'd left her, Supaporn had filled him in on her husband's movements. It turned out the family compound in Samut Sakhon wasn't used much anymore. Khun Pleum needed to be closer to the country's centres of power, and Supaporn needed the better-quality shopping experience that only Bangkok could provide. Plus, their three children had attended private schools in the capital. The real family home had become a place off the Rama III Road. It was a mansion, the way she'd described it, and had been designed according to her impeccable taste. She'd picked out the statues for the garden, decided on the shape of the swimming pool, had the banyan and teak trees planted. But it wasn't central enough for Khun Pleum, so they also had a penthouse apartment on Tonglor, off Sukhumvit Road, a short drive from the headquarters of his construction company. He spent a good deal of time there alone, as she needed her statues and teak trees. ("I'm a person who is close to nature," she'd told Vijay, somewhat unconvincingly.) In the novel, this penthouse flat was how Khun L had managed to have his affair.

For surveillance of this kind, there was a motorbike taxi guy Vijay always used. Following one car with another in the city centre was a nightmare, but a motorbike could slip through the gridlock. And no one ever really noticed the faces of motorbike taxi riders, for some strange reason. Donning a fluorescent orange vest made you anonymous.

Tong was willing to do the work for 1,000 baht a day, and Vijay had found him to be both clever and reliable. He phoned and gave the man descriptions of Khun Pleum's cars: a grey Bentley with the registration "KP 1" and an E-type Jaguar in racing green with the plate "KP 2". "No problem," Tong said. "So easy to spot."

"He's got good taste, hasn't he?" Vijay was sitting with his ankle resting on his knee, mushing up the last of the ice and syrup in the polystyrene bowl, and staring down the road. Oddly enough, a fairly impressive car was inching through the Chinatown traffic towards him, a vintage cream Mercedes with ebony-tinted windows. Edging past a lottery seller on a bicycle and a shirtless guy wheeling a pallet of vermicelli boxes along the gutter, the Merc made Vijay think of a dowager in sunglasses, picking her way past the hoi polloi.

After he finished the call, he put Khun Pleum's full name into Google images, downloaded a couple of up-to-date pictures and emailed them to Tong, just in case he didn't know what his target looked like. By now, the Mercedes had reached *pii* Mo's stall. The hazard lights came on and the car stopped dead, the driver not even bothering to pull up to the kerb. Behind him, a racket of horns began.

A chunky guy in a black suit and black tie stepped out of the driver's side door and glanced at the tailback he'd caused with indifference. He came round to stand in front of Vijay. "My boss wants to have a chat with you."

"And your boss would be who?"

"Get in the car and find out."

People were now trying to drive round the Mercedes, horns still blaring in frustration.

"My mother warned me about getting into cars with strange men."

Still with his back to the road, the man put his hands on his hips, which had the effect of pushing his jacket back far enough to reveal the handgun slotted snugly into the concealed carry holster inside the waistband of his trousers.

"Oh, come on," Vijay said. "You're not going to shoot me here in front of this many witnesses. Everyone in that lane is looking at you right now."

"It doesn't have to be today. Or tomorrow for that matter. But my boss isn't someone to disrespect, and you don't want to spend the rest of your life looking over your shoulder for me. Do you?"

This, Vijay considered, was a fair point. He got into the car.

There was an arctic level of air conditioning and, in the back seat next to Vijay, a farmer in his sixties. The farmer said, "Just keep going." Peering out at a Chinatown darkened by his tinted windows — the weaving motorbikes and the roadside clothes stalls and the gun shops — he added, "We're not going to get far anyway."

As the man gave the instructions, Vijay revised his impression. The blue top might have been cut like a farmer's work shirt, but the soft folds and shine of the material showed it was silk. The jeans were good quality, and on one wrist was a slim Omega. The man had thick, corded forearms though, and dark skin. You could almost believe he'd been a farmer once, and had retired after great success. With his solid, square face, firm jaw and a downward slash of mouth and white hair cut bristle short, he looked like a farmer who'd come out of the sun and put his money to work.

"Hello, Vijay," he said. "You won't know who I am. People don't."

"That's a relief, then. I wouldn't like to think I was missing out."

It didn't get a rise out of him. Staring out of the window, he said, "It used to be when people found out about me it was too late. But that was a long time ago." He turned back to Vijay. "Too late for them, I mean."

Vijay waited.

"Let me ask you something," the man said. "Do you believe in luck? Do you think luck has played much of a part in you getting to where you are now?"

Over the man's shoulder, Vijay could see the brownstone of the Old Siam Plaza, tinted midnight black. "I suppose some odd coincidences have played their part." After all, it was meeting Mana in England during his student days that had brought him to Thailand.

"Luck has been central to my life." The man patted the cream leather seat next to him. "This car, my nice house, my beautiful wife — all just luck."

"I'm so happy for you."

He continued as though not having heard the reply. "All I had to do to get these things was provide a certain basic level of loyalty. And that has never been difficult. You could say loyalty is one of my skills." He gave Vijay a look to see how that was being taken, and then said, "Loyalty to Khun Pleum."

"Right," Vijay said, for the sake of saying something.

"I happened to live in a particular street in Samut Sakhon at a particular time. I happened to have Pleum for a friend. You can see what I mean?"

"I think so."

"We were almost the same age. I left school at eleven, went to work in the fish market with my father. And if it wasn't for Pleum, I'd still be there now. Getting up at three a.m. every day, going down to the port, waiting for the boats to come in. I wasn't an ambitious person, you see. But I had a friend I was loyal to, and his ambition put me in this car." He rubbed the seat again, as though to remind himself it was real. "He had the ideas, I had the muscle. And when the time came, he convinced Sia Heng to take me on. Because Pleum knew he would need someone whose first loyalty was to him rather than to the organisation. And I've always been that person. The one he could confide in, the one who would do anything for him." He opened his palms. "You see?"

"Got it," said Vijay. "You hitched a ride on a shooting star."

The man nodded. "A shooting star. Yes, that's good. I'm telling you all this just so you understand me. I know why you've been hired, you see. I know about this trashy book. I know about the writer who got shot." For one golden moment, Vijay wondered if he was going to confess to having shot the man himself. Instead he said, "Are you married?"

"Nope."

"When you marry, you'll find your wife expects you to provide her with a certain level of comfort." He was watching Vijay in a way that seemed neither friendly nor unfriendly, but consisted of a level of concentrated stillness. It was the gaze of a sniper focusing down a sight. "Mai, for instance. My wife. She's discovered something called aromatherapy. Do you understand aromatherapy?"

Vijay couldn't imagine the man giving a damn whether he understood it or not. But there didn't seem to be anything to do except play along. "It's some business with oils that smell nice."

"She tells me she needs this thing in her life. And so I pay. And she gets her aromas, and they do whatever they do. And then she goes for lunch, and there you are talking to Pleum's wife. About what, may I ask?"

Thinking about it afterwards, Vijay wasn't sure if he'd hesitated or not. It was on the tip of his tongue to tell the man to go and ask Supaporn himself. But just before he said it, instinct told him bluster was the wrong tactic. "It was an odd sort of conversation, to be honest with you," he replied. "She might have wanted something from me, but if so, I'm not sure what." He paused, but got nothing back in either words or expression. "Basically, she wanted to tell me how she met her husband. But you must know that story, right? The bicycle with the puncture?" It was like dropping coins into a deep well and not hearing the splash. "That was all, really. She wanted me to know that about her. Wanted me to know how long they'd been together. Oh, and she told me how she gave him his start in life."

The man snorted. "That's rubbish."

"I'm not making this up. She said she pawned some of her jewellery—"

"I know the story, Vijay, I was selling those lottery tickets. I mean that it's rubbish he needed her help. A man like Pleum — do you think he wouldn't have got into Sia Heng's organisation some other way?"

"I suppose it's possible."

"Of course it is. We both owe him all of our good luck."

"Though she comes from a rich family, right? She had her own *yai.*"

He gave that a look of contempt. "Her family managed a petrol station, that's all. They were rich by the standards of Samut Sakhon in the 1960s. Have you seen the house off Rama III?"

Vijay shook his head.

"That's not a life she was born to. In spite of whatever she's convinced herself."

They'd reached the corner of the Old Siam and were turning right, circling the building. With perfect timing, a man with a wooden tray of state lottery tickets hung from his shoulders was waiting to cross. He was the dutiful, legal version of Khun Pleum's road to success. From what Vijay knew of such things, he would have paid the lottery commission around 35,000 baht for his pallet of tickets, which meant he probably wouldn't make more than a five-baht profit on each one.

The car swung right and their tinted, air-conditioned cabin left the ticket-seller and his impoverished, honest path behind.

"She also wanted to tell me how different he was from the way he is now. 'Hungrier' was the way she put it," Vijay said.

That raised a brief, genuine smile. "In those days if you had touched Pleum's body with a light bulb, it would have lit up. Some people are more alive than others, have you noticed? And he was the most alive person I ever knew." He sat back and stared out of the window. Vijay assumed they'd finished, but then the man said, "Do you think it's possible she wanted to ask you something, but in the end couldn't bring herself to?"

Vijay thought, *Nice try, but I'm not biting the worm on the end of that hook.* Because surely this man had read *Jao Por*

62

by now. Perhaps he even knew who this *mia noi* was. "That doesn't make much sense," he said. "I'm one of her husband's employees. She can ask me anything she likes." He met the man's gaze with what he hoped was a blank look. He thought of how he'd once read that most communication was non-verbal. He wondered how much he'd already given away.

"So she called you all the way over from Chinatown just to tell you some stories about her marriage?"

"I got the feeling — and I don't in any way mean this as a criticism — but I got the feeling she's quite used to summoning people into her presence, irrespective of where they happen to be."

The man stared some more. "The thing to remember, Vijay, is that Supaporn and I are the people who care about Pleum the most." He grimaced. "More than his children, even. But we've helped him in different parts of his life."

He brought out his wallet and extracted a business card. The name on the card was Somchai Charoensawat. It was one of those things you noticed about Thai men of a certain age — they all seemed to be Somchais or Somsaks. "My nickname is Ton. I'm a good person to talk to, Vijay. In my younger days, you could say I talked to people for a living. And Pleum trusted that. He trusted the information I came away with. You might want to talk to me, when the time comes."

Somchai looked out of the window. "You can walk from here, can't you? We haven't gone far."

CHAPTER 5

The next morning, Vijay found himself awake before the alarm. Lying back on the sleeping mat, he took in the fact that there was no light at the edges of the curtains. His phone screen said five thirty-five a.m.

It must have rained during the night because the temperature had dropped and the breeze from the fan was nearly cool. With his hands under his head, Vijay stared up at the ceiling and considered his life.

His philosophy of work had always been that the nearest problem was the only one to bother with. Further worries could be ignored until they came closer. It was a strategy that had worked well for him — if you ignored certain credit-based disagreements with the Thai banking system. And right now, the nearest problem was clearly Lek and the claw hammer. But Vijay couldn't quite lose sight of Khun Pleum. It wasn't just the man's power, or the possible existence of his *mia noi*, but the thought of where Khun Pleum had come from and how he had arrived. "His hunger," Supaporn had said. Scratch the urbane gent in the cigar bar, and the hunger would still be there. After all those decades, it would still make him capable of anything.

He decided that if he was up, he may as well be awake at the office. His one-room flat was only a short drive away. It was possible to go down to the food cart at the bottom of his block, have a breakfast of crisp, newly fried *pa tong go*, and still be in before seven thirty.

Doi had left him a printout of everything she'd done. Vijay set to work, and considered the possibility of never finding Montri's shooter, while simultaneously doing such a good job on the book that an English-language copy found its way onto the shelves at Kinokuniya. *Translated by Vijay Mistry*. There was an outcome to fill Khun Pleum with joy.

He finished a quick grammatical edit of Doi's writing and began pondering how to change Montri's tone. Stuck for ideas, he left the work and did a Google search.

By the time Doi came in, Vijay was sitting back with his feet up on an open drawer, hands behind his head, staring at the opposite wall.

She said, "You're here early."

"I've just realised what's been bothering me about Montri's shooting. It's the wrong kind of threat."

Doi took a carton of iced tea from the fridge. "So what's wrong with it?" She held the carton up. "You want some?"

He shook his head. "I don't mean the shooting itself, I mean the way it escalated. First the bullet with his name, then the shots into the side of the house, then into his leg. An increasingly strong message. As though someone was saying, 'cease and desist'. Except there was nothing to desist *from*. The book was already written. It was already out there. If they wanted to teach him a lesson, why not shoot him in the leg to begin with?"

Doi brought her glass back and settled herself behind her desk. "To create fear. It's not just teaching him a lesson, they want to make him afraid."

"Then why not carry on? Why not send him another bullet in the post and make him fear he's about to get one in the other leg?"

"Because now the police are investigating. So it's more difficult for them. People on the island are looking about more."

"Yeah, maybe. Though this feels like something that really should be happening to the publisher, who is, by the way, an out-and-out rogue: 'Stop publishing this book or something worse happens.'"

"Maybe he *was* threatened and he's been keeping quiet. He doesn't want to scare away other writers."

"It's possible." Vijay told Doi about the Google search he'd just done. "Real publishers only pay ten per cent royalties. Somsak paying fifty is actually a huge red flag. He's not making his money by selling books, he's making it from authors paying for his so-called marketing packages." He thought of Montri and Aim in their old wooden house and Aim's job at what seemed to be an advertising start-up. There was a story to be told about their finances.

Vijay and Doi worked steadily through the morning. It was always the most efficient time of the day — the sun was on the other side of the building. As noon approached, he told Doi he was going to be having lunch with Mana in a restaurant in Chinatown. "I feel I owe him a meal."

"And you want something from him," said Doi.

* * *

"And you want something from me," said Mana, digging white crab flesh out of a shell with his fingers. He was roughly the same age as Vijay and had changed very little in all the time they'd known each other. The thick, precisely trimmed moustache, the short side-parted hair, the guarded brown eyes had all been present in their student days in Bristol, and had the effect of making Mana seem older and more mature than the rest of their drinking group. And unlike them, Mana had a plan. He was going to take his BA in Business Studies back to Ratchaburi and organise his family's fish sauce company on modern, Western lines. That was, after all, the reason his parents had stumped up the extortionate international-rate tuition fees to send him to Bristol in the first place.

Vijay envied him with his ready-made entry into the world of business. Less than one year of a Chemistry degree had been enough to show Vijay that lab work wasn't for him. He was meant to make deals, to read the room. But having failed to get onto any graduate training schemes, he had wound up working for Bristol City Council.

He and Mana had promised to keep in touch. Vijay had looked forward to hearing about the kind of life he'd wanted for himself. But instead, Mana's first email was all about how being a businessman was the wrong life. Too many fishy people, too many fake personalities. "I sit across the table from these characters in the provincial government, and watch their faces getting red from the whiskey I'm paying for, and I think, 'You should be in prison.'" At the time, Vijay took that as one of Mana's typically abrupt judgements of the world, but no. His next email came with a photo attached: Mana looking as serious as possible, in a brown uniform and cap.

His family had been furious, and it had taken Mana the nearly fourteen years Vijay had been in Thailand to work his way back into their good books, helped, slightly, by the fact that he'd made a "good" marriage to a woman his mother approved of.

They were in the Yung Fo Seafood Restaurant, five floors above the noise and fury of Yaowarat Road. It was a room of imperial red wallpaper and lacquered wooden ceiling fans. Waiters replenished their glasses of iced water from cloth-wrapped metal jugs. Vijay helped himself to some more fried rice and took another prawn fried in chilli and garlic. "This is really just a thanks for all the help," he said. He wondered if he could put the meal on expenses. It was undeniably an expense. "Though yeah, there is something you can do for me."

"You see?" Mana held up the shell he'd just evacuated. "People see me in my uniform, talking to someone like you in a place like this, and you know what they think? They think you're bribing me. And you know what's funny? I must be the only cop in Chinatown who's never taken a bribe." He put the shell down. "Other than from you. In places like this."

"Oh come on, this is just shellfish. You can't say bribe when it's shellfish. I'm thanking you is all I'm doing."

"Well don't thank me yet, I haven't agreed to anything."

Vijay brought out a folded sheet of paper with Bundit's full name on it. "I just want to find out about this guy. He will probably have a criminal record. For instance, he was actually calling himself Na Nakhon at one point. He must have done some jail time for that."

"How does this relate to Khun Pleum?"

"It doesn't."

"What — you've solved that case?"

"Not yet, I'm multitasking. That's the key thing in business, you have to stay agile."

Across the table, Mana gave Vijay a long weighty, stare. "Have you got money troubles?"

"No, of course not. Khun Pleum's actually paying me twice my normal rate. In fact, right now, twice my normal rate *is* my normal rate." Sensing a certain degree of scepticism, Vijay added, "Though I haven't actually got that far on who the shooter is," and then described why he thought it was the wrong kind of threat.

Mana sipped some water. "Doi could be right. Give him some fear then give him some pain. That's his lesson."

"Except it looks as though the girlfriend is more worried than he is."

"Of course it does. He's a guy. He doesn't want to show fear in front of her."

Vijay's phone was sitting next to his plate, and now it pinged with an SMS message from Tong.

KP buying necklace!!

Vijay had told him to only communicate by SMS, as he didn't want to get into awkward conversations about the mistress when Doi was present. He texted back, *Promising!*, then said to Mana, "I don't think Montri is that kind of guy."

Mana peered at the phone. "Is KP Khun Pleum? What does his buying a necklace have to do with anything? And who's sending this?"

"I asked Tong to follow him. Any information is good at this point."

"So what's promising about him buying a necklace?"

"I'm giving positive feedback to someone who works for me. Don't they give you management training in the police force?"

Mana gave that another long look. "Why do I think you reckon you've come up with some other good idea?"

"All my ideas are good."

He pointed to his plate. "It's this crab that's good. Your ideas, I'm not so sure."

* * *

Doi and Vijay worked on through the afternoon. The shadow of the venetian blinds stretched across the walls then disappeared as the rain clouds hovered in. Vijay crossed out everything he'd written and decided a hard-boiled thriller writing style would be better. Short sentences. Punchy. It's crime. In the real world.

Doi asked, "So how's Mana?"

"He's a cop. In Chinatown. Eating crab because losers choose fish."

"Vijay, *what*?"

"I'm trying to get a more crime-writing voice. What d'you think?"

"I think you don't need to try so hard. It's just a cover story, remember? They're not even paying us that much."

She was right, Vijay thought. Out of all the jobs he had on his plate, the *Jao Por* translation was bringing in the least

69

money. And yet, having sold Montri on his fake enthusiasm, it had now become real. The dangerous part of working on the novel was that underneath the overblown prose lay a great story. A fatherless thirteen-year-old boy sells underground lottery tickets to the men whose bicycles he fixes. And from there, after who knew how many beatings and deaths, to Khun Pleum's brandy-and-cigar chats with government ministers. It was, thought Vijay, a mark of how badly the thing had been written that no real publisher wanted a tale this compelling.

The thought of a "real" publisher led Vijay to pondering Somsak. What if the man was a route to discovering the source of Montri's funding? It occurred to Vijay that he'd taken the wrong tack. There could be leverage in translating Montri's book into English. He could tell Somsak he now had influence over the choice of publisher. Or why not lose the fake innocence altogether and come at him as one conman to another?

He picked up his phone and dialled. "Khun Somsak, it's me, Vijay."

"Of course. You've thought about the packages. You want to let us help you. I can see the book, Vijay. I'm sitting here picturing it."

"Actually, I was phoning about Montri Tongta's book, *Jao Por.*"

"You don't have to worry about that. It's nothing, a flesh wound. You're not going to let someone else's flesh wound stand in the way of your vision?"

"The fact is I'm putting my vision on hold for a bit. Montri has hired me as a translator. I didn't mention that, did I? I also do Thai to English translation, and now I've landed this project."

"So why are you phoning me?" Somsak's voice had become guarded. Vijay looked out between the slats of the venetian blinds to Chinatown under the grey light of the rainy season, where there always seemed to be more grime on the buildings, more dirt in the gutters.

"Well, once it's done, we'll have to think of what to do with the manuscript. He's not happy, Khun Somsak. Not happy with your lack of marketing. But then, I don't suppose anyone ever has been."

"Of course not. They don't buy the Celestial and then they're filled with regret. I don't want that. I don't want people to be filled with regret."

"He won't be buying any package if I don't talk him into it."

"That's good, Vijay. You can do that, can't you?"

"Probably, but I'm going to need a reason. Fifty per cent off the package, for example, would be a reason that worked."

A chuckle came down the phone line. "Now why would I offer you that?"

"To stop me from sending him to a different publisher, of course. A real one. Which I'd quite like to do anyway, as I think there is genuinely some money to be made from this story."

Another chuckle. Vijay couldn't seem to get the man out of "genial uncle" mode. "I am a real publisher. I've been one for a long time, and I know all about this business. For example, I know how to draft a binding contract. Montri signed over the rights to any and all future translations."

He would have, wouldn't he? "But that's only for this book, Khun Somsak. Don't you want others? Montri's writing another one now. A more literary work. He's not happy about how you've promoted *Jao Por*, but I can make him listen to me. I'm your man on the inside."

"So you say."

"If I get him to sign on for another package, then you'll know it's true. I bet that doesn't happen very often, does it? Writers coming back to you a second time? That's the problem with this business model, you always need fresh blood."

"It takes a particular kind of person to do my kind of work, Vijay. I've talked to you already and I don't know if you've got the skills." And then in an odd moment of honesty, he added, "Or if you realise what it's going to do to you."

"Then teach me, Khun Somsak. Show me the right line to take with these people. And as for what the job does to me, you can leave me to worry about that." He waited. Silence. "Look, I know it sounds like I'm trying to muscle in on something you've got running perfectly well yourself, but if I can get you return authors, that's a win for both of us. And if I can't, then you haven't lost anything anyway."

Finally, Somsak replied, in a voice that sounded strangely tired, "It might be something."

"Of course it is. You give me the name, I go and see them, tell them I found their book, which, by the way, will prove your promotion package is working. Then I say it's ideal for a foreign readership and give them a reduced version of my rates. Basically, everything I did with Montri."

After a pause, a serious Somsak said, "We could talk about this. You could come and see me and we could talk."

"Just give me a time."

"I'm in my car at the moment. You could . . . you could see me at home."

"Where's that?"

He reeled off an address in the north of the city — a *moo baan* called Kunali off Phahonyothin Road. "Vijay, one more thing. Was there ever really a book? When you came to see me?"

"It was a true story. The bronzes and the blackmail and everything."

Somsak gave out a papery sigh and cut the line.

Doi had stopped work and was watching him.

"I'd better leave right now," Vijay said. "This is going to take me straight into rush hour."

"You're not really going to do this, are you? About these writers?"

"God no, it's just a cover story to go and see him again. You don't think I'm that bad, do you?"

Doi gave a long, thoughtful pause and then said, "No."

"But what?"

72

"You've been talking a lot about money lately. I just thought . . . maybe there's a problem."

"Definitely not, we're fine. Robust, in fact. And Khun Pleum's paying me twice my normal rate, remember?"

"Hmm," said Doi, and went back to her translating.

* * *

Bangkok rush hour was the slow death of hope, as always. Vijay inched along in second gear under the low black lid of the sky and at some point the quick tropical night fell. Above the rumble of the pickup's engine, he could hear the muffled boom of thunder. Dark clouds were thrown into sudden, dramatic relief as the lightning backlit them. Below the height of the expressway, diamond-white trails of light snaked away in permanent gridlock.

When he made it off, things were initially no better, but the traffic gradually thinned and skyscrapers and malls were replaced with shop-houses separated by dark gaps of wasteland. Vijay was on Phahonyothin Road looking out for *soi* 126 when his phone went. He checked the number and said, "Khun Somsak, I'm just coming. The traffic's been really bad."

"I used to be a real publisher, did you know that?"

"I had no idea."

"You thought I was always this conman type of person?"

"Well, I wouldn't go that far. I mean, there's no need to put yourself down." Vijay didn't want to drive all the way across Bangkok just to find Somsak had evolved a conscience.

"My father left me a lot of money, you see. And I created S & K Books. Both are me, by the way. In case you were wondering. Som-*sak*, the beginning and the end. The who-ole thing."

"Khun Somsak, are you drinking right now? Not that there's anything wrong with that." In fact, he thought, it might be useful, provided Somsak wasn't under the table by the time he arrived.

73

"It's not easy for a small independent publisher. Not so many people in Thailand read books, but ever-*ry*body thinks they can write one."

"Sure, I understand." At that moment, the sky broke open. Vijay turned the wipers to full speed and that still wasn't enough. The rain was slamming down so fast the view beyond the windscreen had dissolved into blurred streaks of light. Meanwhile, he was steering with one hand while the other pressed the phone to his ear. "Khun Somsak, are there any landmarks near your *soi*? Is there something I should look out for?"

"The first marketing package was for a real book. I believed in it, he believed in it. But it was very experimental, you know?"

"I think I'm seeing . . . a petrol station, Khun Somsak. It might be an Esso, is that any good?"

"You know *Ulysses*, Vijay?"

"Not personally. There's some kind of pub thing now, looks like. I think it says Cow . . . Cowboy, something in English. Does that ring any bells?"

"It was going to be like that. A Thai *Ulysses*, but I didn't have enough money to promote it. And so he put up his own cash and I told him, 'I'll give you more royalties for this.'"

"I'm going to have to ring off, Khun Somsak. I need to concentrate on the street."

"The fact is, the Thai people weren't ready for Thai *Ulysses*. And you know what? After that, he quit fiction, ended up going into PR. By now he's probably got a wife, a kid and a Toyota Fortuner. But what about me, what have I got?"

"I'd love to hear what you've got, Khun Somsak. Tell you what, why don't you pour me out a glass of whatever you're having, but maybe don't have any more of it yourself until I get there?"

"You know, I don't even read the manuscripts anymore. I'm scared I'll find a good one. I don't want to do this to someone who can write."

"That's great, Khun Somsak. I'm going to ring off now."
He went back to peering at the street. A blue sign reading
soi 122 appeared and dissolved and reappeared to the beat of
the wipers. Vijay counted out the next two turnings and then
went in without seeing anything for 126.

It was a narrow lane and he bumped the pickup down it
wondering if he'd turned in too early. It could just be a sub-
soi of 122 after all. But then on the right was a high archway
with Kunali written on it. Vijay swung in and the guard in
the wooden hut raised the barrier without bothering to come
out and ask for an ID card.

Inside the *moo baan*, the drains had already blocked up
and the water in the lanes looked to be ankle height. Vijay
drove slowly, searching for *soi* eight, and noted they were all
large houses set back from spacious gardens. He wondered if
this had come from the money Somsak's father had left, or
was the writer-scamming business really so good?

His phone went again.

"Khun Somsak, I'm in the *moo baan* now, just on the
way to your *soi*."

"You just get here, Vijay, and I'll tell you what this job is
like. I'll tell you what it's going to do to you. I'll tell you how
it's going to feel in ten years' time when you wake up and lie
there staring at the ceiling because you can't make yourself
get out of bed anymore."

He ended the call before Vijay could ask for directions.
The *moo baan* hadn't been built in anything as simple as a
grid. Instead, sub-*sois* wound into one another in ways that
made no sense. For instance, *soi* 6/3 brought Vijay out into
soi 7/2. He considered calling Somsak back but didn't want
to get into a long, involved conversation. Plus, he was loath
to waste this alcohol-soaked, rueful mood on house directions. There was so much better information to get out of
him.

After going past the same jackfruit tree twice, Vijay realised there was actually a right turn just beyond it. A lightning
flash illuminated a sign reading *Soi 8* and somewhere ahead

of him, a car revved furiously and screeched away into the rainy night.

As he pulled up in front of Somsak's house, the thunder cracked and a next-door dog howled in response. Incredibly, the storm was getting stronger. Vijay cut the engine, steeled himself, then got out and splashed across to ring the bell above Somsak's house number. Being out of the pickup was like standing under a shower head. He tugged on the metal gate, found it wasn't padlocked and rattled it back.

Another flash threw the garden into relief — large old trees and a flagstone path winding through the grass. He ran to the shelter of the porch, rapped on a sliding glass patio door and called Somsak's name. No reply.

Vijay peered into a large, dark front room and considered going back out and ringing the bell again. *What the hell*, he thought. He tried the door. It slid open.

He stepped in, dripping onto the parquet floor, and called, "Khun Somsak, it's me, Vijay." A thunder crack swallowed the second half of that, so he called again and waited. Still nothing. He made his way through the dark room, calling. Lightning flashed a crooked shadow of a tree onto the wall. He passed the humped shapes of a sofa and an armchair, bumped his shin on the edge of a coffee table, then went right and found himself in a dark kitchen. He switched the light on and considered making the strong coffee Somsak would surely need. Then he decided he ought to find him first. He came back out, passed through the unlit living room and went on.

There was an archway here, then stairs and beyond them, a closed door with a wedge of light under it. Vijay knocked, called out Somsak's name and swung the door open.

There he was, passed out at his desk. Vijay had a moment of déjà vu and realised he was looking at the scene from the website photo, the brass table lamp, the bookshelves behind him. So Somsak wasn't wholly fake after all. And then as Vijay came closer, he thought, *Not "wasn't" but "hadn't been"*. Because now he could see the deep red stain in the back of his sky-blue linen shirt and the blood seeping out from under his body and dripping over the edge of the polished rosewood onto the parquet floor.

Vijay's trembling fingers searched uselessly for a pulse in the man's neck. His first confused thought was that he'd arrived too late to stop Somsak from killing himself. He should have said something encouraging down the phone. But for a suicide, there would have to be a gun in one hand, or dropped on the floor at least, and here there was nothing but the awful red wound with its black centre and Somsak's dead body.

Overhead came a crack of thunder, as though something gigantic in the sky had been irrevocably broken.

CHAPTER 6

"So nothing was locked, is what you're saying. Not the gate, not the house?"

The questioner was a Lieutenant Colonel Apichart, according to the triangular plastic sign on his desk. It was just past ten p.m. and Vijay was in the man's office. He was giving his story for the second time, but there was a guarded politeness about the whole procedure. After phoning the police, Vijay had phoned Mana. He outranked Apichart, though not his boss. ("My boss is . . . unavailable," Apichart had said, and his face had twitched.) After having his fingerprints taken, Vijay had been brought a mug of Nescafé and a towel for his hair. Meanwhile, for now, Apichart was keeping his accusations in check.

"It was all open," Vijay told him. "But then the killer had just left."

"That's what you said," Apichart reminded him. "A killer had left." He was probably in his mid-thirties, with a receding hairline above a narrow face and cheekbones so prominent it seemed he wasn't eating enough. He performed a minute adjustment to the position of the pad on his desk. Here in his office order was going to prevail, never mind the world's chaos. "But of course we don't really know that." He paused. "The killer could have still been in the house. Or did you look around?"

The pause, Vijay thought, was for them both to register the possibility of the killer being him. Mana's rank would keep Vijay from manufactured trouble he'd have to pay his way out of, but it wasn't going to absolve him of suspicion.

"I looked around his office a bit. And the living room. But I didn't go upstairs and I didn't touch anything."

"You looked — why?"

"Curiosity. I mean, he'd just been killed."

"And you were there to talk about a book? Was he going to publish a book you'd written?"

"Not written as yet — thinking of."

"So why were you doing that at his house? Why not see him at work?"

"I already had. We talked about the process, including the marketing costs he wanted. When I thought about them some more, it sounded like a scam, so I phoned again. He said he was in his car, on the way home and that I should come and see him. Discuss the whole thing."

"What were these marketing costs?"

Deciding he'd probably find out anyway, Vijay gave him the details of the Exclusive, Royal and Celestial. Apichart snorted. "And you didn't know it was a scam to start with? What kind of private detective are you?"

"A part-time one. Most of my work is translating, the rest tends to be cheating spouses."

He nodded. "You're a translator and he's a publisher. You have more of a connection that way."

"His books are all in Thai."

"And you drove all the way up here from Chinatown, instead of waiting till tomorrow to see him at Makkasan Junction."

"I liked the idea of meeting him at home. I thought away from the office, I might get some truth out of him."

Apichart made an adjustment to the pen above his pad. Vijay was starting to think he didn't use either of those items but, like a Zen stone garden, they existed purely for his con-templation. "That's why I wouldn't expect him to invite you to his home," Apichart said. "That kind of person. They want to keep a distance, a front."

"There was the car I heard, remember?"

"But didn't see. And no one else in the *moo baan* saw it either. So that's not helping me." He pursed his lips and took a long look at Vijay. "Okay. You can go. But you might have to come back." In the tone of describing an outcome neither of them wanted, he said, "You might have to talk to my boss."

* * *

The next morning, the clouds had gone and the sun was beating in. Vijay was woken at seven by his mobile bleating next to his pillow.

"Vijay, turn on the TV."

"Doi? I don't have one, remember?"

"Guess what happened to the publisher?"

"He's dead, I know. I'll tell you about it when I get in."

He drove to work thinking about Somsak. In fact, he had gone upstairs at Somsak's house, and considered it per-fectly reasonable under the circumstances. Before phoning the police, he'd snooped around the whole place, taking pic-tures. He'd used a towel from the downstairs bathroom to wipe up the water he was dripping and to open door and wardrobe handles.

He hadn't learned very much, other than that Somsak lived alone and didn't have people staying over very often: his two spare bedrooms were used for storage. One contained a running machine with a film of grey dust on the running belt. In the other were pieces of DIY equipment on a trestle table — a Bosch drill and a case of drill bits, a Phillips screwdriver, a spirit level, and a sheet of paper bearing what seemed to be the diagram of a bookshelf. The paper was weighted down by a metal tin of screws and Rawlplugs, and had yellowed with age, which made Vijay think it was another unrealised plan. Like the running machine and Thai *Ulysses*.

Beyond the spare rooms, the house was a comfortably appointed place of cream walls and parquet floors. On the landing were a couple of nice oil paintings of southern Thailand, and in the bedroom was the echo of a woman who'd once been in Somsak's life. Expensively framed pictures showed the couple posing outside an autumnal Japanese temple, by the railings of Buckingham Palace, holding hands in a European city with cobbled streets and glinting tram tracks. But it was a much younger man in all of these photos. He had more hair, and the same cheer he'd displayed in their meeting. Except, perhaps back then, it had been real.

"And the killer didn't look for anything," Vijay told Doi, back in the office. "He would have been dripping like me, and wouldn't have had the time to wipe anything up."

"So, it's like you said. They should shoot the publisher, not the writer."

"Except he hadn't received any threats. I'm sure of that. He was far too relaxed. And who the hell had even read this book before Montri was shot?"

Doi went back to translating *Jao Por* and Vijay picked up his pen, then put it down and took his phone out. He swiped back to the picture he'd taken of the crime scene.

"There's no bottle here," he said. "In the study, I mean. Where he was killed."

"So?"

"He was drinking when he phoned me and was shot not long after he put the phone down. By someone who then rushed out of the house. But apparently, he wasn't in such a rush he didn't first direct Somsak away from wherever his bottle was and into the study. Why?"

"Because he wanted something in that room?"

"Right. But the study didn't have the look of being searched, which means the killer knew its location. Or Somsak simply handed it over, whatever it was." Vijay swiped through the rest of the pictures, but couldn't find a bottle or beer can in any of them. However, he hadn't bothered taking a photo of the dark living room. Somsak could have been sitting there drinking with the light off, sunk in melancholia, when someone rang the bell. And he'd gone out to open the gate, believing it was Vijay.

He went back to the crime scene photo. It occurred to him that if he'd taken it from a slightly lower angle, and closer up, it would have made a grim counterpoint to Somsak's website picture. Before and after.

Vijay was still pondering that when he and Doi went to their usual noodle shop for lunch. Doi gestured to the mirrors on the walls, reflecting the lunchtime crowd shoulder to shoulder at the narrow wooden benches. "We always come to the same place," she said. "And order the same thing."

The shop was just beyond the intersection. *Pii* Nuch had been a hairdresser for most of her working life, but now, in her sixties, had found she couldn't keep up with the styles the young people wanted. So she had sold off her reclining chairs, put in tables and benches and started cooking up noodles. From her old days, only the mirrors along both walls remained. They captured everyone's reflections to show a crowd of diners receding into infinity. Doi was right, Vijay thought. They did always have the same thing. He always ordered large noodles, dry. Doi always had small noodles in a soup she reddened with copious amounts of dried chilli flakes.

"It's good to have a regular routine. It frees your mind up to think about other things." That set Vijay wondering how regular Somsak's routine had been. He knew so little about him. Just one face-to-face encounter with his public persona, and a brief alcohol-tinged phone chat with the troubled man underneath it. What he needed was to speak to the people who saw him regularly.

"I'll see you in the office a bit later," he said. "I'm going back to Makkasan Junction."

The electronics shop was just as busy as before, the *mor lam* music still thumping out into the roar of the traffic. Vijay had the gloomy sense of the street not even knowing Somsak had gone.

He rang the buzzer ready with a story that wasn't needed. The door unlocked, absent of any questions crackling out of the intercom. As Vijay mounted the stairs, Oot's cyclops eye turned to look at him. The man pushed up the magnifying lens. "Somsak's dead." And then: "I thought you were the police again."

"I heard about it on the TV this morning. Can we have a chat?" Oot had only one chair, so Vijay went into Somsak's office for something to sit on. The police had already cleared it out, and there was a feeling of vacancy now that the computer was gone, along with all the paperwork from his desk, though on the metal shelves by the walls, they'd left his manuscripts untouched. Vijay picked up the title page of one. Gritty with dust, it read, "*A Statement of Rectitude* by Khunying Thanaporn Charoensuk."

He carried out the chair he'd previously used and set it opposite Oot's desk. The man had another metal case with *Sony* on the side. So, either very unobservant cops had passed through here, or the shop was paying them off already. "I just want to find out a bit about him. I realise that probably sounds odd—"

"Because you're a private detective?" Oot added, "I heard everything he said in there, you know. It's a thin wall."

"Right, that's it exactly. Obviously, the police are looking into this, but I feel a certain duty. To Somsak."

"I don't think *he* ever felt much duty," Oot said. "Just promises, that's what I used to hear. It was like having a radio on in the next room, always playing the same song."

"And recently?" Vijay asked. "Had he been busy placating anyone over the phone?"

"That's what the police asked, but I told them he did that all the time. Before yesterday, it wasn't any different."

"What about in person? There must have been some furious people coming through here."

Oot shook his head. "He didn't let them in. The camera outside went straight to his computer. I used to hear the bell ringing and ringing. Then his mobile would go and he'd say, 'I'm in Chiang Rai at the moment, on top of a mountain. Very bad signal.'"

"And did he seem different at all in the last few days? Moody? Worried?"

"We didn't really talk, just did our own jobs. Most mornings I'd be here before him. He'd come up the stairs with a cup of iced coffee in one hand and say my name in a certain way. Oo-ot. Or, Oot-Oot-Oot. Or some other thing. It was his morning joke and maybe I was a joke to him too. He'd leave very early at times, not yet four and already locking up. Then he'd say, 'Still slaving away, Oot-Oot,' as he went past. He couldn't understand a person doing a regular job. I always felt he looked at me and saw something that didn't make sense."

"For what it's worth, he had regrets underneath it all," Vijay said. "I talked to him shortly before he died and I would say there was definitely a part of him that wished his life had taken a different direction."

"I wonder what that could ever have been."

"You didn't like him much, I don't suppose?"

"It wasn't about liking. He couldn't talk without building fantasies. Bestseller lists, SEA Write awards. I'd hear him on the phone saying things like, 'When the offers come in, you can leave me to negotiate the film rights.' He'd drop names like Phranakorn Films, Sahamongkol Film International. And then before four, he was out the office, looking pleased because he'd avoided being someone like me for one more day."

"Was it always work calls or was there anything personal?"

"It's hard to say. Everything he said sounded personal. Every time he answered the phone, you'd think a long-lost brother was on the line." He paused. "I heard what he said to you in there. About my work. But our hardware is just as good as Sony's. We use Chinese op-amps instead of the

Japanese ones, that's all. But apart from that, it's the same circuit."

Vijay gave Oot one of his business cards in case he remembered something important, and then went out to look for a taxi. While he was standing on the kerb, his phone went.

It was Aim. "We want to discuss the project with you, immediately or as soon as possible. Nothing is negotiable." And with that, she cut the line.

As Vijay stared at his mobile, a taxi pulled up. He got in, directed the man to Chinatown and called Aim back.

"Sorry, but what?"

He could hear her saying to someone, "He wants to know but what." She said into the phone, "That's not negotiable."

"Aim, what's not?"

"Anything you might want to negotiate."

Feeling as though he was climbing the kind of staircase Escher used to draw, Vijay said, "Is this about Somsak's death?"

"Yes, it's about that. Well . . . not 'about' about. But about." A muffled something away from the phone ended in her muttering, "This is really stupid." And then to him, "Vijay, it would be good if you could come out to Ko Kret. I've taken the day off as it is."

He gave the driver the change of direction and wondered if his travel expenses were getting out of control. He then called Doi. "Just lock up and leave if I'm not back before half five."

"So where are you going now?"

"Ko Kret. I've just had a call from Aim. My guess is they want to pull the plug on the translation."

Leaving the taxi at the Sanam Nuea temple, it was less hot but more humid than his last visit. Grey clouds were gathering and the Lat Kret River was running fast as it ferried water hyacinths downstream. This time, Vijay went straight to Montri's place without stopping at the stalls. Again E-yen announced his presence, barking furiously. And, again, a committee was waiting to meet him, but this time by the hammock, under the shade of the house, there were three of them. The addition was a man who looked to be about Montri's age. He wore black skinny jeans, a black silk waistcoat over a white shirt and a black Borsalino with a white band.

As Vijay approached, he stepped up and put out his hand. "Hello," he said in English, and then in Thai, "I'm saying that because you're the translator. I know all about you." He had a smooth, lean face, thin lips and, behind red-framed spectacles, eyes that seemed to need something. Vijay shook his hand and introduced himself.

"I know, they gave me your business card." The man seemed primed for a particular reaction. It was as though he'd been told Vijay was a great eccentric and now he was waiting for that eccentricity to manifest itself.

Aim said, "His name's Lam." Again the quick, hurtable gaze, as though to check how his name was being taken.

Vijay said, "Pleased to meet you," and *wai*ed.

"The idea is," said Montri, "that we could have a talk about the project. Why don't we sit down and have a coffee?" He looked hopefully at Aim.

"Why don't we?" she said, giving no indication of going anywhere near the gas cylinder.

"I'll make some then," said Montri after a pause.

"I'm okay with the plan," said Lam. "We can do that."

Montri busied himself with the tin kettle, while the other three went over to the wooden platform where they'd had their last chat.

"If you and Montri are having second thoughts about the translation, don't worry, I understand." Vijay said, wondering what excuse he could find for staying in touch with them.

"Not now," said Lam. "We can talk about all this when Montri's here. It's going to be a proper business discussion."

Vijay glanced across at Aim and she turned her palms up and looked away. Meanwhile, Lam was studying him in detail

— jeans, watch, shirt, face — a steady, unceasing stocktake of everything Vijay represented. He would be very easy to wind up, Vijay thought. The kind of person who would bite on anything. And running against his usual instincts, something told him it would be a bad idea to try.

Montri came over to the platform.

"That kettle doesn't whistle, you know," Aim said, and he went back to stand over the gas cylinder. Lam took out a crumpled packet of Gauloises and set them down in front of him. For the sake of making conversation, Vijay said, "It can't be easy to get hold of those here."

"It is for me. I have contacts."

Vijay had an itch to reply, "Wow, can you score me some brie?" and only a monumental act of self-control stopped him. Instead, he said to Aim, "I suppose you're moving — from this place?"

She nodded. "We're getting off the island. My parents want me to come home, but they're in Dao Khanong. I can't commute that far."

"So, what's the plan?"

"I've given the landlord our one month's notice. We'll move to a cheap guest house tomorrow, and then get our stuff out as soon as we find an apartment."

Vijay said to Lam, "Do you live on Ko Kret as well?"

He looked surprised at getting the question.

"He's on the mainland," Aim said.

"So, just visiting?"

Aim drummed her fingers on the wooden boards and then called out to Montri, "There's only four of us, how much water did you put in?" Vijay had the odd thought that she didn't like being left with Lam. He asked her, "So how's work?"

"Oh, it's the usual, fighting for contracts. We're trying to get an account for sunglasses at the moment. We visited the marketing department and it was all men in their fifties using teenage slang. I think they felt if they didn't talk to us in a certain way, we wouldn't understand them."

Turning to Lam, Vijay said, "And what do you do?"

He blinked behind his red specs. "I'm a visual artist. Mixed media." And then abruptly: "But we're here to talk about you."

Vijay opened his palms. "Ask away."

Aim looked over her shoulder and Montri came across with two mugs in each hand. "You're spilling," she said, taking them off him. From his shirt pocket he pulled out four Starbucks sugar sachets and said, "There's no milk, I'm afraid."

They positioned themselves on the platform as compass points with Vijay opposite Lam. One after the other, Lam tore open each sugar sachet and then emptied all four into his mug. There was a slight tremble to his hand as he stirred the coffee.

"Did you want any sugar?" Aim asked Vijay.

"No, I'm fine."

Lam put his spoon down. "So this is really a business meeting. But I'm not a businessman full time," he added, as though accused of something shameful. "I'm a visual artist."

"That's great," Vijay said. "I've never had the chance to talk business with a visual artist."

The anger ignited behind Lam's eyes and his nostrils flared. "Are you trying to be funny?"

Vijay kept his face as blank as possible. "No, I meant it. I don't come across artists in my world, I don't get the chance to meet creative people. It's one reason I wanted to get into translating fiction."

"That's what we're here to talk about," Lam said.

Vijay had the sense of him placated but on guard now, ready for not being taken seriously. He looked from Montri to Aim. "Does this mean we're carrying on with the project?"

Aim rested her elbow on her leg, cupped her chin in her palm and stared pointedly at Montri.

"Yes," he said. "We're going ahead."

"That's why we're all here," said Lam. "We're going to discuss the big picture."

"And how are all of you 'we'?"

"Lam is a backer for my writing," Montri said. "He's a kind of silent partner."

"But not actually silent," said Lam. "There's no point being a partner if you're silent."

"Is this Somsak's marketing package we're talking about? You mean you helped pay for it?"

"And we didn't get anything in return," Lam said. "Zero publicity."

"And look what still happened," Aim put in. "Can you imagine if he'd actually publicised Montri's work?"

Montri reached across the coffee cups and rubbed her knee. "Tomorrow morning we're out of here."

"Somsak does look like the kind of person who'd have a lot of enemies," Vijay said. "Given how little he did for your book, it's possible none of his other marketing packages were real."

"I don't remember telling you his name," Aim said. "Or that there was a marketing package, for that matter."

"From the TV," Vijay said. "The news report."

"This is what we've got to do better next time." Lam looked at Vijay. "We've got to find people we can trust, not just those who look at us like we're a bunch of kids and think they can get away with anything."

"He could have been involved in all kinds of shady stuff," Montri said. "In the news they said a private detective discovered his body. That shows you the type of person he was."

"Why does it?" asked Aim. "Maybe he hired this detective because he was being threatened."

"So do you support a lot of other writers or is this a one-off?" Vijay asked.

"I might do, I might support other writers," Lam said. "I have different plans."

"So it's actually you who's paying my translation fee?"

"Now you've got it."

"And why this book, can I ask? Did you all agree on Khun Pleum together?"

"It's an important subject," said Lam. "It's significant. Plus, it can sell big if we do it properly." Vijay found himself watching Aim as he spoke. "That's what we want to talk to you about. This needs to be done in the right way. There's a tone of voice you've got to get."

"I can send you samples of my work," Vijay said. "I'll do that as soon as I get back."

"Right, right, right. But we're talking about fiction now." He said in English, "I can speak your language, you know. So I can read what you've written. That's the idea."

"Sure."

"He means as you're writing it," Aim said to Vijay without looking at him.

Lam nodded and went back into Thai. "Regular updates is what I'm talking about."

"Fine, I could do that. Just give me an email address and I can send them on."

Lam reached into the pocket of his waistcoat and took out Vijay's business card. He ran his thumb along the edge. "Or I could just come and see you, couldn't I?"

Trying to sound nonchalant, Vijay said, "Sure, if you don't mind fighting your way through the traffic, you can visit me anytime." He added, "Was this how the original book was written, by the way?"

"Exactly," Lam said.

"So it's essentially something you commissioned?"

"Not commissioned exactly," said Aim. "They thought it was an important subject."

"That's it," said Montri.

Vijay looked over at Aim and she met his gaze with a plea in her eyes. It obviously wasn't the time to mention her rewrite request. At that moment, his phone pinged with an SMS from Tong.

Shangri-La Hotel

Vijay texted back, *Great*, then said, "Sorry about that, a work thing. But anyway, this is fine, I can send my pages.

90

Though I should tell you, I'm still looking for the right style. But once it's there, we're full speed ahead."

"I'll look at that." Lam made a careful adjustment to the way his Borsalino was sitting. "I can judge the style. I read creative *farang* writing all the time."

* * *

Vijay got back to the office at five, just as Doi was packing up to leave. She'd printed out the next few *Jao Por* pages and left them on his desk. "So what happened at Ko Kret?" she asked.

"I solved the mystery of Montri's finances. He's got a backer. A guy called Lam." Vijay explained who Lam was, and found himself needing to describe the man's strangeness. "Imagine an actor who's been told to improvise the part of an artist, but is too angry to carry it off properly."

"And what do you think he's angry about?"

Vijay thought of Lam's quick, furious eyes taking him in. "No idea. Yet. I think I need to get him on his own. Come to think of it, I should also talk to Montri without the other two around."

After Doi had gone, he made himself a coffee and set to editing. After a while, he pushed his chair back and thought about Somsak and their last phone call. How little the man had expected his ending. There'd been no fear in his voice, only alcohol-induced sadness. And yet his study had possibly contained something worth killing for.

His phone buzzed with an unknown number.

"Is this Vijay I'm talking to? Vijay Mistry?" When Vijay said it was, he continued, "Khun Pleum is not happy with you."

"Sure, I can understand that. This is about Khun Somsak, right?"

"Have you seen the news? They're calling him the publisher of *Jao Por*."

"Perhaps you could tell Khun Pleum that I was the one who found his body? I think that will demonstrate how pro-active I'm being."

"Is this true?"

"Sure. Both things. Being proactive and finding the body. I went to his house as part of my investigation."

"And what did you discover?"

"Well, nothing really. He was dead."

"I don't think you understand what it means to make Khun Pleum unhappy."

"No, sure I do. But let's not throw the baby out with the bathwater here. I wouldn't say Somsak being dead is mission critical. Well, it is for him, obviously—"

"I have no idea what it is you're saying, but you should stop talking and listen. Khun Pleum didn't hire you to make things worse. And if he ever thinks you've been taking his money and not doing anything, you're going to be visited. Do you understand?"

"Sure." Vijay reflected on how he was developing a great deal of expertise in being visited by goons with attitude. You could put it down as one of his core competencies.

"I don't think you do. I don't think anyone in your life has ever taught you a real lesson. But we are the people who will. We teach lessons that no one ever forgets. Remember that."

"And do you think it's possible that someone—"

But the line was cut before Vijay could finish. He'd been going to say, was it possible one of Khun Pleum's friends had decided to teach Somsak a lesson? But then it didn't seem likely, given the strength of Khun Pleum's feelings on the subject.

Vijay put the phone down and drew Doi's pages back towards him. With grim timing, she'd got to the part about Sia Heng's assassination and Khun Pleum's terrible revenge on the gang boss who'd organised it. As if the phone call wasn't enough, Montri's book was a further reminder that the silk-shirted man with the gold cufflinks was the prod-uct of a deception decades in the making. Here was his true past: a world in which business rivalry consisted of Claymore mines detonated by remote control. And shrieking out of that world were who knew how many restless ghosts.

That idea made Vijay want to talk to Khun Pleum's friend from Samut Sakhon again. Besides, he thought, getting Somchai on board with the idea that he was busy investigating would do him no harm.

He dug his business card out of his wallet and phoned.

"Khun Somchai, it's me, Vijay. You remember?"

"Of course."

"I was wondering if I could come and have a talk with you about this case. Are you free tomorrow?"

"I could be, if it was necessary. What exactly do you want to talk about?"

"Khun Pleum's background. I get the impression he's convinced it's not his friends who are threatening this writer."

"It's not."

"So that just leaves his enemies. And I can't believe a man of his status would have enemies who would stoop to something like this. I can't really explain it in a logical way, but this feels like something that's come out of his past."

There was silence. "I'll tell you what we'll do," Somchai said at last. "I'm travelling back out towards Samut Sakhon tomorrow for a meeting. Take the Rama II Road out of the city, drive for maybe an hour and a half. Something like that. There'll be a turn-off for Route 2041, eventually. Garden Mansions, you'll see it. Why don't we say three o'clock?"

He ended the call, Vijay's agreement not being something he needed.

CHAPTER 7

"He's really something." Mana jerked his thumb at the bulging manila file at the side of his glass-topped desk. It was ten in the morning and Vijay was in his friend's small, air-conditioned office. Mana had had a clear-out for some reason, and the desk was clean, other than this file and the inevitable pile of pistachio shells.

"He must have done a lot of jail time, for that many arrests."

"Not as much as you'd think." Mana slid the file across the glass. "He had his particular contacts, I would say. Just under six years, if you add it all up."

Vijay leafed through the arrest sheets. Forgery seemed to have been a big part of Bundit's schemes, especially fake land certificates. He'd also run his own political party for a while, "The Pure Aspiration Party" and had been elected to parliament during the time Banharn Silpa-archa was prime minister. One of his arrests had been for siphoning off the party's funds, but that was another charge he'd escaped. Then eight months later he had been brought in for using the royal surname Na Nakhon, but he'd dodged that one as well.

"He was a fixer of some kind, I suppose," said Mana. "You know how it is, get the right people on your side and then feed off the nobodies." He cracked open a pistachio shell. "And nothing comes to court."

Vijay thought of Ploy in his office, the heavy gold around her neck, the gold teardrops at her ears. "It doesn't look like a nobody who's coming after him now. She looks like a really angry somebody. And she's young, mid to late twenties, I'd say."

"She wants him for what?"

"For a scam he pulled on someone else. A person she cares about, for some reason, but won't name."

"I don't know why you need another case."

Vijay was partway through an explanation of the importance of agile multitasking when his phone rang.

"Any progress?" Supaporn asked.

"Not yet, but these things take time. However, the person I've hired is very reliable."

"What person you've hired?" Mana said.

"You haven't got anything, is what that means," Supaporn said.

"Trust me, this investigation is on the runway. Our seat backs are upright."

Supaporn gave an impatient click of her tongue and put the phone down.

Mana was still watching him. "You've hired someone to do what?"

"I haven't as such. But it's important in business to put up the right front. I'm making sure we're front-facing."

"Meaning you're lying to Khun Pleum now?"

"I wouldn't say lying, it's more like polishing the truth. Plus, that wasn't him, it was an associate. He's phoned before. He wanted me to understand certain things."

"Such as?"

"Khun Pleum probably likes good news."

Mana sighed and shook his head. "Vijay, Vijay. And you're here working on a second case. What do you think he's going to do if he finds out?"

"How's he going to find out? Hire another private detective to investigate me? And then what, another investigator to investigate that one?" Vijay flipped through some more pages of the file. "This stops at 2004. I wonder what he's been doing for the last eleven years? Gone clean, d'you reckon?"

Mana snorted. "With a record like that?"

The last two arrests had been performed at an address in Bangmod. Vijay keyed the address into his phone, along with the name of the arresting officer, one Banchorn Chevatakul. "Do you think you can get me a contact number for him?"

"I could try, I suppose." Mana reached for another pistachio and squinted at Vijay. "Why does it feel as though I'm helping get you into further trouble?"

* * *

Back in Chinatown, Doi and Vijay decided to push the boat out for once and drove to a southern Thai place where they had a 250-baht lunch — rice and three eye-wateringly hot curries.

"See, we don't always do the same thing."

"Imagine if we could afford to eat like this every day," Doi said. "I'd probably get so fat."

Vijay dropped her back to the office and then began the long haul out to Somchai. As the Rama II Road snaked out of the city, apartment blocks above shops and the gated entrances of *moo baans* gave way to an industrial sprawl of factories separated by scrubland. Later came flat planes of light, glinting in the harsh sun. These were salt farms, where sea water was funnelled out from the gulf and left to evaporate in shallow pools.

Not far past one of these farms, Vijay's phone flagged up Route 2041. It turned out to be a bumpy road running through scrub, past the long concrete wall of a plastics factory, and finally dry, dusty ground supporting a granite sign reading *Garden Mansions*. But there were no mansions, just bare earth, and the brown puddles of last night's rain. Further back was a lone concrete skeleton, ten storeys high, with building rubble on each floor and a staircase winding up the far side. The pickup bumped up to it, but Vijay couldn't spot Somchai, or any builders, for that matter. It was still a quarter to three, and so he settled in to wait, keeping the engine going so that he could run the truck's air conditioning.

To kill time, he took out his phone and scrolled through Pantip, Thailand's biggest internet forum. Sure enough, there was already a thread titled: "Is this Khun Pleum's work?" Most of the posters had replied, "Yes of course it is, who else would be responsible?" He pondered that, and then found himself thinking about the *jao pors* in general.

His journalist friend Petch had once explained it to him like this: when Thailand constructed its state system at the turn of the nineteenth century, almost all the power — political and military — was concentrated in Bangkok. Beyond the capital, order depended on poorly resourced provincial governors, who had to rely on the odd garrison of soldiers and a handful of cops. It only really worked because the provinces were so poor. But once the economy rose and money washed in, there came a level of crime no one could cope with. And out of all that entropy and lack of enforceable law, a new class of citizen emerged — the *jao por*. This was the man who didn't just run a province's organised crime network, but also took responsibility for the province's upkeep, who would see to it that a school roof got fixed, that a needy temple was renovated. Both Sia Heng and Khun Pleum fit the mould exactly, right down to being the sons of Chinese immigrants and having spent little time in school.

The difference with Khun Pleum was that he'd managed to find success in Bangkok. And that set him apart from every *jao por* Vijay had ever heard of. Because these plain-speaking provincial hardmen weren't built for entry into the city's business elite. They couldn't just shoulder their way in on threats and violence — not in the capital — and the business leaders weren't susceptible to charm. They didn't want to share. The world of politics was an easier route for them to influence, either through becoming MPs themselves or by buying enough votes to get "their" people elected. Petch was fond of saying it was what had turned Thailand's parliament into gangster land. (And, Vijay supposed, if you wanted to join the dots up, it was the existence of so many weak, corrupt governments that had made people do no more than shrug when yet another coup rolled in.)

But Khun Pleum had done it, somehow. That afternoon in the cigar bar, he could have been conversing with the result of ten generations of inherited wealth, Suankularb Wittayalai or some other prestigious private school, and the whole package rounded off by an Ivy League or Oxbridge university. Vijay pictured a young boy squatting on the pavement with his greasy hands and looking up at Supaporn, this emissary from the world of privilege with her *yai* and her American bicycle. It was as though in that moment of longing, he hadn't just chosen the future he wanted, he'd chosen his past as well.

Vijay glanced up from his phone and saw a fragment of Khun Pleum's true past rocking towards him. Somchai's vintage cream Mercedes was swaying over the earth, trailing a dust cloud. The car pulled level with the pickup, but some distance away.

Vijay shut off the engine and got out into the silent, breezeless wet heat. As he approached, the same driver as before stepped out in his black suit and opened the passenger door. Inside, Somchai was alone.

Vijay climbed into the car's chill. "Thanks for seeing me. Is your meeting finished then?"

"You don't have to worry about that." The man was wearing cream slacks and a collarless silk shirt of burnt orange. It was a conventionally respectable *pu yai*'s outfit, but it didn't quite suit him. With his stocky figure and his hard, watchful stare, he still had the look of an off-duty sniper. "So. Pleum's past. What is it you want?"

"Well, like I said on the phone, I can't imagine him currently having enemies who would come up with an idea this . . . off-centre. So that just leaves the people he came from."

Somchai seemed to weigh up the honesty of that reply. "What do you want to know about them?"

"Take this gang war, for instance, after Sia Heng was killed. What about the other brother? The one who's called Lertchai in the book?"

"That *was* his name. He died a few years ago. And by the way, Pleum paid for everything. Food for the mourners, new robes for the monks, all of it."

"So, what? They were on friendly terms again?"

"Of course. Lertchai conceded once he saw the situation was hopeless. Most of his best men had already defected to us. And Pleum welcomed him back. Don't forget, Sia Heng had been like a father to Pleum and this man was Sia Heng's son."

"And just out of curiosity, what happened to the other son? The one on your side?"

"He's still alive, in his late eighties. But in a home. He has Alzheimer's, I'm afraid. They say he no longer recognises his own children."

"That's the odd thing about this case. I get the feeling all the relevant facts, and all the relevant people, are lost in the mists of time."

"Then maybe they're not relevant."

Vijay stared out through the windscreen's tint. In the premature darkness, the tower block looked abandoned. "I've just thought — you must have known Supaporn when she was a kid."

Somchai shook his head. "I never met her back then. Pleum came and said this girl was going to pawn some of her jewellery for him. And it just seemed like one other piece of the magic he could do."

"So, when did you two meet?"

"She was maybe nineteen, twenty, something like that. We were going to a new club that had opened. It was the place to be in Samut Sakhon, back then. They had air conditioning, and a Filipino band that knew all the Western songs."

"And what was your first impression of her?"

Somchai frowned. "Why does this matter to you so much?"

Vijay said honestly, "I really don't know." And then: "There's just a feeling of long-dead ghosts that comes with this case. I can't explain it."

"Well, she was pretty. Thai women were getting more Western by then, wearing shorter skirts." He shrugged. "She had good legs."

"I meant more what was she like as a person? The two of them came from such different worlds, I can't picture the attraction."

"I would say that *was* the attraction." Somchai stared out of the tinted window, into his past. "When Pleum told me, 'The girl we're going to meet, it's *her*,' I didn't understand at first, and then I realised he meant the jewellery, all those years ago. He made it sound like a great achievement, bringing her along. And this club, it was popular with Sia Heng's people, you see. And not just them — there were other *nak leng* there. And off-duty cops, still wearing their pistols, getting drunk and looking for disrespect. It had an edge, that place."

"Wasn't she scared?"

"She was with Pleum, remember. She'd be there on his arm, sipping her Black Label and soda and admiring him as he managed his way around people decades older. It gave her a thrill, I think, to step into our world. And love. I would say she loved him," he added, as though in reluctant concession.

Vijay thought about that. He pictured a twenty-year-old Supaporn in a short skirt and a seventies hairdo, in thrall to Khun Pleum's plans while a Filipino band did "Satisfaction". He followed Somchai's gaze out of the window. "I didn't know Khun Pleum had projects going so far out. I thought he only built in the city centre these days."

Somchai snorted. "Look at that thing."

Vijay didn't reply.

"See how small the rooms are? You don't think Pleum builds like this, do you?"

"If it's not his, then why are you here?"

"To help someone. A more or less honest man with a construction firm had some questions about a strange contract."

Vijay wondered where the honest man was. And the construction firm, for that matter. "Going back to the gang war, what about Lertchai's foot soldiers? The ones who didn't defect. I'm thinking Khun Pleum didn't show them the same levels of kindness he showed their boss."

That raised a thin smile. "You would be right. But the ones he left alive are old men now. We're all old men," he said, with the satisfaction of having reached a destination he'd long been travelling to.

"But what about the killing of Sia Heng himself? What about the people responsible for that?"

Somchai took on the expression of someone sucking on a lime. "A fool. A fool with ideas beyond his abilities. He wasn't even from Samut Sakhon, you know. Chonburi, that's where he came from. But of course, he couldn't establish himself there, Kamnan Poh had that place sewn up. So he comes to our little town and thinks we'll be no match for him."

"What was he doing?"

"Small stuff. He had a place where he sold second-hand pickups, and around the back he organised cockfights. The police chief of Samut Sakhon would go there sometimes and this man, Neung, would give him money to bet with. He thought that made him a big shot. Apart from that, he had an underground lottery going, a small one. Also, most of the pickups had Chonburi licence plates. I think there was some money laundering thing." He waved a hand. "That's what someone said. It was all a long time ago."

"It's funny, he doesn't even sound ambitious."

"Exactly. Sia Heng didn't think he was worth bothering with, and that's where he made his mistake. You become top dog by killing top dog, that's what these nobodies convince themselves."

"Except for Khun Pleum."

Somchai looked across at Vijay and said with deadly quiet, "Pleum is not a nobody."

"Right, right, sure. I mean . . . I didn't mean it like that. Obviously. I just meant he didn't want to kill the top dog."

"Of course not, he didn't need to. He had brains and ability. He could work his way up the organisation. We were doing well by then. We had money, we had all the good things." He ran his hand over the cream leather seat between them. "All the good things in my life, just because he was my friend."

The comment reminded Vijay of Somchai's beginning — working in a fish market from the age of eleven. "Would I be right in thinking you haven't read this book yourself?"

"You mean, would you be right in thinking I can't read? Yes, Vijay, you would."

"And Khun Pleum?"

"Oh, he can. He made a point of learning once he went into the construction business. He can read *and* write. He tried to get me to learn as well, but as I told him, the things he needed me for didn't involve little pieces of paper."

"So the *Jao Por* book . . ."

"When the shooting happened, I asked my wife to read it for me, and tell me everything it said."

Vijay thought of how his wife and Supaporn must have known each other for decades, and yet at the spa café, they had sat at separate tables. This woman would surely have enjoyed telling him about the *mia noi*. She wasn't going to leave out that tasty morsel. "Getting back to Sia Heng's killing, how did you know this Neung guy was responsible?"

Somchai put his hands on his knees. "Let's get out of this car. I'm tired of sitting down."

They stepped out into the muggy heat. The driver came with them, having first removed his suit jacket and placed it with great care on the seat next to him. Somchai set off towards the tower block. Vijay went with him and the driver fell in behind, having first taken a dawdling stroll across

Vijay's path to make sure he saw the handgun nestled inside his waistband.

Vijay said loudly to Somchai, "I hope he's got the safety catch on. I wouldn't want him to trip and turn into a ladyboy."

Somchai looked Vijay over. "Imagine thinking I need protection from you."

"Sia Heng, then."

"This man Neung, one of his people got cold feet. He realised they'd bitten off more than they could chew. So he went to Pleum, confessed everything, and begged for his life."

"And Pleum did what?"

"He spared him — in return for being told where to find Neung."

They'd reached the foot of the tower block by now. There was a cock and balls spray-painted on one of the inside pillars, and no sign of work in progress.

"There was a bar called Brown Sugar," Somchai said. "They played all that Western music from the sixties. It was an easy location, out at the edge of town. No cops around, just truck drivers who knew better than to talk. This fool was in there drinking, thinking he was a big deal now. I went through the door first. I used a Mauser machine pistol in those days. I took care of Neung's people. Then Pleum took care of Neung." There was no boasting or drama in his tone, as though he'd just said, "And then we painted the skirting board."

"So Pleum killed him?"

"He spoke to him first. I'd never seen Pleum like that before, never seen him so angry. He was always someone who stayed in control. He said, 'This is the second time I've lost a father.'"

"And what about Neung, what did he say?"

The sour look came back. "He wasn't a man. Do you understand? When you do something like this and it doesn't work, then you take the consequences. But he couldn't do that. By the end he was crying like a baby, begging for his life, pretending he didn't do it. Saying anything he could think of to make Pleum spare him."

"And then Pleum shot him?"

"Once, in the head. And afterwards he said, 'This was no kind of ending.' Not Neung, you understand. He meant Sia Heng. He shouldn't have died like that. Killed by a nobody." Somchai added, "Let's go this way," and went left around the block. Moving briskly over the uneven ground, he seemed unaffected by the heat. Again, Vijay had the idea he could have been a farmer, with a body trained by decades of toil.

"There's one thing I wondered about Sia Heng's death," Vijay said. "A Claymore mine detonated by remote control. That's really quite sophisticated, isn't it? For a guy who runs cockfights and does a bit of money laundering? I'm thinking the military had its fingers in this killing."

Somchai stepped over a pile of broken bricks. "Of course they did. Bound to have. He found a soldier who had the knowledge and could steal the equipment. You just need contacts. And he came from Chonburi, remember. A big mafia town like that. He could find someone."

"And Pleum didn't try to get the soldier's name before killing Neung?"

Somchai turned and smiled mirthlessly. "Who's running the country right now? Were you here in 1992?"

Vijay shook his head. "Still in England."

"But you know what happened? The coup and the soldiers shooting the protestors, and how the king stepped in and saved us?"

"Sure, I've heard about it."

"Afterwards people said, 'This is the last time. Now the army will stay in their barracks.' But I knew that wasn't true. There are unwritten rules in this country, and number one is: No one picks a fight with the Thai military. Not even elected politicians. Certainly not Pleum and me."

He went round the next corner, so that they were now opposite the side their cars faced. There was a mesh metal cage, external to the building, connected to thick steel hawsers running up. Somchai undid the latch on the door and swung it open. "Are you scared of heights?"

"No, I like them."

"We'll go up then."

The driver climbed in with them and pressed the green button on the simple grey control box. The cage shuddered and slowly rose to a faint shriek of steel. Vijay looked over at the goon and was gratified to see patches of sweat under his armpits. "What about him? Does he like heights?"

"He likes his job," said Somchai.

As the ground fell away, the plastics factory came into view, then as they rose higher, the hot tarmac ribbon of the Rama II Road and the cars racing down it in silence. A breeze blew through the cage. "That's more like it," Vijay said.

Somchai was still enjoying the view. "What I like about being high up is that it lets you think. It gives you a perspective." He looked back at Vijay. "You can decide what you really want."

"That's easy enough. I want to do a good job for Khun Pleum."

As though in reply to that comment, the driver hit the red stop button. He'd pressed it a bit too soon and they had to step up to get off. On the top floor, none of the internal walls were up. It was a single open-plan space of dusty concrete, and when Vijay looked out in any direction, he saw nothing but pearl-white sky.

Somchai went over to the side they hadn't yet walked around, and stood staring into space. The driver placed a hand on the butt of his automatic. Vijay raised his palms to show he posed no danger, and joined Somchai.

The man had set his sturdy frame at the building's very edge, the wind flapping at the legs of his cream slacks. "You can't see it, but the city is in that direction."

All that was visible was patchwork flat land, some of it being worked and other sectors lying fallow. And further back, the exact glinting rectangles of the salt farms.

"A man in your business, I suppose you have friends in the police," Somchai said.

"Sure."

"And they know you're working for Pleum?"

"I've told some of them."

"*Some* of them," said the driver with a snort. He'd come up to stand a short distance away, and still had one hand on the grip of his automatic. "Listen to Mr Well-Connected here."

Somchai put up a palm to stall further comments. "And I suppose they like the idea of you getting access to Pleum? I would, if I was a cop. Is that what this is, Vijay?" He widened his stance and crossed his arms in front of his chest. "Do you think you're going to go rummaging around in Pleum's past on behalf of your friends?"

"No, definitely not. Look, if I wasn't capable of keeping my client's confidentiality, I wouldn't be able to make a living from this." *Unless I was being paid to investigate them*, Vijay thought. *But let's not get into that.*

Somchai's hard, flat stare appraised the comment, then he looked back at the horizon. Vijay pictured him up here on his stomach, squinting through a telescopic rifle sight.

"That's where you'll find your answers, out there in the city," Somchai said.

"I'll bear it in mind."

Somchai regarded him, and something in his expression suggested Vijay had missed the point of going up there. And then he looked down.

The mangled body of a man was lying at the foot of the tower. A human puppet whose strings had been cut. The limbs were horribly twisted, and in one leg, the calf was at the wrong ninety-degree angle to the thigh. The shock of seeing it made Vijay cold in the heat. Inexplicably, he laughed, and the sound of his laughter shocked him further.

The alien laughter, which didn't really come from him, but from something strange inside him, told Vijay what he was looking at. "It's a mannequin."

Somchai shrugged slightly, as he pushed his bottom lip up in faint dismissal. *Okay, so you spotted it.*

"We'll go back down," he said to the driver, who made a point of watching Vijay walk back to the lift, still with his hand on the automatic, radiating disappointment that he hadn't been required to unholster it.

* * *

By the time Vijay got out to Bangmod, it was past five. He drove all the way to the city thinking about Somchai on the tower, and the body below them. When he'd got back into the pickup, his hand had shaken as he'd tried to fit the key into the ignition, and he'd understood the shock of the discovery had affected him more than he'd first realised. Meanwhile, Somchai's Merc engine had gunned into life, and the car had sat there idling, waiting for Vijay to leave. On the long drive down Rama II, the Merc had stayed no more than one car length behind him, and had only peeled away after he'd reached Pracha Uthit Road.

As he drove, Vijay replayed Somchai's response to his mannequin comment. After a while, it became less of a dismissal of Somchai's plan and more a dismissal of Vijay. *Tell yourself it's a mannequin if you want.*

Surely not?

Vijay found himself picturing the body and couldn't tell if his imagination was filling in details that hadn't existed. Natural variations of skin tone, for instance. But, Vijay thought, I couldn't have really seen those variations on a body ten floors below me. *Could I?*

He turned the pickup off Pracha Uthit Road and edged down a long, narrow *soi*, while the motorbikes and scooters weaved around him. When he got to it, Bundit's building turned out to be not so different from Vijay's own. It was in a U-shaped block, five storeys high, and the courtyard formed by the U was coming to its evening life. Young children were out on bicycles, a woman was wiping off the metal table of a food stall, an old man was laying pieces of chicken on a smoky charcoal grill. It felt like a return to the safe and normal world.

Vijay parked, checked the numbers on the concrete stairwells and trudged up four floors. The doors on each block opened onto a single, continuous balcony, and each apartment had a window next to the door. At 483, there was a thin blue curtain drawn with no light behind it. Vijay knocked.

There was no answer. He tried next door. That was opened by a middle-aged woman, who told him someone called Nisara lived in 483. She worked at the shoe factory, you just carried on going down the *soi* and there it was. Got home around eight most days. No, she didn't know who was there before, Nisara was here when she moved in.

Vijay had no luck on the other side, either. A young guy in a vest, a tattoo of a tiger on his bicep complained "I have to leave for work in five hours and you're waking me up, *hia*."

Back at the bottom of the building, there was a coin laundry next to the stairwell. A woman was sitting on a stool just outside the door with a pouch for change around her waist and a settled look of boredom. Vijay asked her about Bundit and she remembered the name, but had no clue where he'd gone. She remembered him as a friendly guy though. And also that he would sometimes be dropped back home in an old red Mercedes. Vijay gave her a business card and asked her to get in touch if she remembered anything important, either about Bundit or the red Merc.

He then went round the courtyard asking the same question. Two different food stalls, a photocopy shop, a guy repairing computers, a noodle cart on wheels. No one knew where he'd gone, though a picture emerged of someone gregarious, generous and unreliable.

"Oh, he was a friendly guy, all right. But if I'm going to speak straight, not an honest one. I'm not saying that to gossip, but he owed money to people. Take *pii* Gung, he borrowed 10,000 baht from her, that's what a person told me."

"Well, I liked him. Yes, I did, and never mind what anyone says. Look, I'll give you an instance. There's a temple in my home town and I was collecting money to repair the stupa. You know, he took out his wallet and he gave me a 1,000 baht note. Just like that . . . No, of course he didn't owe me 10,000 baht! Who told you that? Actually, it was 5,000. But the way I look at it, he was someone who made merit when he could. So I'm making merit by lending it to him, aren't I?"

"That's it, right. An old red Merc dropped him here. What of it? Sure. You could put it that way, if you want. The old red Merc started coming and then he vanished."

"Had some problems with his wife, I recall. Because of the gambling. We were sitting there drinking one time and she turned up shouting, 'You're pissing our money away on cards, you old fool!' Not happy . . . Oh wait, *Bundit*. No, no, he didn't gamble. Or have a wife, come to think of it. And his boxing days were long behind him. He wasn't a good boxer, but he was an honest one. Every time he went down, someone had actually hit him on the head . . . Oh, wait, wait. I'm thinking of someone else. Bundit wasn't a boxer. Now I remember, he worked in an underground casino, a high-stakes place somewhere round here. He told me one night when we were drinking. He was a greeter. He said to me, 'Gold, *pii* Chechawan. Gold has fallen into my lap.' And I never saw him again."

"Actually, no, I don't know what he did for a living. And he came and ate my noodles every morning for over a year. People are like that, aren't they? They come here and they eat and they go, and I think, what do I really know about them? A casino? Oh, I wouldn't trust anything *pii* Chechawan tells you. He's on the Leo by ten in the morning. Comes here for noodles to line his stomach and then it's the beer again. He used to be a handyman, you know. Now he barely works and lives off his wife. I don't know why she puts up with it. I suppose he must have a *really* large penis."

Vijay went to the building's maintenance office and told them he'd heard the landlord of 483 had other places going and was a good person to rent from. They gave him her number and he called, sitting in the cab of his pickup with the engine off.

No, she had no idea where Bundit had gone.

"Can I ask, did it occur to you to call the police?"

"They won't do anything. Just say it's my job to chase the rent down."

"I don't mean for the rent, I meant the fact that he's obviously gone missing."

"Well it's not obvious to me. Three months, he owed. Just because I'm a kind person, just because I listen to him telling me a sad story. And there we are. He planned the whole thing."

"What did he leave in the room?"

"Nothing of value."

"Could you be a bit more specific? If you help me find him, I can get your money."

"Really, for tracking him down, there wasn't anything useful. Just a wardrobe full of cheap clothes, a sleeping mat, one of those low Japanese tables and a desk lamp. That was it, as I remember. My daughter took the lamp for her university dorm. There was one good suit I could sell, dark blue with a red silk lining. The rest of his stuff was rubbish."

Well, there was an epitaph for you. Vijay asked her to phone if anything occurred to her, and she replied by pointing out he had a duty to phone *her* if he discovered Bundit.

* * *

Vijay inched back to Chinatown thinking about the man's disappearance. It was seven by the time he swung into Yaowarat Road, but he was too restless to go home. And since he'd broken up with his girlfriend, he wouldn't be doing anything there other than using his phone to watch *Alan Partridge* clips on YouTube.

She'd left him for a Chinese–Thai guy who drove a BMW. At least, that was the way Vijay had phrased it to

110

Petch. Though he knew he was doing Malinee a disservice by putting it like that. She hadn't left him *for* the BMW, she drove one herself. The fact was, she left Vijay for Vijay.

It had happened at a party at the apartment of a friend of hers, a large place of angular, weapon-like metal furniture and floor-to-ceiling plate glass windows revealing a glittery night in the city centre from thirty floors up. By some odd, unplanned way (not consciously planned, Vijay was sure of that much) he'd ended up alone in a kitchen of white tiles and steel Swedish efficiency. Alone that is, other than for a friend of Malinee's who'd given him the vague impression she liked him. Her parents had sent her off to a private school in Oxford and whenever the two of them met, they found themselves talking about things they missed in England.

She had told Vijay she was thinking of finding an *ajarn* to give her a tattoo that would protect her from evil. It was a notion that had become fashionable to Bangkok's Hi-So ever since Angelina Jolie had got one. With that announcement, she had swivelled on her toes, running one hand down her hip, and asked what part of her body he thought she should get it. Vijay had said that for the *ajarn*'s spells to work, she'd have to stick to the five Buddhist precepts, which would mean, among other things, no more alcohol. He had pointed that out because she'd had a mojito glass in one hand, complete with little cocktail umbrella.

She had replied that she could give up drinking easily, it was the pain of the tattoo that bothered her. And where did he think would hurt least? It was then that Vijay had had the bright idea of taking the umbrella out of her glass and using the point to find out where she was most sensitive, an experiment that was facilitated by her dress not really having much in the way of a back. Or right thigh, for that matter. And that was when Malinee had come in searching for ice cubes. She had never forgiven him the look of triumph her "friend" had given her and, the fact was, he'd never forgiven himself.

So instead of home, Vijay headed back to the office. The regular night's rain had begun, and the whole of the building was dark. He found the stairwell light bulb had gone and, using the flashlight on his phone, made his way up the stairs and let himself into the office. Doi had left the next sheaf of *Jao Por* pages on his desk, under his stone tortoise paperweight.

He made a coffee, opened the windows to let in the cool breeze the rain always brought, then put his feet up on a drawer and thought about Bundit. For a conman, lighting out without paying his rent was nothing strange. But why do it in a manner that risked the police treating him as a missing person? And why leave an expensive suit behind? Surely only because someone very bad had gone after him. And he was still on the run now.

Vijay put his feet down and turned his attention to Doi's pages. She'd got to the stage of Khun L's ascendancy. He'd set himself up as a businessman in Bangkok and, for all Montri's accurate details, here was one piece of the jigsaw he hadn't placed. He couldn't explain how Khun Pleum had done it. The book simply described him muscling into Thailand's booming construction industry. ("Khun L's unholy, unfillable hunger saw him slithering into Bangkok.") Money was passing under tables and contracts were sliding over them. Meanwhile, Supaporn had given birth to two sons and they were described as spoiled brats with *yais*, wanting for nothing.

Something bothered Vijay about that detail, but he couldn't think what. Finally, he put his pen down, went over to Doi's table, picked up *Jao Por* and, with the rain whispering outside, did what he realised he should have done days ago. He read his way steadily through from beginning to end.

CHAPTER 8

The view from Vijay's pickup, as it bumped down Kheha Non Road, was of exhaust-blackened apartments whose narrow balconies were enclosed by wire cages, a furniture shop where the chipboard wardrobes had spilled out onto the pavement, the spark of a welding torch throwing restless shadows in a small, dim garage, and then a shopfront with *Deep Blue Advertising* stenciled on its glass door.

Inside, there was no reception desk as such, just a partition that Vijay rounded to find an open-plan area with four cluttered desks. Beyond them was a kitchenette and staircase. On the whitewashed walls, a couple of Salvador Dali prints had been mounted with Sellotape. At the desk farthest away from him, Aim looked up and her eyes widened in surprise.

"Hi, sorry for not calling beforehand," Vijay said. "Could we go and have a chat, do you think?"

She came round the desk to stand in front of him. She was wearing black leggings and a loose white T-shirt that came down to the top of her thighs, and looked as chic and guarded as before. "About what?"

"Just a few things I want to get straight in my head."

The room's three occupants were watching them. She frowned. "I suppose so." And then to the room: "It's about Montri. I'll be back soon."

Vijay opened the glass door for her. "My pickup's parked just down there. We can go back to the Be Trendy building if you like."

She gave that a questioning look. "There's an *oleang* stall over the road." She then led the way without waiting for a reply.

Set out on the pavement, it was just a wooden booth with a couple of stools in front of it. Aim perched on one of them, crossed her legs and yanked her shirt down. The woman in the stall put ice into two plastic cups and then poured in the sweet black coffee.

"Diabetes in a glass, this stuff," Vijay said, and was met with a thin, impatient smile. "Okay, so, I was reading the rest of the book. I mean, obviously I've read it once, but I think there were things that I, you know, missed on the first pass. It's quite detailed in a lot of ways. The compound in Samut Sakhon, for instance. I found it on Google Earth and it's just the way Montri describes. Likewise, characters who haven't even had their names changed. Sia Heng being a case in point."

"It's art based on reality." She sucked up some *oleang*. "Montri explained all that."

"Right, but I just wondered why he had to follow reality quite so closely. I mean, what's the betting Khun Pleum's wife really is driven around in a white Mercedes by a driver wearing a black tunic with white cuffs?"

"I have no idea, and why is any of this bothering you? I thought you liked the book. That's what you told us."

"I liked the story, I'm just not sure about the writing style."

"But we've discussed this already. You're going to change it, aren't you?"

"Sure, but now I have to pass it by Lam, don't I? Your backer."

"Don't worry about him. Just make it sound like a proper novel and I'll talk to Lam afterwards. Or Montri will."

"I've read some of Montri's other work. The thing he did about hot towel shaves for that lifestyle magazine. I found it on the internet. He writes quite well, actually. The light, slightly ironic tone. He managed to quietly poke fun at the expense of a hot towel shave while at the same time making you want the luxury of having one."

"I told you, Montri's good."

"Which makes me wonder about the unreadability of *Jao Por*. I'm guessing it's because he had to get the pages past Lam, just like I'll have to, and Lam demanded rewrites until it came out sounding the way it did."

"Vijay, you seem to think we hired you to investigate us. Well we didn't, we hired you as a translator, and you still haven't shown us any work."

"I know, I know. But it's not threats anymore with this book, is it? It's murder now."

"I'm well aware of that. We're now living in a one-bed-room apartment on the mainland, after all."

"What about Lam? Is he worried?"

"In his own way. Why do you keep going on about him?"

"I just keep thinking of his role as Montri's backer."

"They're friends. He was at Silpakorn with us."

"And Lam's rich, obviously. Given everything he's had to pay for."

"He is. What of it?"

Vijay paused. The booth had an awning, but even under its shade the heat was fierce. He could feel the sweat trickling down the small of his back. It occurred to him that he could possibly get more out of Aim if they went somewhere air conditioned. But she didn't seem to trust him enough to get into the pickup.

"In the whole book, with all of its painstakingly accurate details, the compound in Samut Sakhon, Sia Heng and the rest, there's only one thing Montri and Lam missed. They gave

Khun L two sons, whereas Khun Pleum has three. But then that's understandable . . . given the third son is Lam. Isn't he?"

Aim gave him a long stare and put her sweating plastic cup down on the counter. "Why are you asking me if you already know?"

"Well it's a pretty weird thing to do, isn't it? And given everything that's happened since . . ." Aim wiped the sweat off her forehead with the back of her hand. "Do you want to go somewhere with air conditioning?"

She shook her head. "That's not necessary. We can stay here."

"So. What's he up to?"

She started to speak, then paused. "Lam came to Montri with the idea. Like you said that time, he commissioned him. And we were having trouble with the rent. Deep Blue just weren't getting accounts in. It looked as though we'd have to leave Ko Kret and get somewhere cheaper." She wrapped her arms around her body. "So that's ironic, isn't it?"

"Why did Lam say he wanted this?"

"At first, he tried to pass it off as performance art. Though obviously it wasn't. He was very specific, gave Montri all these details he wanted included. Then he kept bringing his pages back, saying the tone wasn't right. It had to be more critical." She added, "This was very hard for Montri," as though Vijay had questioned the fact. "That's why I wanted you to edit the whole thing before showing it to anyone. I thought if Lam read the finished work, he might change his mind about how it should sound. And then the translation would be more like the book Montri wrote to begin with."

"But now Lam wants regular updates."

She sighed and looked away. "I know."

"So what *was* Lam's motivation, do you think?"

"To get back at his father. He imagined the whole of Thailand reading the book and laughing."

"Get back at him for what?"

"Not letting him be an artist. His older brothers, the twins, they're doing everything his father wants, running

116

parts of the business. Lam was supposed to follow them. The whole Fine Arts thing at Silpakorn was meant to get being a bohemian out of his system. But Lam didn't see it that way. There was a gallery space he wanted his parents to pay for. He was going to make an installation with these huge mirrors."

"So it's an act of revenge?"

"I suppose. Like I said, when he first came to Montri, he told him he had an idea for a piece of performance art that would exist outside a conventional gallery setting. But yes. Revenge is mostly what it is."

"I couldn't help noticing, in the book Khun L has a *mia noi*. Is that from reality?"

"No idea. He might know something, or he might have just guessed."

"And why did he pick Montri for this project?"

"Because they were friends. And Lam didn't have many of those at Silpakorn by the time he'd finished."

"So he's a hard person to get on with?"

"At the end he was. Or hard*er* — it was never easy."

"Except Montri managed it."

"Montri gets on with everyone." She added, as though it was a particular quirk of his, "Montri likes people."

"So what did Lam do to lose his other pals?"

"No idea, he was closer to Montri than me. It could be the woman he split up with. That seemed to affect him, I remember. He was very bitter about it."

"Would you have her full name, by any chance?"

"For *what*? You're going to track her down, are you?"

"People are getting killed here. I need to know a whole lot more about this situation."

"Well honestly, I don't think it's her who's been shooting anyone. Plus, I don't know her full name. It was Anuttara something."

"She was a Silpakorn student as well?"

Aim grimaced. "Hardly."

"You didn't like her, I'm thinking."

"She was a gold digger, simple as that. She latched on to Lam for his money and probably left him when she found someone richer. In fact, she more or less admitted that to me once. We were in the toilet at a club. She was redoing her lipstick and asked me what Montri's parents did. When I said they ran a food stall in Ayutthaya, she gave me a look. I told her, 'If you're going to live with someone, it won't work unless you really love them.' And she said, 'Money makes men loveable.'"

Vijay finished his *oleang*, which by now was more melted ice than coffee. He promised Aim he'd soon be sending some pages to Lam. "It's straight back to Chinatown and down to work."

She met that without comment. Aim didn't necessarily like people, but she had love and loyalty and work ethic where her boyfriend was concerned. What a lucky guy Montri was, Vijay thought.

He stood up, expecting her to leave the *oleang* stall also. But instead she sat on in the heat, with her melted ice and her thoughts, and by the time he'd got to the pickup and ignited the engine, she was still there, twisting round in her seat, playing with her straw. He drove away, and in the rear-view mirror he watched her watching him go.

* * *

It was just past two by the time Vijay got back to the office, and Doi had already angled down the slats of the venetian blinds. He poured out some iced tea for both of them and told her about Lam.

"Modern children," Doi said. "This is what our society's turning into." And then: "Are you going to tell Khun Pleum?"

"I don't think so. He wants to know about the shooter, not the author. Plus, if he thinks his son's in the firing line, he might want to hire someone better equipped than the two of us."

"But what if someone shoots his son, and then he finds out we knew all this time?"

Vijay thought about Montri's brave (foolhardy?) argument to Aim: if the shooter wanted him dead, by now he would be. "Lam should be okay. No one knows it was his money, other than Montri and Aim."

"The publisher knew, and now he's dead."

"Assuming it was connected. Somsak must have collected so many enemies over the years." Although it had to be said, the timing of the shooting did seem to be a little too coincidental.

Vijay's phone went, with Supaporn's name on the screen.

"And when can I expect to hear some progress?" she asked.

"We are 110 per cent laser focused on this," Vijay replied, then mouthed "Khun Pleum's wife" at Doi and carried the phone down the stairs to the second-floor landing.

"And you've got?"

Vijay considered telling her about the necklace and decided against it. If she went to Khun Pleum with questions, it was going to be the end of two lucrative jobs at once. Not to mention what Khun Pleum's reaction was likely to be. "At this stage, the investigation is ongoing. It's progressing in the sense that it's going on."

"Which is another way of saying you've got nothing."

"You know, this kind of work, it's a lot like being a big game hunter. You're out there in the bushes waiting for the lion or whatever to come to the watering hole. It can be days before it breaks cover."

"Yes, but you're not in the bushes, are you? That's the whole reason I hired you, *detective*. You're already working for my husband. Talk to people. Use some initiative."

"This is something I don't usually tell my clients, Khun Supaporn, but do you think you'd be better off discussing things with your spouse? You could talk about your feelings . . . and his feelings . . . and how your feelings are making you feel."

"No, I don't think I'd be better off. A marriage requires certain responsibilities from two people, and I've been true to mine for almost forty years now. If the same isn't true for Pleum, then he's going to have to take the consequences."

This no doubt meant she'd already loaded an expensive divorce lawyer into the chamber and was pulling the hammer back. Vijay gave her some more reassurances about the reliability of Tong's work, and pointed out that her lawyer was going to need photographic evidence anyway.

With that, he rang off and thought how Supaporn had read the whole book but hadn't picked up on Khun L only having two sons. In its way, that told him about the strength of her feelings over the *mia noi*. Presumably, she'd read Montri's descriptions of Khun L "slavering over her smooth, young body" and the red mist had descended.

He went back upstairs to find Doi staring at him. "What's so secret you can't talk to her here?"

"Nothing much, it's just that she sounded a bit odd. Drinking in the afternoon, if you know what I mean." He made a glass-downing gesture.

"You had to go outside for that?"

"Not only that. It sounds as though they're having marriage problems."

"And she's phoning you?"

"That's what I thought — the woman's got marriage problems and she's phoning me? I feel like an idiot talking to her. What am I supposed to say?"

Doi sniffed, went back to her work and gave Vijay the cold shoulder for the rest of the day, just to make it clear she didn't believe a word he'd said. For instance: "I've just thought, why don't we do the whole thing in rhyming couplets?"

"If you like."

"Because it's all quite Shakespearean, really."

"If you think so."

At around four Vijay went down to *pii* Mo's and bought an iced cappuccino as a peace offering. After only light rain yesterday night, they were in for a deluge today. A low, dark bank of cloud was already hovering over Chinatown, which seemed to compress the wet heat. By the time Vijay got back to the office, Doi had the light on.

At five — darker, but still no rain — an old man with a walking stick shuffled in. Possibly in his seventies, he was wearing a checked shirt, faded jeans and a white straw boater that had greyed with age. He removed the hat and his mild gaze took in the room. "You're a detective," he said. "I expected more."

Vijay gestured to the chair in front of his desk. "What can we help you with?"

"I don't think you can," he said, but sat down.

Doi brought him over a glass of iced tea. "Uncle, why don't you tell us anyway?"

"People come into my house at night," the old man said. "They steal my things."

"What kind of things?" Vijay asked.

"There's so many. It could be a comb that's gone, or one of my shoes. Or the next morning, they've taken the sofa."

Doi and Vijay exchanged glances. "Have you ever seen any of these people?" Vijay asked.

The man shook his head. "By daylight they've vanished. But my things are missing, that's how I know."

"And have you gone to the police about this?"

"Oh, many times. They used to send someone round, but now they don't bother. Just tell me to stop disturbing them. Call me an old fool. But all the pieces of my life are disappearing. They can't deny that."

Doi said quietly, "Uncle, do you live by yourself?"

"For the last seven years now. Since my wife died. And her picture, they took it off the wall."

"Did the two of you have any children?" Vijay asked.

"I have a daughter, she's married now. A grandson as well."

"Do you speak to her much?"

He looked away. "I suppose she does okay."

121

Doi's mouth was a thin, angry line. "Uncle, give me your daughter's number. I'll speak to her."

He patted his shirt pocket and then those in his trousers. "My address book, I must have forgotten it. I have a book where I write things down." He gazed around the office — the safe, the fridge, the fan — as though the book might appear somewhere. "It must be at home. I'll go and get it — why don't you come with me? I can show you how it's all gone. Because the police, the police won't come anymore."

Behind him, Doi was giving Vijay a pleading look. "Is home far?" he said.

"No, it's just a short walk from here. That's what happened. I was out walking, I can't remember why, and then I saw your sign and I thought, 'That's what I need, I need a detective.'"

Vijay stood up. "No problem. We can get your address book and you can show me everything that's happened."

They ambled down to Ban Mor Road in the early gloom. The tables had gone from under the acacia trees, in anticipation of the coming downpour. The old man went on, past the Brahmin temple, and a bright-yellow block of apartments over shopfronts. He turned into a narrow alley where the awnings on either side met in the middle to form a ceiling.

They pushed their way through the crowd, past the clutter of stalls — T-shirts, upright bolts of cloth, sewing materials — all the while, the man keeping up a stream of talk. Most of it was about his wife. As in many Thai marriages, she'd been the organiser of the home. He had handed over each wage packet and she'd parcelled out everything: the money for food, how much they saved, how much he could go out drinking with. Vijay couldn't work out what he had done for a living, though. As the man shuffled along with the crowd, his mind went into it, and they weaved down alleyways of his memories. For instance, in front of them at one point, there was a woman pushing a pallet trolley stacked with boxes of donuts, selling them as she went, and the old man started on about Noot and his insatiable sweet tooth.

"Did you work with Noot?" Vijay asked.

"Noot didn't work, he just sat there licking the sugar off his fingers. Noot's father on the other hand . . ." And he was off, describing how Noot's father had been a tobacco farmer and what a hard job it was.

They came out of the alley onto the neon blaze of Yaowarat Road. The slivers of sky between the black clouds had darkened to blue ink, and with the bright Chinese signs, it felt as though they'd left Thailand completely. They passed gold shops, Double Dogs Tea Room, and then turned right into a quiet *soi* of apartments over what must have once been shopfronts. Other than a single shark fin place, they were now all closed, their metal railings gated and padlocked. On the second floors were rows of peeling wooden shutters, looking as though they hadn't been opened in decades.

The old man brought out a key and fumbled with a padlock.

"So you owned a shop?" Vijay asked.

"We should have. For most of our life, this place owned us." He rattled the metal gate back and swung open one panel of the accordioned wooden door behind it. They stepped out of their shoes and entered his home. The man closed the panel behind him, padlocking it from the inside while muttering about keeping his things safe. In the pitch dark, Vijay heard him click a light switch. When nothing happened, he gave a wheezy sigh. "Well, the fuse has gone again. Do you know about fuse wires?"

"Sure. Why don't you show me where the box is?"

Vijay took out his phone and switched on the flashlight. The small bright circle revealed the discoloured plaster of a bare wall.

"Ah, you've got a torch. You're a bright fellow, aren't you? Having a torch."

Vijay tracked the beam down and found floor tiles grey with dust. Set into the grey was a clean white rectangle that could, conceivably, have been left by a recently removed sofa. As he rotated the phone, its beam revealed other bare walls and nothing but bare, grey floor. They seemed to be in an empty room.

"Your things—" Vijay started to say, when there was a metal clatter from the direction of the old man. He swung the flashlight back and found the gentleman picking a revolver up off the floor.

He lifted his right trouser leg to reveal an ankle holster. "They told me it was the right size, but I don't think so. I think it's really meant for a .22. And this one's a .38."

"And what would you be carrying that for?"

The old man dropped his walking stick and held the gun in both hands. "Why, to point at you, of course."

Vijay brought his arms out away from his body. "Hey, look, there's no reason to do that. I'm not even armed. And I'm not the one who's taking your stuff. I came here to help you, remember?"

"Why don't you take a couple of steps backwards?" the man said, in a voice that was no longer slow or confused.

Vijay followed his instructions, still with his hands held out. He angled his phone.

"No, no, no! As soon as that light shines in my eyes, I'm going to pull the trigger. Do you think you're so fast? Do you think you can jump out of the way of a bullet? That would be a sad cause of death, wouldn't it? Trying to act like the hero in a bad film."

"I'm pretty sure the cause of death would be bullet lodged in body," Vijay said.

"Ah, that's good. You can still make a joke, even though you're so scared. I like that. Why don't you reach back with your hand now?"

Vijay did and found nothing.

"Step back and farther to your right and try again."

This time, Vijay touched a thin metal pole.

"It's a lamp. Find the switch and turn it on."

Vijay did so with unsteady fingers and a cone of amber light illuminated a metal chair.

"Now you can take a seat, and switch off your phone light without doing anything else to it. Good. Now put it in your pocket."

Vijay heard the scrape of another chair being dragged over the floor, but the standard lamp had a very weak bulb. The amber cone of light revealed no more than the dusty floor, the man's walking stick and the dim outline of his body.

"You didn't really need the stick."

"I do when I'm wearing the ankle holster. The weight of the gun makes me limp."

The furthest clear thing Vijay could see was the black hole of the barrel. The man had positioned the chairs exactly right.

"But there we are. Get me onto something neutral and then pretty soon you'll be talking about yourself. Making yourself human so that it's harder for me to shoot you. Yes, you're a bright fellow. A bright fellow who turns up in Bangmod, asking questions, handing out business cards as though they're invitations to his daughter's wedding. And thinks it's not going to get back to me."

Vijay's mouth was very dry, and when the word came out, it was a hoarse croak he didn't much like the sound of. "Bundit?"

CHAPTER 9

It was the second time in Vijay's career someone had pointed a gun at him. The first had come not long after he'd started his new line of work. Before hiring Tong, he'd followed a man called Sumate back home in his pickup, and had made the mistake of thinking he hadn't been spotted. In the early evening light, Vijay had parked under a mango tree some distance from the house, and was sitting in the cab with the engine off when Sumate came out with a handgun levelled at the windscreen.

He'd thought Vijay was a burglar casing the joint. When Vijay had explained the man's wife suspected Sumate was using her business trips to have an affair, the man looked comically surprised. "She's figured that out?" They had sat together in the cab and had a chat about how she didn't care about him anymore. Vijay had pointed out she'd cared enough to have him investigated.

Other than the shock of the guy emerging from the foliage of his garden, it wasn't all that frightening an experience. Sumate had cradled the pistol in both hands, and had seemed oddly shamefaced about his actions. He said he'd never aimed it at a human being before, and explained they had a lot of gold in the house. "*Her* gold," he added hopefully. "So I was protecting her stuff."

Sitting in Bundit's darkened room, under the weak beam of the standing lamp, was a very different experience. The black eye of the revolver didn't waver, and everything about the room's arrangement felt lethally professional.

"I want you to answer my questions simply and truthfully," Bundit said. "No long speeches, no wandering off the point. What were you doing in Bangmod?"

"I've been hired by someone who wants her money back."

"From what?"

"You sold her a fake land certificate, in Rayong. It was supposed to be for beachfront real estate."

The black eye jerked. "Try again. Tell me the truth this time."

"I am telling the truth. We're on the same page here."

"You're going to make me shoot you if you carry on like this."

"Carry on like what? Come on, it's what I do for a living. She could have said, 'He killed my daughter's cat' and I would have taken the case."

"This is a scam from ten, fifteen years ago. Why is she only hiring you now?"

"I don't know the answer to that."

"You're making me impatient. Which will make me pull the trigger. It's going to hurt and you're going to bleed a lot."

"Okay, okay. Let's not jump the shark here. I do know the answer. But you're not going to like it. I'm putting that on the table. I haven't been hired by this woman, I've been hired by a third party who's angry at how her friend was treated. The victim herself doesn't even know I'm on the case."

"You're right, I don't like it. That's a ridiculous story."

"Exactly. There you are then. If I was lying, don't you think I'd come up with something more credible?"

Possibly the revolver was getting heavy. It was a chunky-looking snub-nosed piece with a barrel that was horribly wide. Bundit rested his elbows against the sides of his stomach, which had the effect of bringing the gun's elevation down to Vijay's crotch.

"Is the bloody safety catch on that thing?"

"Which one of us is holding the gun? That's the one of us who asks the questions." Bundit added, "This woman gave you a ludicrous story and you still took the job. Why?"

"I need the money. I'm in debt to a loan shark."

There was a pause while Bundit seemed to evaluate the truth of that. From the safe, unthreatening world beyond the door came the sound of a pickup rumbling down the street.

"Describe this person who's hired you."

"She's in her mid-twenties, spectacularly beautiful and from the looks of things, rich."

"Now it's getting even more ridiculous. You're describing someone from one of those books."

"Right, sure. Exactly. If I was making this up, I'd tell you it was a middle-aged guy with a scar on the back of his right hand or whatever. But it's actually a beautiful woman called Ploy and I can't change that."

"She's looking for h—" Bundit began, and went into a heavy coughing fit. Vijay waited for him to recover and he continued, "If this person is real, then describe them in more detail."

"Yellow skirt, black sleeveless top, fair-ish skin, heart-shaped face, shoulder-length hair curled at the ends, full lower lip." Vijay paused. "That's about it, really. I'm not going to say there was a beauty spot under her right eye or something because there wasn't."

"That doesn't make your story any more believable. And you're saying she didn't tell you anything else about the mark?"

"Only that the victim loved you."

"We'll leave love out of this. And you shouldn't say victim. Those people knew they were breaking the law. They thought they were paying bribes to real officials for real certificates. We just happened to give them something else. It's always like that, you know. It's always a person's own greed that does it."

128

"So now they can't go to the cops, but they might just want revenge. Is that why you had to clear out of Bangmod in such a rush?"

"I'm not here to provide you with answers. How did you get my address?"

Vijay explained about Mana pulling his record and going through the arrest sheets. While he talked, no questions came back at him, and he had the odd sense of Bundit's interest having been disengaged.

"That was all? You didn't have any other leads?" the man asked.

"No, just your arrest sheets." Vijay noticed how the tone of angry interrogation had dropped. There was a disappointment the man's voice couldn't hide. He took a leap in the dark. "You're not Bundit. You're someone who's looking for him."

"Don't try and get clever. I'm the one with the gun."

"I'm not trying anything. And by the way, you said, 'We gave them something else.' So you helped Bundit run these scams is what I'm thinking."

"I told you, I'm the one asking the questions."

Growing in confidence, Vijay said, "That wasn't a question. It's obvious enough. And by the way, since you're in touch with someone in Bangmod — it does seem like he's gone missing, doesn't it? I mean, his clothes are still in the wardrobe and all that."

The man rallied himself and the revolver's elevation raised, so that it was back at chest height. Vijay's toes curled up into the balls of his feet, and then in a voice that sounded suddenly tired, like the baffled old man he'd pretended to be, the stranger said, "I don't know. There's no telling with Bundit. He may have gone missing, but he may have wanted it to look that way." He sighed. "There's no telling at all."

In the innocent street, another pickup rumbled by.

* * *

The next morning, Vijay described it all to Doi. "So basically, someone else is hankering after Bundit. Except this guy was an accomplice rather than a victim."

"Or maybe Bundit sent him after you? To make you believe he can't be found."

"I don't think so, it felt genuine. Though having said that, there was something I missed in that house."

"Missed how?"

"I don't know, it's just a feeling I had after it was all over. Something he said, or the way he said it."

"And this place off Yaowarat, it wasn't his?"

"No, he was pretty cagey about who it belonged to. I could probably find out, just go back there and ask around. But what's that going to tell me?"

"And then he'll come back here with the gun, because he'll have heard you've been asking questions again. You see, this is what happens when you do two cases at once."

This reminded Vijay of actual case number two. He sent Tong a text asking for progress, then decided it would be good to find out more about Bundit's unseen victim. He phoned Ploy and asked for a meeting. She gave him the address for a *soi* off Sukhumvit Road, deep in the city centre. "It's the half-built shop, Vijay. You can't miss it."

In the meantime, however they were going to be received by Lam, he did owe Montri some pages. He had settled for telling Khun Pleum's story as simply and as clearly as possible, which meant essentially giving Aim what she wanted, and cutting out most of Montri's sneering digressions. After a while, Vijay stopped work and scanned through the rest of what Doi had done.

"It's weird doing this while knowing one of his sons is responsible," he said.

"That's how our society's going now. Children don't respect their parents anymore," Doi replied.

"Yeah, but this is more than just a lack of respect. Aim told me he kept bringing Montri's pages back, so he must have *really* wanted it to read this way. There's a certain kind of loathing here, not just for where his father came from but for where he is now. Except that's where Lam is himself, given he's living off his dad's wealth. Didn't he also grow up with a *yai*? Didn't he also go to an expensive private school? In which case, he was as spoiled as he makes the twins out to be."

"Probably thinks he's so clever, using Khun Pleum's own money to make him look bad."

"Yeah . . . maybe. You know, Aim told me he had an idea for an art installation involving a huge collection of mirrors."

"So?"

"I just wonder what he was going to do with them. Because I don't think this is someone who likes their own reflection very much."

* * *

At close to eleven, Vijay reached Sukhumvit Road and went winding down one of those *sois* where all the money lives. Luxury condominiums towered over the high, metal-spiked walls of old family homes. The number Ploy had given him turned out to be another family place. The gate was rolled back and a flatbed pickup parked directly in front. A group of men were manoeuvring large panes of glass out the back of the vehicle and carrying them into the grounds.

Vijay parked his own pickup behind theirs and followed them into a small courtyard of old, cracked flagstones. At the centre was a huge banyan tree, its trunk wrapped with holy cloth. Beyond the tree was a long two-storey house with intricate wrought iron balconies, wooden eaves and tall, open ground-floor windows. Through one of these, Vijay could see Ploy.

He found her in what seemed to be a formal sitting room. She was dressed in a chic take on workman's clothes — spotless white jeans, a tight oxblood T-shirt that matched the red of her Doc Martens boots, and a fiery orange silk scarf knotted over her hair. When she saw Vijay, she smiled. "Do you know anything about pianos?"

There was a wooden upright Steinway behind her, the brand name running across it in gold leaf. "Not really. You mean 'know' as in whether it's in tune?"

"I mean whether it's worth keeping." She swivelled in her boots, hands on hips and scanned the room. There were sofas and armchairs of old, dark wood, with the look of having been reupholstered many times down the years. Against the walls stood glass-fronted mahogany display cabinets, all of them empty. On the rose wallpaper, rectangles of a slightly lighter shade indicated pictures now gone.

"Well, I suppose that depends on what you're planning on doing with this place."

"They're going to tear it down, I'm afraid. This will be the site of a very modern restaurant doing Thai–Japanese fusion cuisine."

"And the owners of the house?"

"They gambled and lost. From what I know about it." She raised the piano lid and pressed a single key a couple of times, producing a lonely, plaintive sound against the thumps and clangs of the workmen. She looked across at him. "The rich are pitiless, aren't they?"

"I wouldn't know." Vijay wondered where she was setting the scale mark for "rich" given her workman's get-up hadn't precluded some pricey-looking earrings. "So what's your role in this, can I ask?"

"I'm here on behalf of a friend. They've been told they can have anything they like, before the building starts."

"And is this friend Bundit's ex-mark?"

"No, it's . . . somebody else. And stop digging for information about her."

"Just so you know, she was actually doing something illegal. She thought she was paying Bundit to bribe an official at the Rayong Land Office." Ploy's expression didn't change. "You already knew that."

"I wouldn't say knew, but suspected."

"And you still want to find this guy for her? You're still willing to pay?"

She closed the piano lid. "Since it seems to matter to you so much, it's not my money. It's hers. She's the one who wants him found, I'm just a go-between."

"And she couldn't come to me herself because?"

"Her reputation is important. She doesn't want it known she was trying to bribe government officials."

"So this is someone in the public eye?"

"Not her, the husband. She doesn't want it reflecting badly on him."

"And is she paying you for this service? And if she is, are you sure you can trust her?"

"Oh, definitely." That came out with no hesitation at all, and felt like a small island of truth in a dark sea of falsehood. She regarded the furniture. "I wonder if these cabinets are worth taking?"

"What will your friend do with them?"

"It's for a coffee shop. The idea is to give it a retro look. We could stick one of these in the corner and fill it with fake antiques."

"And you get to just go off with anything you like here? It's very generous."

"That's Thailand, Vijay. Everyone's kind to the influential." She didn't sound pleased about it, Vijay thought, despite clearly doing very well out of being some influential woman's public face.

"The other thing is," Vijay said, "this scam would have taken place ten to fifteen years ago. Do you know why she's only coming after him now?"

Ploy considered that. "I expect she spent that time thinking about him. I know, she's married. But still. I think she decided if she can't have Bundit back in her life, there's going to be a price to pay."

"Okay, well this is what you can take back to her." Vijay described the man's thick police file, his very few convictions, his disappearance from Bangmod and finally the visit from "Uncle". The last part brought a softening in her expression. "And this old man's been waiting for a trace of him all this time?"

"Bundit seems to have a gift for that, doesn't he? People not abandoning him. I got the feeling most of the people in Bangmod liked him. Even the ones he owed money to."

"So what's your plan now?"

"One of those people told me he was working in an underground casino. The old man didn't say anything about that. So either he was keeping his cards close to his chest or he didn't know. It could have been the latter, as this seems to have been something Bundit let slip when he was drinking."

Ploy gave him a look of delight that was almost payment in itself. "And do you know where this casino is?"

"No, but there are ways of finding them. It takes leg-work but it can be done."

"Good. That should keep her happy." She added, "Why don't we go upstairs? I heard they had some nice wardrobes."

"For a coffee shop?"

"Why not? It will look different. Or we can take the doors off and put things inside."

It turned out they did have nice wardrobes. Smooth, varnished teak from the look of it. The beds were still there, as well as the mattresses, nightstands and chests of drawers that Vijay couldn't resist opening.

"Looking for clues?" asked Ploy.

"I'm just wondering about the family that left all this behind. They weren't even allowed to keep or sell their furniture?"

"It's what comes of losing to the wrong people." She was sitting with her legs crossed on the bare mattress of a king-size four-poster bed. Leaning back with her arms out behind her, the T-shirt tight against her small, high breasts and a dreamy, faraway look in her eyes, she had a dangerous, unintended beauty. Like a loaded gun designed for other targets, she could shoot you all the same.

Ploy brought her attention back to the room. "Do you think people ever really change? Even if they did something in their past, could they become a different person?"

134

"Because the arrest sheet stops in 2004, you mean? Do I think Bundit's gone straight?"

"If you like."

"It's one possibility. Another is that he found a better scam."

"So people don't change is what you're saying." She began swinging her leg.

"Is that going to be a problem? If we find him and he's still liberating people from their savings, will it affect how this woman pays you?"

She stopped and sat upright. "Oh, it's not going to affect *me*, Vijay. Finding him is not going to affect me at all."

* * *

On the drive to his office, Vijay thought about how he was finally living out his fedora-and-raincoat private detective fantasy of coming to the aid of a beautiful woman. And that fantasy could have held if only she'd been able to lie better. Or at least pick a cover story that didn't need readjusting halfway through.

Back in Chinatown, he went to the usual place and had his usual bowl of dry noodles. It was close to two by now and the lunchtime rush had passed. *Pii* Nuch at the cooking pot had time to tell him Doi had already eaten and gone. Which was a good thing, as Vijay didn't want her turning up and overhearing him.

He phoned Tong, told him he could leave Khun Pleum and gave him the *soi* number in Bangmod where Bundit had lived. It seemed a good place as any to start.

He then went to an ATM. Having extracted the money he owed Tong so far, he got back into the pickup and set out for Bangmod himself.

Clustered at the mouth of any long *soi* in Bangkok, there will be a group of motorcycle taxi riders in their fluorescent orange jackets. And it is a given that these men will know far more about the life of that *soi* than the *soi*'s inhabitants realise. Tong spent a large amount of his time ferrying passengers to and from a large, middle-class *moo baan*, and could pass Vijay precise intel on who was having an affair with whom, who was no longer visited by his children, who had been phoning out for "massage" services ever since his wife left.

When Vijay got to Bangmod, Tong hadn't yet arrived, so he stayed in the pickup, listening to the radio. The news came on but there was nothing about Somsak, who'd dropped off the current affairs cycle. Instead there was more about the Junta cracking down on their critics. A politician from the last government had recently called out one of the generals for making sexist comments about Yingluck Shinawatra, Thailand's last, ill-fated prime minister. The result was that he'd been brought to a barracks for "attitude adjustment". Vijay found himself thinking of Sia Heng's death and Somchai's comment that you couldn't fight the Thai army. It was an argument backed by thirteen coups.

And yet something about the Claymore mine tale bothered him.

Shortly after the news finished, Tong arrived. As usual, he was wearing his hair short except for a very thin ponytail that came down to his shoulder blades. When Vijay had first hired him, three years ago, when he had barely just turned twenty, he had said the motorcycle taxi job was temporary. The problem, Vijay suspected, was that he couldn't think of what else he wanted to do. He was too clever for factory work, too restless to stand behind the counter of a shop all day, and too independent to become a company driver. And his brief temple school education hadn't provided him with the qualifications for anything else.

Tong parked behind the pickup and came round and sat in the cab. Vijay handed him the roll of thousand-baht notes. "This goes up to the next three days. I expect one way or another, it's going to take us at least that long."

Without counting it, Tong slid the roll into the pocket of his jeans. "Your guy's really something, you know that?

Guess who he had lunch with yesterday? The Transport Minister. And guess where? The Shangri-La Hotel."

"I know. You texted me, remember?"

"You should have seen him. Dark suit, tie, handkerchief in the top pocket, and a guy goes behind, carrying his brief-case — never walks alongside him, always a couple of steps behind. He looks more like a minister than the ministers do. They look like they're selling something to *him*."

"Which makes sense, really. Khun Pleum must have been at the centre of power longer than most of the people he's meeting." Vijay then explained about the casino, and on his phone map they divided up Bangmod between them.

Tong climbed back onto his bike. "If it's here, one of these motorbike *win*'s will know."

Vijay trundled the pickup through his section of the borough, stopping at each *win* he came to. It turned out to be a long job, and an unreal one. Far out from the city centre, Bangmod was a less hectic, less built-up, less Chinese version of Chinatown. The same paint-peeling apartments sat above shopfronts, the same metal grilles fenced in narrow balconies, a tyre shop, an internet café, a coffee shop of small, low tables edging out onto the narrow pavement and the customers all university students or younger. Vijay had to remind himself that hidden somewhere in this mundane urban flora was a high-stakes casino.

But that was the way it went. Only the state lottery was legal, but everyone wanted to gamble. Everyone believed in the transforming power of luck. A dream containing a num-ber was a reason to go looking for a lottery ticket. At a tem-ple, the shape of ash on an incense stick burning down could be a clue. Likewise, when the wax from a candle dropped into a bowl of holy water and made a shape. If you rubbed powder into a holy tree trunk, the spirit in the tree might cause an outline to form. Numbers were everywhere. The universe spoke in signs. If an acquaintance was in a car crash, you wrote down his licence plate. If he was hurt badly enough to go to hospital, you noted down the room. Petch once went to the cremation of his cousin and bet on the serial number of the coffin.

Most of the motorbike guys Vijay spoke to were friendly, and most laughed when he told them what he was looking for. Which was understandable, he thought, given he hadn't dressed like a high-stakes gambler. But no, nobody had any idea about where a casino might be. After an hour, Vijay had started to wonder if *pii* Chechawan's beer-pickled memories hadn't mixed up Bangmod with somewhere else.

His section of Bangmod went up to the district of Tungkru, and it was here, just inside Tungkru itself, that he finally got lucky. At the mouth of a *soi*, a motorbike guy with a big, thick *Jatukam* amulet looked him up and down and said, "I'd pick something smaller, if I were you." Vijay told him he was asking on behalf of a friend, and was met with scepticism. "Your 'friend' needs to know people. He can't just walk up to the door and think they're going to let him in." Vijay told him he'd bear that in mind and for twelve baht the man agreed to show him the building.

It was almost four and the rain was starting to patter down. Vijay climbed onto the back of the bike and in the day's greying light they wound down the *soi*, past ageing apartment blocks of small, lit rooms, bumping over broken tarmac, skirting the puddles in the road. The man drove for almost a mile, over a humpback bridge that crossed a small *khlong*, and turned left into a sub-*soi*. At the end of this was a huge mansion behind a high wall. The gate was a steel mesh with a sky-blue metal plate at the centre, bearing a white gothic "P", beyond which was a gravelled courtyard and what looked like the edge of a fountain. A CCTV unit on the wall angled down to the gate's intercom, which was presumably why the man had stopped where he had. Any closer and they would have been in the picture.

"You should see the cars parked out here in the evenings," he said. "Mercedes, Porches, BMWs."

"And you're busy writing down the licence plates, am I right?"

"Think that would get me anywhere? This place pays the cops on time. And these gamblers aren't the kind of people the police arrest."

Vijay dismounted and walked parallel to the gate. There was indeed a fountain, with a couple of fat cherubs laughing under the water spray. Beyond the courtyard were steps leading up to two huge doors of black glass. "You always wonder why people this rich need to bother setting up a casino."

"*Pii*, it's because they want to get more rich. The bank always wins. You should tell that to your 'friend'."

CHAPTER 10

"And you're asking me?"

Kritisak leaned back in his chair, savouring the idea as though it was a slice of particularly good roast duck. It was just past ten in the morning and he and the goons were ensconced at their usual table, engaging in what was either a late breakfast or an early lunch. Bowls of rice, pork fried with garlic, and sections of spring roll were being rotated in the centre of the table. Kritisak sipped his glass of Chinese tea and said, "For Khun Pleum?"

"Absolutely. Like I said, the shooter seems to be tied into the people behind this casino. But I don't know how." Vijay drank some of the tea Kritisak had insisted on pouring him. "You see, the thing is, Sia Geng — and I'm saying this in confidence—" Kritisak nodded and looked around the table: the goons promptly nodded. Vijay's confidences were now a serious business.

"Khun Pleum doesn't want me to tell anyone I'm investigating this case," Vijay continued. "He doesn't want people to think he cares about some nonentity writer. Which means, obviously, I can't use Khun Pleum's name to get me in. I do that, and they're going to put two and two together."

Kritisak was bubbling over with agreement before Vijay finished. "I get it. And I'm the only other influential person you know. Of course I am." An expression of pain then crossed his face. "But Khun Pleum doesn't want you to tell people you're investigating. That means you can't tell me." His eyes creased with a look of angina. "Khun Pleum isn't going to know I helped him."

"He didn't mean the likes of you, Sia Geng. He doesn't mean those in the same world as him. Which you are, obviously. He just means I can't tell the little people."

Kritisak beamed at Vijay. "In that case, you can leave this in my hands. I'll make some enquiries. That's something you can let him know. Straight away. You can tell him right now."

* * *

Back in the office, Ploy returned Vijay's call to tell him she would transfer 50,000 baht by the afternoon. He promised her he wouldn't blow the whole stack, and she said, "By five, Vijay. You'll get it around then."

"That's very quick. She's not short of cash then, your boss?"

"Of course not, she's rich. I thought I made that clear?"

"I'm just wondering what the land certificate cost ten years ago."

"This has never been about the money. And anyway, if she'd cut her losses, you wouldn't have a job."

Fair enough, Vijay thought. *You can't argue with that logic.*

After he'd put the phone down Doi said, "That's a lot of money someone's sending you."

"It's never been about the money. Apparently." One of those truth islands that bobbed up every so often in Ploy's conversation. He slipped his phone into his pocket. "Let's get an early lunch before the rush starts. I've got to go and have a difficult conversation this afternoon."

* * *

Stepping around the partition, Vijay found the Deep Blue office emitting that familiar vibe of "not enough work to keep busy".

All four desks were occupied, but this time the guy sitting opposite Aim was reclining his chair to an almost horizontal position, while tossing a tennis ball up and down. Next to him, a woman with a barrette in her hair was leafing through a glossy magazine and spinning a pen in one hand.

Vijay said to the room, "Hi, me again. Can I borrow Aim for another chat?"

She came frowning out from behind her desk. "About what, Vijay?"

"I've got quite a long, involved story for you. Let's go and get a coffee."

"Is this about your wanting to quit the project?"

"No, it's not."

"You want more money?"

"Not that either. Come on, let's take a walk."

Outside he gestured to his pickup. "It's going to be quite a long talk, let's go somewhere cooler than the *oleang* stall." He got in, leaned across and unlocked the passenger door. She hesitated and then entered. "Any ideas where we could go?"

"If you want cooler, we can go to the same coffee shop as last time. I'll give you the directions."

"As a copywriter, would you have named it the Be Trendy building?" he asked, his eyes on the road.

She thought about that. "I suppose so, why not? Does it sound strange to you? 'In trend'," she said in English, "is one of those things Thai people know. It sounds more sophisticated if it's in English."

"In England when we want to make something sound sophisticated, we put it in French. It's funny, isn't it? No one uses their own language."

In the Starbucks she ordered a cappuccino and insisted on using her own money. Vijay could imagine her dates with Montri going like this, Aim determinedly paying her way through everything.

They took a couple of low, red leather armchairs. She was wearing her usual attire of black leggings and a shortish T-shirt, and again gave the impression of a sleek pedigree cat, reserving judgement.

"Basically, I've got some good news and some bad news. But let's start with the good." He took out his wallet, extracted a business card and slid it over the table. "I've actually got two different cards for my work. This is the second one."

Keeping her arms crossed, Aim scowled at the card as though it was an unwanted proposition. "'Translations — Detective'? What is that supposed to mean?"

"It means I do a certain amount of private-eye work. We were a translation bureau before we were anything else, but it wasn't always easy making ends meet. One day I met this guy called Edwin who'd been scammed and I got a cop friend of mine to help me help him. Even though I didn't ask for it, Edwin paid me ten per cent of the money I'd recovered. It made me see there were opportunities out there."

She was watching him with cautious, unsmiling attention.

"Now in your case, obviously I'm employed as a translator. But when you said it seemed as though I was investigating you, that's also true. You see, the thing is — and this is actually good news, if you think about it — someone hired me to investigate Montri's shooting."

Her young face tightened with anger. "Hired you to investigate *us*? Who did?"

"Khun Pleum."

Her mouth opened and closed silently. "Is this a joke? It's not, is it? He's been paying you to spy on us?"

"Not spy, investigate. If I was spying on you, that would be watching your house through binoculars or something."

"How do we know you're not?"

"Why would I want to do that?"

"Why would someone like you not want to do that?"

"You know, you're answering my question, which was already an answer, with another question."

Her hand clenched around her coffee cup and for a moment, Vijay thought she was going to fling the contents at him. "I knew you weren't to be trusted. When you sent Montri that message on Facebook, I said, 'His rates are too low'. I knew you were up to something."

"Look, just for the record, you're not the first person to say that about me. But the fact—"

"Oh, I'll bet. I'll bet if you line up all the people who think you can't be trusted, they go from here to the Cambodian border."

"Jesus. One ex-girlfriend is what I was talking about."

"I just can't believe you're shameless enough to sit there admitting it to me."

"You're missing the point here. Khun Pleum hired me because it bothered him that people thought he was responsible for Montri's shooting. He said to me, and these are his words not mine, why would he be bothered by some nonentity? I'm the proof that Khun Pleum's not responsible."

"Oh really? And how do you know he's not using you to create an alibi for some other sick thing he's got planned for us? You should hear the stories Lam tells about his childhood."

"Lam's not exactly Mr Balanced Opinion."

Her knuckles whitened against the coffee cup again, and again Vijay wondered if she was going to throw it at him. But Aim had better control than that. She thumped the still-full cup back onto the table and a small cloud of froth oozed down its side. She said with icy politeness, "You can return the money Montri paid into your bank account. We still haven't received any pages from you, so I expect the whole amount back. And don't bring it in person, I don't want to see you again. Put it in an envelope between some thick card and send it by recorded delivery to Deep Blue under my name." She uncrossed her legs, pushed her chair back with a jerk and stood up.

"You haven't heard the bad news yet," Vijay said. "I think I know who shot Montri."

She glared down at him. "Oh really? Who?"

"Lam."

She put her hands on her hips. "Honestly, Vijay, don't be so ridiculous."

"It makes more sense than you'd think." He gestured to her chair. "Actually, it makes more sense than anything else."

She hesitated, then plumped herself back down in the seat. "Okay, what? And don't bother coming up with some other tall story."

"I don't mean Lam shot him in anger, obviously. I mean they cooked it up between them."

She'd recrossed her legs, had her chin on her fist and was staring at him with flinty scepticism. "Put it this way. If we say Lam didn't shoot Montri, then who the hell did? Someone who's read the book? We know Somsak's business plan didn't require him to sell any books, just marketing packages to the gullible or the desperate. And obviously Lam was one or both of those things. So then having been cajoled into parting with half a million baht just to discomfort his family, he sits back and finds nothing's happening. So he and Montri try to drum up some publicity between them. First, they try the name on the bullet thing, but that doesn't work. So, then they fire a gun into your house, and when the press don't bite on that either, Lam convinces Montri to take a flesh wound."

"Montri's not that stupid. He'd never agree to such an idiotic idea."

"I imagine Lam sold him on it by describing how the publicity would help find a publisher for his real work. You know, name recognition. Which does seem to be happening, by the way. He gets mentioned now in threads on Pantip. Not just about *Jao Por*, either. Politics, corruption, all that stuff."

"If this is all you've got, it isn't much."

"There's also the shooting itself. The gunman hit Montri in the leg and then left, rather than finishing him off. Which means he didn't intend to kill him."

"That doesn't make the gunman Lam."

"No, but it does mean he didn't fire from where Montri claims. The sun was shining on the path while his target was standing in the shade. It's a ridiculously good shot from that distance."

"Which could just as easily mean the gunman meant to scare Montri by shooting near him and ended up hitting him by mistake."

"One of the first things Montri said to me about *Jao Por* was that he was suffering for his art. Which doesn't make much sense, given he didn't think this book *was* art. He was writing it to order. What he meant was that he's suffering for the work to come."

He could see the first glimmers of doubt in Aim.

"He's not that desperate for a book deal."

"Maybe it's more guilt than desperation? Here he is, sitting at home while you're slaving away at Deep Blue. For a lot of men there's this feeling that if they're not the bread-winner, then there's something wrong with them."

"But why would he think . . . I don't mind being the one who works, he knows I don't mind. I've always believed in Montri's writing, ever since I read his short stories."

"When Lam was at Silpakorn, was he interested in guns?"

"Not as far as I know."

"But he could have been, right?"

"Vijay, anything 'could have been'. This isn't much of an argument."

"It's not all — there's more," he said. "When I asked Montri, he told me he heard Leung Tor's dog bark before the shooter appeared. I think he thought he had to say that for reasons of credibility. But when I went to see him, Leung Tor told me he hadn't heard any such thing."

"If you're going to trust that drunk old—"

Vijay put his hand up. "Wait, wait. I think Leung Tor's a lot sharper than you give him credit for. Sure, he drinks a bit too much, mainly because he's figured out his yuppie son would rather put money into his bank account than suffer the boredom of having to come and visit. But he's no fool. And was a pretty decent potter back in the day. You said yourself E-yen doesn't bark at the *pla salit* woman. And that's because he's used to her, right? So who else was always at your place? Who kept turning up with Montri's pages, wanting them redone?" He saw her eyes flicker.

"He was getting tired of all the rewrites," she said.

"Leung Tor also told me a full five minutes went by before Montri called for help. Why wait so long other than to give Lam time to disappear?"

Aim's face said she still wasn't convinced. "When you say the dog didn't bark, that could just as easily be because the shooter didn't leave by the path. Maybe he went through the bushes."

"Right, and that's the story Montri should have set up by telling me he didn't hear anything. But he's too inexperienced at this business and didn't realise I'd go and talk to Leung Tor."

Aim sat back and uncrossed her arms. "Just so you know, I still don't actually believe any of this. But if *you* think it's true, what are you going to tell Khun Pleum?"

"I don't know yet. I suppose it depends on what his reaction is going to be. Say he and Lam have a touching father-and-son bonding moment where they talk about their feelings and hug." He paused. "But that's not going to happen, is it?"

"You've got to give me some time, Vijay." Aim ran a hand through her hair, looked away and then looked back. "For the things I said about you being untrustworthy, I'm sorry."

"Forget it."

"I've got to talk to Montri." She paused and then in a quick, catlike movement, reached across and squeezed his arm. "Until then, don't say anything to Khun Pleum."

CHAPTER 11

It was a Chinatown mid-morning, with the sunlight glaring off gridlocked cars. Vijay was on foot, making his way down Ban Mor Road, on the gold shop side of the street. He was heading to Kritisak and the Restaurant With No Name. It was two days after his chat with Aim. Nothing of importance had happened to him the day before, other than Aim phoning and saying, "You were right, Vijay, about the person I was going to marry."

"*Was*? You're still planning to, aren't you?"

"Oh, I don't know. Probably. I suppose. I'm just not sure who I'm living with anymore."

"Someone who was trying very hard to secure a future for the both of you."

She sighed down the phone in a way that sounded far too world-weary for her years. "Well, that's one way of looking at it."

Vijay had spent the rest of the day trying to come to terms with his promise not to tell Khun Pleum. It had been easy enough to make it in the coffee shop, with Aim curled up opposite. In fact, he'd felt quite noble about the whole thing. But back in Chinatown, the price of the man's impatience was impossible to ignore.

I don't think anyone in your life has ever taught you a real lesson. But we are the people who will.

The problem was that while Khun Pleum might not do anything to Lam, Montri's fate was another matter. And if Vijay couldn't hand him over, then he needed a credible, hardworking way of coming up empty.

On the other hand, when it came to ruining Khun Pleum's marriage, the investigation was steaming ahead. Tong had begun sending Vijay promising text messages. The man's method for meeting his *mia noi* seemed to consist of using his business discussions as cover. His people would book out a meeting room at some high-end hotel and then when they all broke for lunch, Khun Pleum would head up to one of the hotel rooms. The suits would disperse without waiting for him and two or three hours later, he'd be driven back to his office on Sathon.

Vijay had told Tong to keep him informed of everything, which had resulted in Tong's messages becoming increasingly abstract. *Lift!*, for instance, had turned out to mean that Tong had taken the risk of getting into the same lift as Khun Pleum ("He won't remember me. We're invisible.") and had got the hotel room number but couldn't see who'd opened the door. He told Vijay later on the phone, after Doi had gone home, "You could tell from his face, here's a guy about to have sex."

Kritisak had phoned and asked Vijay to come and see him today, which had made a nice change from being summoned in person by one of his goons. When Vijay got there, the man had again been ensconced at a well-catered brunch. It had made Vijay wonder why Kritisak hadn't put on more weight. Or perhaps it was all for show rather than consumption? Maybe this was what Kritisak thought success looked like? Unhindered access to roast duck.

Seeing him, Kritisak shooed the two goons away. "Sit, sit." Putting two spring rolls on a plate, he rotated it towards Vijay. "Try these, they make them just right here. They fry the pastry crisp and it's not too thick. Lots of filling."

Vijay bit into one.

"So, I got your information," Kritisak said. "There's a guy I know, I used to run into him at cockfights out in Bangkhuntien. He's a much bigger gambler than me. Crazy for it, in fact. Anyway, he knows this place. He's been there." Kritisak squinted at Vijay. "You really picked some casino."

"You mean big money goes there? I've arranged for a stake of 50,000 baht. That should be enough, shouldn't it?"

Kritisak nodded, still looking sober. "More or less. At least it probably reaches the low end. You know, I asked Sawang — that's my friend's name — I asked Sawang what he knew about it. He said it's run by the Phuttaraksa family."

"That would be the owners of the house."

"Right. They set it up something like thirty years ago. And the thing is, it's right between Bangmod and Tungkru."

"Just inside Tungkru, according to the GPS on my phone."

"Right. So they're paying off both sets of cops. And paying them up to a *really* high level. This is a place that won't ever be raided."

"Always good to know," Vijay said with a grin.

Kritisak didn't smile back. There was a toning down of his personality that Vijay hadn't encountered before, and it occurred to him that for once the man wasn't acting out the role of a Channel Three Mafiosi. He might even be engaging with Kritisak's true self. "They're real estate people, Sawang said. Or that's what he'd heard. They own resorts down south — Phuket, Krabi, places like that. But it's not the whole story, you understand?"

"I don't think so, Sia Geng."

"It's the feeling Sawang had, about these people. Their family has all these resorts going for them and then thirty years ago, they open this big money casino and pay off every cop in sight. So what's the deal? He didn't know the whole story."

"Just that the house always wins, right?"

"Sure. It always wins . . . Anyway, he got in touch. You can go there and use his name — *pii* Sawang, he's older than me — and that will get you in. He's told them to expect you. But the thing is . . ."

He squinted at Vijay again. "You know, I like you." This, Vijay thought, was coming from the man who'd threatened to make his ankles freely rotating along the x-axis. "I don't know how your shooter's connected to these people, but what I know about them, what Sawang knows . . . it's not the whole story."

* * *

Back at home Vijay dug out the suit he'd brought with him from England (dark blue, polyester, Primark winter sale purchase). He'd worn it to the offices of Bristol City Council where he'd interviewed for a "graduate training" position and then found himself typing numbers into Excel spreadsheets day in, day out. The sheer tedium of the job had made Vijay dream. Not just of a better training scheme with a different employer, but of another life completely. And it was into that stale space that Mana's emails landed. Vijay asked about employment opportunities in Thailand, and Mana told him there was always English teaching. So Vijay had spent the autumn getting his TEFL teaching certificate from evening classes at the same university he'd done his degree. But it was clear in his mind that an English-language school would only be a first step. As soon as possible, he would find a way to work for himself. No more performance reviews, no more key performance indicators. From then on, and for the rest of his life, he would be the master of his own destiny.

Kritisak had told Vijay the casino got going at around eight and ran till the early hours of the next morning. So, with his jacket slung over his shoulder, wearing his good black shoes, and feeling pleasantly successful as a result of the get-up, he went looking for a taxi. It was seven thirty when he found one and past eight by the time the taxi's yellow headlights were sliding down the long *soi* in Tungkru to finally pool up against the big gothic "P" on the Phuttaraksas' gate.

Having paid off the driver, Vijay approached the intercom in the wall, making sure to turn his face to the CCTV camera when he spoke into it. Three Mercedes were already lined up on the grass verge outside the compound walls. A man in a white shirt and dark slacks was leaning against the bonnet of the middle one, smoking a cigarette.

"Yes?" crackled a voice from the intercom.

"I'm a friend of *pii* Sawang's," Vijay said. "I'm here for the game."

There was no reply, and for a while nothing happened. He waited and finally heard a bolt being scraped back. A man in a black collarless jacket opened the door and looked Vijay up and down, *wai*ed and led him past the cherubs in the fountain. They were now lit from below, starkly white against the moonless night.

The factotum went left from the house, taking Vijay past metal awnings sheltering a Mini Cooper, a couple of BMWs and plenty of free space. "So these are the house cars," Vijay said. "They don't let the gamblers park here?"

"No, sir."

Beyond the high, imposing mansion was a wide single-storey building. A broad wooden veranda led to double doors guarded on each side by waist-high stone Chinese lions. The factotum came as far as the top step, *wai*ed and retreated. Vijay pushed one of the doors open and found air conditioning arctic enough to let him slip his jacket on. Laid out in the chill were all the money games — a hypnotically spinning roulette wheel, the dice, the hopeful green baize of the card tables. And coming towards him across the parquet floor, a smiling man in a dark suit, with the yellow splash of the silk handkerchief in his pocket matching the yellow of his silk tie. "I believe you're *pii* Sawang's friend," he said, simply beaming with joy at their meeting.

"That's right."

"And how *is* Sawang these days?"

"Oh, you know, just the same. Still travelling down to Bangkhuntien for his cockfights and then betting on the wrong bird."

The comment elicited an indulgent chuckle, although Vijay had a feeling he could have said, "He's still running naked through the paddy fields with his face painted blue, trying to bayonet field rats" and would have got the same genial "isn't that the Sawang we know" reaction.

"And this is the first time you've visited us, I believe?" the man asked, making it sound as though Vijay was bestowing a great compliment upon them by his presence.

"It's the first time I've been in any casino for a while. Things haven't been great with me on the business front, to be honest."

"And business is?"

"I'm a translator. Just lately I made some very good contacts at the UN and work has started to flood in. And the thing is, I made them purely by accident. So I thought to myself, you know what? My luck is back."

Another benevolent smile. "I'm very glad to hear that." He gestured to the tables. "Please. Enjoy yourself." He moved away to speak to a woman with a bright orange wrap around her shoulders.

At one side of the room was a granite-topped wet bar. Thinking it would help him look the part, Vijay went over and spent 300 baht on a martini.

Drink in hand, he surveyed the room and wondered where to start. Up to now his only gambling experience had consisted of card nights in Petch's apartment. At first they'd played poker (draw and five-card stud), and then Petch returned from a two-week holiday in France insisting they switch to baccarat. He'd seen the Monte Carlo casino at night through a tour bus window. Possibly excited by the tour guide's exaggeration, Petch had come back announcing that baccarat was the game of the French aristocracy, now played by European millionaires. The four of them — Petch, Pasara (his girlfriend), Prem (a fellow journalist) and Vijay — had regularly sat on the floor of the flat pushing one-baht coins across Petch's low Japanese table. Even when switching to poker they could play for five hours straight without any-one winning or losing more than 1,000 baht. The point of the evenings was really to drink Leo, eat salted peanuts, and set the world to rights. And to satisfy the hunger brought on by Petch's glimpse of golden light spilling out of a casino window. "And a bit of a chandelier," he'd told Vijay. "You could see the edge of it."

Looking around the Phuttaraksas' set-up, Vijay couldn't help thinking the best cure for Petch's casino yearnings would have been to visit one. Because this wasn't what he'd expected. He'd imagined a place of indulgent luxury, peopled by glamorous women in evening dresses carrying cigarette holders and tough guys in suits, and for the whole thing to have had an air of romance and mystery. In fact, the atmos-phere was far more functional. The walls were painted a basic white and could have done with another coat. There were marks of discolouration under the windows and around the light switches. The cards being flicked over tables had a new, shiny look, but the green baize surfaces were worn. And the sparse crowd had an air of joylessness. These people hadn't come here for a social gathering. They might not have even come to enjoy themselves, such was the rapt, unsmiling way they were placing their bets. They were, however, mainly an older group, most in their mid-fifties or above. Which gave Vijay the hope he could find some regulars who would remember Bundit.

At a marble-topped counter to one side of the room, he handed over 20,000 bahts' worth of Ploy's friend's money, and received sixteen chips: one black (5,000 baht), two green (3,000 baht each), five blue (1,000 baht each) and eight red (500 baht each). It would be a good spread, Vijay thought, in terms of letting him bet frugally but also appear rich should the need arise. Although it was sobering to convert so many grey notes into a cylinder of plastic he could just about grasp in one hand.

With the chips weighing down his jacket pockets, Vijay went looking for a game. He found himself drawn to the roulette wheel. It was the call of "No more bets please" above the quiet murmur of the room, and also the fact that casinos had always meant roulette to Vijay, for some reason. At the table there were just three people seated. A woman in her sixties was twisting and untwisting her pearl necklace with one finger. Opposite her was a man of similar age, sitting with his forearms protectively around his stack, as though guarding it for an owner who would soon return, and next to him, a woman in her fifties. She had a much smaller pile of chips, all blue or red, and was pouting at the wheel. There was a group of onlookers though, and from their air of hushed expectation, most clearly had stakes on the table. Some chips, Vijay noticed, were directly over a number, while others were on the line between two, or at the intersection of four, which made him wonder. He caught the eye of the man standing next to him and something of Vijay's uncertainty must have communicated itself. The man said, "They use European rules here."

The white ball went spinning round the wheel's rim, dropped, hit a metal blocker, bounced twice and came to rest on twenty-four black. The man chuckled and pointed to a green chip sitting below a column of numbers. The croupier placed a second green chip on top of it, and the man pocketed both of them with a beaming look of satisfaction. He was in his fifties, no more than five foot five and pear-shaped. A portly ball of pleasure in dark green silk. He rocked on the balls of his feet and surveyed the room. "I always move off the table after my first win," he said. "Later I'll return. That's the kind of relationship we have, me and the spirit of this wheel."

"Just remind me again, how do European rules work exactly?" Vijay asked.

The man sized him up in a kindly uncle sort of way, and went through the complete rules of roulette — what it meant to place your chip on the intersection between two numbers, four numbers, at the bottom of a column, and so on. The greeter in the yellow tie gave an indulgent smile as he went past. Vijay put a red chip at the top of the grid, at the intersection of the zero line and that of numbers one, two and three.

"An old friend of mine used to work here," he said. "Bundit, he was a greeter. Maybe ten years ago."

The ball spun, bounced and landed on seven red.

"I don't notice them much," replied Green Silk. "It's the table that counts. You have to get a feeling for the spirit of the wheel."

After he'd gone, Vijay placed some more red chip bets, going for the intersection of four numbers at first and then placing chips at the bottom of columns. It was a fun thing to do with someone else's money — watch his luck take physical form, spin round the circumference of the wheel and then drop, rattle and bounce. And then he'd think, *Next time. Next time it will come to me.*

In between placing bets, Vijay chatted with the onlookers, who turned out to be business types that had all reached a certain level of financial security. One man ran a recycling company converting PET bottles into solid pellets of plastic, which he sold to factories in Vietnam. Someone else owned a fleet of the big trucks that mix concrete. A woman with a silver-tipped walking stick owned a private hospital on the Rama III Road. Now her children took care of day-to-day business, while she gambled during the week and made merit in temples on the weekend. "I liked Bundit," she said. "A cheerful man." But she knew nothing about what had happened to him.

Vijay lost three more red chips during all of this and in desperation used a fourth to simply bet on the colour red. The ball bounced three times, landed on six black and he decided to move on. Scanning the card tables, he had to remind himself he'd just parted with 2,500 baht. Such was the deceptive effect of those plastic counters. You divorced your wrestle with luck from the money it was costing you.

Vijay scanned the card tables and decided he didn't want poker. These would be serious players, studying one another's gambling patterns and calculating the odds. He couldn't see them appreciating the distraction of someone jabbering on about his pal the greeter. Punto banco baccarat or black-jack were better options, but instead he found himself in the magnetic pull of a kidney-shaped table and a sign in gothic script reading *Chemin de fer*.

This was Petch's major obsession. The game of James Bond, he told them. Petch had even gone out and bought extra packs of cards, just so that they could play it with the full six decks. They didn't have a shoe to put them in, so stacked them onto an unwieldy pile on top of a red silk hand-kerchief, and then dragged that round Petch's Japanese table to signify who the banker was.

Here there *was* a shoe, a tall gunmetal thing with a lip to let you slide the cards out. It was currently parked in front of a man in a dark blue blazer with wide gold buttons. He was younger than most of the casino crowd — perhaps mid-for-ties — and was sitting with one elbow over his chair back, his other arm on the baize, as though presenting to this col-lection of old folk the size of his stake. Which was huge. Tall columns with plenty of green among the red and blue. He now began picking up cylinders of chips and tossing them into the square that represented the banker's bet.

In a way, it was what Vijay had wanted from the casino. Not Bundit — or not *just* Bundit — but this. A moment of high-stakes drama. And because he was so entranced by the action at the table, he didn't see her coming until it was too late.

"Vijay, what are you doing here?"

He turned to find Malinee next to him. She was wearing a pair of figure-hugging black slacks with white pinstripes and a shimmering white silk blouse. Her hair was longer than it had been when they'd been together, and curled at the ends. And while she wasn't on Ploy's scale of megawatt film-star beauty, her dark eyes still filled him with longing for everything he'd thrown away.

"Oh. Right." Vijay found he was conscious of the people around him. Admittedly they probably weren't interested in this conversation, given they were serious gamblers, watching the construction of a serious bid. And yet he felt suddenly trapped by his surroundings, and by everything he'd wanted to be when he was with her. "I've made some good contacts, believe it or not, and work has started to flood in. At the UN," he said. "And I said to myself, you know what? My luck is back."

She looked at him with dismay and put her hands on her hips. "You can't, can you? You just can't—" She turned on her high heels and marched off across the parquet floor to the granite-topped bar.

So that was that situation dealt with. Now he could go back to enquiring about Bundit.

Vijay left the game. Malinee was collecting a glass of something red with ice cubes and Vijay knew it would be a vodka and tomato juice. She saw him coming, stopped, seemed to steel herself and then tilted her chin up.

"Okay, so that wasn't totally true," he said.

"Nothing in your world is totally true."

"No. Right. Well . . . some of it is. Look, thing is, I'm on a case."

"Let me guess, a beautiful woman came to you for help?"

"That's actually pretty much it."

She gave an irritated click of her tongue and began to turn away.

"No, I'm working. Malinee, come on. What else would I be doing here? I'm not of these people."

That, at least, got a reluctant smile out of her. She reached out and fingered the sleeve of his suit. "What is this? Polyester?"

"D'you like it? This was my graduate training scheme suit, back in England."

"I thought you didn't get on to any graduate training schemes?"

"Yeah, I blame the suit."

That got another smile, which made him feel good. After all this time single, it was like rediscovering a lost power: he could still make her laugh. He took the cocktail stick out of his martini and said, "These drinks are something, aren't they? One hundred baht per olive, this works out as. If it came with more than three, I wouldn't have been able to afford it."

"They've got mojitos. If you ask nicely they might even give you one of those little umbrellas."

Vijay didn't say anything in his defence. She had the right to see that particular arrow land. "Whose name did you use to get in here?" he asked.

The ghost of a smile came back. "We used our own. Chu is a regular." With the hand holding the Bloody Mary, she pointed back to the chemin de fer table. Vijay realised the guy in the dark blue blazer, and giant pile of chips, was Chu. He had only seen the man once before, and that was at a distance, opening his car door.

"Oh, right. I didn't know that was your boyfriend."

"Fiancé, now." She splayed out the fingers of her free hand to display the ring, a decent-sized glittering diamond, set between two smaller ones.

"That's great. Congratulations." Vijay paused. He felt himself dropping soundlessly through space, and reached blindly for words to break his fall. "It looks good on you."

"Thanks."

"So what do you usually play here?"

"Oh, I don't even come all that often. When I do, I usually just keep Chu company. He says I bring him good luck."

"You know, Petch should be here. He loves chemin de fer."

She looked at him in a sad, resigned sort of way, the way you'd look at a room you'd never re-enter. "I liked Petch."

Vijay knew at that moment he wanted to keep Malinee with him more than he wanted to find Bundit. "I have to go and play blackjack. I mean, for work," he said. "Why don't you come and bring me some luck?"

"I don't think the two of us ever brought each other much luck, Vijay."

"Well . . . there's a first time for everything." He took the chips out of his jacket pocket. "This is all I've got. I'm going to need some good fortune to stay afloat here." Her gaze skittered over him. With Malinee, even under her irritation, there was always a kindness you could appeal to.

"Okay, just for a bit," she said. "Is that your own money?"

"No, it's from an unknown client via a go-between."

"Very good. Very mysterious."

They headed for the blackjack table.

"This is actually one of strangest cases I've ever had."

"Have you forgotten? You always said that to me. Every time you phoned and explained why you couldn't make dinner, or the film, or the party. It was always 'the strangest case you'd ever worked on'."

He grinned at her. "Look at this place. Look at you. I'm living in strange times."

"Look at me? What does that mean?"

"Oh, I don't know. Just . . . the fact of us meeting. Not now, even the first time. If Ning's father hadn't had his Indian bronzes stolen . . . Here." He placed three blue chips on the table in front of her. "You've got to have something to bet with."

The croupier smiled at them and began shuffling the cards in sections.

"I don't like betting on things much," Malinee said.

"Come on, live a little."

Having completed the shuffle, the croupier restacked the deck and pushed the pile across the baize for Malinee to cut. She then inserted a blank plastic marker close to the bottom and dropped the whole stack into the shoe.

Vijay tossed a blue chip into the betting area and Malinee followed suit. The croupier slid them each a card face up — jack of diamonds for Malinee, three of hearts for Vijay — and then dealt herself the seven of spades.

"If you don't bet, what do you do all evening?" Vijay asked.

"I told you, I keep Chu company. Which I *enjoy*." She reached over and pinched his arm. "Don't look like that."

The croupier dealt Malinee a five of clubs and Vijay a six of diamonds.

"I'm not looking like anything."

Malinee took her second card face down and stared at the baize. "Fifteen . . . Well, hit then, I suppose." She received an eight of hearts and sighed. "Busted."

Vijay asked for another card and got the queen of spades. "So how's life at River City?" It was the site of the auction house where she worked.

"Hectic. We've been getting lots of Chinese buyers lately and they're all paranoid about us selling them fakes."

Vijay took another hit and got the ten of clubs — twenty-two.

"If they're worried, why don't you give them my number?"

"You mean employ *you* to investigate *us*?"

The croupier turned over her second card to reveal the king of diamonds. Seventeen meant she had to stick, which meant she'd won.

"You see, Vijay, I said we weren't good luck for each other."

"Minor setback. Come on, let's go again." He dropped his last blue chip onto the table. Malinee hesitated before following with one of hers.

"I could investigate your company, why not? I'll give the Chinese a discount rate."

He received a seven of hearts, Malinee a ten of clubs. She rested her elbow on the table, cupped her cheek in her palm and turned to look at him. It was exactly the look he still couldn't get over. A liquid stare, serious and challenging, that went right through him. "Vijay, do you think you could find out one single thing about me?"

"If I take you on as a case, you won't have a single secret left."

At that, she seemed to remember herself and turned back to the croupier, whose face-up card was the five of diamonds.

"Hit," she said.

"You've only got one card."

"Yes, I'm aware of that."

The croupier slid Vijay a four of spades and Malinee a nine of clubs to match her ten. He went chasing her score of nineteen and ended up on twenty-four. The croupier turned over her other card to reveal an eight of hearts. She slid herself cards out of the shoe until she reached eighteen, and from dealer's rules had to stop. Smiling at Malinee, she placed a blue chip on top of her stake and pushed it back.

"You should have these," Malinee said. "It's your money."

"Yeah, but it's your luck." Vijay tossed two red chips onto the table.

"I should get back to Chu soon." She pushed another blue chip out. The croupier slid out cards over the baize. They both had royals — the king of clubs for Malinee and queen of diamonds for him. The croupier then gave herself the ace of spades.

"Well," said Malinee, "this is ominous."

Her next two draws — a five and a two — gave her seventeen. "Do you think I should stick?" she asked the croupier.

The question elicited a bright, professional smile and nothing approaching an answer. Malinee chewed it over in that way she had, mushing her full lower lip up against her top lip. A lonely question wandered into Vijay's mind: was there anything about him she'd remember, the way he remembered every little detail about her?

"Are you thinking about your case?"

"Sorry?"

"You've got that squinty, faraway look you get."

"No, not really . . . I mean, yeah, I was."

She laughed. "Vijay, *honestly*."

He pointed to the croupier. "She's waiting for your decision."

"Oh. Right." Malinee pushed her palms onto the baize in the manner of someone summoning spirits to a table. "I'll stick."

"No, I was really thinking about the case," Vijay said. "I'm here working."

"I haven't seen you do any work."

It was a fair point. The problem was, his last round of questions had conjured up that old "uncle" with a gun. What if this time they produced whoever Bundit was fleeing? Vijay knew he couldn't risk Malinee appearing involved in his search. And yet, the fact was, he knew he would rather spend the evening with her than do any work.

So again he went chasing her score, but this time reached twenty. The croupier flipped over her second card, a nine of hearts. And now he was in luck. Playing to the dealer's rules, she busted out at twenty-two.

"You did it," said Malinee, as the croupier set two red chips on top of his stake.

"One each," he said. "Next game's the decider."

"I should get back to Chu."

"Right."

"But then we still have to find out who wins the Great Tungkru Blackjack 1,000 Baht Face-Off."

"Maybe you should get back to Chu."

"Fine."

"I mean, not immediately. You know, at some point."

"No, no. I'll go now," she said, looking away from him. "Here you are, Vijay." Still without meeting his gaze, she placed her remaining blue chip on top of his pile. "You can go back to your important work."

She left and Vijay watched the shimmer of her white blouse wind its way back through the crowd to the chemin de fer table. He gave a long, weary sigh and said to the croupier, "In English there's a saying: 'Lucky in cards, unlucky in love'. But I don't seem to have much luck with either."

He received a look of genuine sympathy, and remembering himself, Vijay chased the opportunity it gave him. "You know, a friend of mine actually used to work here. Bundit. He was a greeter. I'd love to find out what happened to him."

The woman said nothing, but let her gaze flick sideways to a balding gentleman in rimless glasses, sitting alone at a banco baccarat table. Vijay gave her a quiet "Thank you" and scooped up his chips.

Vijay set down the remains of his martini at the table where Rimless Glasses was the only one present, which meant he'd be playing against him with one of them ceremonially designated as the bank, assuming Petch had got the rules right. He always complained if the four of them switched to punto banco, as he said there was no skill in the game — both the players and the bank had fixed rules about when they could draw and when they couldn't. Though in fact, Vijay liked it just for that reason. Pure luck was the ultimate level playing field. "Me against you then," he said.

"And I'm the bank, it seems." Rimless Glasses had a lean face, prominent cheekbones and long, thin pianist's fingers that he held steepled together, as though the shoe in front of him was a mathematical problem requiring careful consideration. He nodded to himself and dropped a single green chip into the betting square. Vijay matched the bet and found himself wondering if he was going to burn through the rest of Ploy's cash before he found out anything.

The croupier dealt him a card face down and then gave one to Rimless Glasses.

"My name's Vijay, by the way."

The man blinked, seemed to evaluate the idea of Vijay having a name, and then said, "Pin." A second face-down card slid over the baize to each of them.

"What I like about this game is that it's out of your hands," Vijay said. "You don't sit here with a migraine working the odds."

The comment produced a brief but brilliant smile. "You come to this table to escape considerations," Pin said, and turned over his cards. Nine of hearts and eight of clubs.

The goal of baccarat is to get as close as possible to nine (a lucky number in Thailand, appropriately enough). Tens and court cards count as zero. So Pin had a score of seven. Vijay flipped over his to reveal a three of diamonds and a seven of diamonds: zero. "You sound like a businessman," he said.

Face up, the croupier slid over the card Vijay was obliged to take — the queen of spades had followed him across from the blackjack table.

Pin looked over his steepled fingers. "I'm one of the few exceptions to this crowd. I don't deal in business. And I don't deal in luck."

"Banker wins." The croupier pushed both chips out to Pin, who immediately tossed one back into the betting square.

"You could say my job is to hold bad luck at bay," he continued.

Vijay matched his bet. "Now you've got me. I can't guess what that is."

The croupier slid the shoe across, signifying Vijay was now governed by the banker's rules. Pin turned his head and for a moment the ceiling lights were caught on his glasses, making his lean face utterly unreadable. And in that pause, he could have said anything — that he was a hitman, a drug dealer, a grave robber — and Vijay would have believed it.

"I'm a surgeon," he said, and in the chill of the room, with the martini going to Vijay's head, somehow that felt just as sinister.

The croupier slid their cards across the baize, this time starting with Pin.

"That makes sense," Vijay said. "I can see why you'd want to get away from consequences once in a while."

Pin turned over his cards to reveal a six of hearts and a king of clubs. So six in total. Vijay flipped over his to find the worst possible combination — a two of spades and a three of diamonds. High enough to make overshooting nine a real possibility, but less than seven. As the banker, he had to draw. He signalled for the card and received a seven of spades.

"Player wins." The croupier and sent Pin the chips. Again, the automatic toss back.

Vijay matched his bet again (now just one green chip left). "This must be because of all the merit you make in your job. All those lives you save."

"It doesn't work like that," Pin said. "I can have someone die on the table, then come here and have a good evening."

Well great, thought Vijay and considered giving him Kritisak's phone number in case he fancied a change of career. Maybe he could get into the ankle-rotating business as well. "You've been playing here a while, it sounds like."

The croupier had shifted the shoe back to Pin's position. She slid out Vijay's first card.

"Since I qualified," Pin said, "I needed somewhere to park all my luck. My good luck and my bad luck, it's all here in this room. I leave it behind when I go home."

The croupier slid Pin his first card.

"That's an interesting perspective." Vijay drained his martini. "A friend of mine was a greeter in this place, way back when. Bundit, his name was. You must have come across him."

Vijay's second card slid over the baize. "I don't remember the names of these people," Pin said.

The croupier snatched his card out of the shoe so quickly it flipped over: jack of diamonds. Immediately she apologised. In punto banco getting the cards face up or down made no difference, given the absence of betting options, and yet such are the obsessive rituals of long-term gamblers, Vijay could see it bothering Pin. He was staring at the jack as though it was a doom-laden message about his future. Vijay turned his own cards over to reveal an eight of clubs and a five of hearts. A score of three.

Pin pursed his lips with distaste and flipped over his remaining card: four of clubs. Vijay started to wonder if the man's hesitations were well-founded after all. Perhaps the croupier's flip really had disturbed the delicate threads of luck crossing the table. Vijay looked up at her and signalled for the card he had to take. She was older than the other women working there, possibly in her late forties. Her hair had been dyed auburn but was starting to grow out, and you could see strands of grey among the black. Tired eyes and a lipstick smudge at the corner of her mouth. She met his gaze briefly and without emotion, and then dealt him an eight of diamonds. So much for cutting Pin's luck then. A win for the banker without his having to draw.

"I'm going to get another drink. I don't think this table's spirit likes me," Vijay said.

Pin nodded.

Vijay used Ploy's friend's cash to order another three-olive martini and then stacked his chips next to the glass, just to remind himself of where he stood: one black, three blue, two red. He'd gone from 20,000 baht to 9,000 in just over an hour. On the plus side, he still had almost 30,000 in banknotes. And he'd got to the point where it was no longer luck he was betting on.

So he sat back and sipped his martini, and Pin played against the croupier. Vijay chatted with the barman to try and distract himself from the sight of Malinee at the chemin de fer table. She was sitting to the right of Chu, and was leaning forwards with one hand on his shoulder.

Meanwhile, the barman was a friendly, good-looking guy called Nic. In his twenties, he wore his short hair gelled into lethal spikes and had a brass stud in one ear. He told Vijay he'd previously worked in a bar on Sukhumvit. Compared to that, the casino was less hectic and Nic received the same salary, but in this case cash in hand, so no taxes. It was the casino manager who paid him, once a month in the small office at the end of this long room. Nic pointed out the metal door with *Staff Only* written in red. He'd never been to the main house, never seen the Phuttaraksas.

"And what about the manager?" Vijay asked. "How much contact does he have with them?"

Nic didn't know. He had no curiosity about the owners, or about what went on behind the black glass doors of the main house. He only knew they'd never be raided. "Thirty years it's been here. Something like that. And the police haven't come round once. Or that's what everyone tells me."

Vijay raised his glass in a toast to Nic's good fortune and turned his attention to Pin. He was playing in the same automatic way as before, one green chip each time, and taking his losses and wins with the same air of diligence.

"That's the surgeon guy," Nic said, following the line of Vijay's gaze. "He'll go over to the roulette wheel soon. Everyone here sticks to their own pattern."

For a while it looked as though Pin was breaking his. Taking tiny sips of the martini, Vijay had got two thirds of the way down and eaten all three olives before Pin moved.

He carried his glass back to the baccarat table and set it up next to his diminished cylinder of chips. Without saying anything, the croupier began sliding cards out of the shoe. The rule seemed to be that she'd play as the bank. Vijay thought, *What the hell*, and put all three blue chips in. His cards slid over the baize. "Now that Pin's gone, maybe I'll get some of the luck he was hogging," he said.

The croupier met that without comment and dealt for herself. He turned his hand over to find a five of spades and a seven of spades. A total of two: no sign of luck coming his way.

He tried again. "It's nice how people here remember Bundit."

She hesitated and flipped over her cards. A queen of diamonds and a five of clubs.

"Okay, so not Pin. But other people seem to," he continued. A six of hearts came to him. Luck at last, but no longer what Vijay was betting on. He tossed another conversational chip onto the pile. "They all think of him quite fondly, don't they?"

That did it.

"Think of. I don't know where you get that idea." She dealt herself a five of hearts. He'd won, finally.

"They do at least remember him, so that's nice."

She topped his stake with three more blues and pushed it back. "Remember what? They'll struggle to tell you a single thing about him. Their chips and their cards and their drinks are all they care about."

Vijay dropped in three blues for his next bet and she sent the cards across. She was thin-lipped with anger now.

"And he remembered everything about them. Someone could walk in here after six months and Bundit would ask, 'So, did your son get into Chula?'" She dealt her own two cards.

Vijay turned over his hand. A seven of hearts and a six of clubs: total of three. "I'd like to learn more about him."

She slid a four of diamonds out of the shoe and sent it to him. "Because?"

"There's someone who wants to find him."

That produced a sad smile. "Of course there is. And this someone is female, I suppose?" She turned over her own cards to reveal the ace of spades and a six of spades. The ace counted as one and banker's rules meant she had to stand on seven. They'd drawn.

"She's female, but it's not like that."

"Like what?" She pushed his stake back to him.

"She's not a wife or a girlfriend."

Another smile, this time with a degree of self-mockery. "Are you sure? He had plenty of both."

Vijay picked up the three blue chips. "I'm guessing you'd like to find him yourself. Why don't we pool our discoveries?"

"You know something?" For a moment, the hope was alive in her face, then she composed herself and raked the cards away.

"A bit," Vijay said. "But it's not stuff I can go into here. When do you get off work?"

"We shouldn't be talking anyway. They don't like it."

She told him she lived in Phra Pradaeng, gave him the address and said she'd be back there by about three in the morning.

Vijay went off to cash in his chips but then couldn't resist looking over at the chemin de fer table. Malinee still had one hand on Chu's shoulder. As Chu's card flicked over the baize, he said something and she tilted her chin up in that way she had.

Vijay decided he may as well try his luck on one more game. The polished wood of the roulette table carried a clutter of red, blue and green. He set down his black chip at the intersection of sixteen red, seventeen black, nineteen red and twenty black.

"No more bets, ladies and gentlemen. No more bets."

The ball gave two rattling bounces and landed on twenty-eight black. Time to leave. He received 7,000 baht from the cashier in exchange for his remaining chips — 13,000 down from what he'd started with.

Although Vijay had been sure his attention was elsewhere, as soon as he headed for the door, the greeter in the yellow tie came gliding up. "Going so soon?" he asked. "I hope we haven't failed to live up to your expectations." He gestured with his open palm to the card tables and their moneyed crowd. "As you can see, we're really a modest little affair."

"Oh, sure. I like it here just fine. But I sometimes get a feeling about my luck. Sometimes I know it's gone for the evening. I don't know why, it just does. But I'll definitely come back. This is exactly the kind of place I've been looking for."

"I'm so pleased to hear that," the greeter said with a well-oiled smile. "And please allow me to call you a taxi." Which meant, Vijay thought, the man knew he'd arrived in one. He waited on one of the bar stools for the car to turn up but didn't order another drink. The martinis were starting to fog his thoughts, and he needed to sober up.

When the taxi came, the same factotum as before appeared, *wai*ed, and escorted Vijay out to the car. Walking back to the front of the house, Vijay took off his jacket and rolled up his sleeves. In the hot, humid night the main building was unlit.

"Does anyone actually live there?" Vijay asked and received a polite, stretched smile as his only reply.

* * *

Vijay had told the taxi to take him back to the office rather than to his apartment. He wanted to rest, but didn't want to get too comfortable and oversleep. By the time he was back in the silent, empty building it was almost a quarter to eleven. He sat down at his desk, set the alarm on his phone for two a.m. and dozed with his head on his forearms.

Aware of the need to wake soon, it was a fitful, uneasy sleep. At one point, Vijay dreamed he was back in the casino, playing blackjack alongside Malinee. They were both on nineteen, but the croupier seemed to somehow keep drawing cards from the shoe without reaching twenty-one. Vijay said, "You have to stop on five cards," and realised the croupier was Supaporn.

She said, "I can do whatever I like."

"She can, actually," said Malinee, and then her phone went off. Knowing it was Chu, Vijay told her to ignore the call, but the ringtone became louder and louder and turned out to be the alarm waking him up.

He felt more dislocated than rested, and for a brief moment expected Malinee to still be beside him. Then the evening's successes and failures seeped into the room. He thought of the first time she'd visited his office. Her auction-house-trained eyes hadn't missed anything. The water stain on the wall, the dent in the filing cabinet. But she'd seemed oddly impressed. "I like how you're making a go of this."

And what the hell, I still am, he thought to himself, switching off the light and locking up. He was still making a go of it.

He drove fast on the nearly empty roads and was in Phra Pradaeng by two thirty. The GPS led him to a court-yard off the main road. Around him were ageing five-storey apartment blocks, whose windows were nearly all unlit. The courtyard itself was deserted, with the exception of a stray dog curled up asleep and, in one corner, like a single hopeful thought in a dark mind, the fairy lights of a *ya dong* stall.

Vijay's pickup engine was loud, so he cut the ignition and rolled the window down. A light rain started, bringing up the smell of wet concrete. The dog woke, shook himself and loped off to a stairwell, where he curled up again. At some time past three — the rain gone, and the night now cooler — a taxi curved into the courtyard and Mae the croupier got out. Vijay left the pickup and went over.

She gave him a tired look. "We'll get a drink."

At the *ya dong* stall there were three metal tables set out. Mae must have been a regular, as the woman put a *pec* (a shot glass's worth) of the herbal whiskey on the counter without being asked.

"I'll have the same," said Vijay. A twenty-baht note paid for both drinks. Carrying them over to Mae's table, he said, "This is a bit better than the casino prices."

She gave a sigh and eased her feet out of her heels, then took the glass off the table and drained it in one swallow. "I have two of these every night since Bundit left."

Vijay took a sip and found it had a slightly sweet taste, and less alcohol heat than the martinis. "I don't know if 'left' is correct," he said. "It seems like he's been disappeared, doesn't it? I mean, all his stuff was still in the apartment."

She frowned. "That's not what the landlady told me. She said it was empty."

"That's because she wanted his things in lieu of unpaid rent."

Mae stared at her empty glass. "Typical. That's typical of how people treated him. And he was better than all of them."

"Better at what?"

She raised her eyes to his and a spark of defiance flashed out of her tiredness. "At being a human. At being bigger than his surroundings. At having dreams and ideas and plans."

"How much do you know about Bundit's life before the casino?" Vijay said.

"What's that supposed to mean? He did terrible things, is that what you're going to try and tell me?"

"I wouldn't say 'terrible', though he did liberate a few people from their money, by all accounts."

"Don't try and impress me with that. I know all the stories, and do you want to know how? Because he told me them himself. The Pure Aspiration Party and having dinner with Banharn Silpa-archa back when he was prime minister, and arranging meetings in the Dusit Thani Hotel between people in the Ministry of Education and a firm wanting to import computers. And yes, forging land certificates in Kanchanaburi and some other places. And some other things I've forgotten. But he was living in one room in Bangmod when I knew him. He made more money for other people than he ever made for himself."

"Why do you think that is?"

"Because he was too generous. He cared about people, and when he won he wanted everyone around him to share the blessings. That's what made him such a good greeter, you know." She made a face. "Much better than Taowachi. He just sucks up to a few high rollers and keeps his beady eye on everyone else. Bundit cared." She picked up her glass. "I need another drink."

Vijay took it back to the counter and returned with another *pec*. "Did he have any projects on the go, in the time you knew him?"

"You can't just come here and suck all the information out of me," Mae said. "Where's your side?" She drained her glass. "You told me you knew something."

"Well, apart from how sudden his disappearance was, I know someone wants him found. And it relates to a fake land certificate in Rayong."

She rolled her eyes. "In other words, you don't have anything."

"And I know his good pal from his land scam days is still hoping he'll turn up. Maybe you know his name? The old guy with the grey hair, balding on top?"

"He had a lot of good pals." And then quietly, with wry self-awareness, "Bundit made us all feel special."

"So, his current project, what did that involve?"

She rotated her empty glass again. "Look at you, you're just sipping yours."

"Those martinis in the casino were pretty strong."

"You've got a funny idea of strong." She added, "I might as well go."

Vijay threw in his last chip. "I know that before he disappeared, he started getting visits from a guy in a red Mercedes."

She gave that a look of distaste. "And what did he want?"

"You know who I'm talking about?"

"He turned up at the casino sometimes."

"You make him sound like the proverbial bad penny."

"That's what he was. He used to drink Black Label with soda and finish up drunk by the end of the night. Bundit had to try and talk him out of driving home. He'd say, 'I'll speak to the people in the house. You can park the car in the compound and get it tomorrow.' But the man always refused. A couple of times, Bundit got into the Mercedes and drove it himself."

"That was nice of him."

"He . . . indulged him, I don't know why. Extended him credit, as well. It was part of his job, he could do that if he wanted."

"So this guy lost a lot of money then? He wasn't a good gambler?"

"It's not just that he wasn't good. He didn't gamble like a normal person. Sometimes, when I was on the blackjack table, he'd twist on nineteen. Once he twisted on twenty. I said to him once, 'Are you sure you want to do that?' Which by the way, is breaking the rules. You're not supposed to advise them."

"And he did this while drunk?"

She paused. "Not always. It could be before he got drunk. It was as though . . . as though he wanted to prove money didn't matter to him."

"So he was rich then? D'you know his name?"

"It was Sanserm something. And no, I don't think he was rich. He was a colonel, Bundit told me. That's not so high up, is it? We've had generals at the casino."

"From a rich family then? Or with a good sideline in something or other?"

She picked up her glass again and rolled it along the table. "I don't think so."

"Do you want another drink?"

"Okay." And then: "No, I don't. If I have another one, I'll have one more. And this is no better than drinking alone." She looked up to the dark apartment windows above them. "When he was here, I didn't need alcohol. Bundit was my nightcap."

"Why do you say Sanserm wasn't rich?"

"He didn't look the part. You observe people, you know. When you've got nothing to do but stand there in your heels and slide cards over the table, and they're controlling your toilet breaks, we notice things." She added, "Like you — you didn't look the part either. Turning up in your cheap suit and your cheap watch. Holding a martini and thinking it made you look like a high roller."

"He had a red Merc though, right? I don't suppose you remember the licence plate?"

"Why would I do that? And yes."

"Sorry?"

"I will have another one."

He went over and got her another shot.

"Did you ever ask Bundit why he indulged the red Merc guy? With the credit, I mean."

"He felt sorry for him, that was all. He told me, 'There's an unhappiness in that man's life. And he's not doing any harm.'"

"That's an odd reason. I always thought they did it for regulars who were guaranteed to pay up." Vijay finished off the remainder of his *pec*. "You know what it sounds like to me? It sounds like this guy was Bundit's new project."

"No. Bundit shared everything with me, so he would have shared that. He was a generous person, that's all. I told you, it's what made him a good greeter. He enjoyed seeing people win."

"Did you go to Bangmod much?"

She shook her head. "He didn't want me to see where he lived. He was proud that way. Any time I said, 'Why don't

175

we go back to your place?' he'd start telling me how it was somewhere temporary." She smiled. "He'd talk about the house he was going to buy us. A big house in a *moo baan* with security guards and a barrier at the entrance. Each time he described it, he'd add another detail. A carp pond in front, a mango tree in the garden. And then I'd say, 'No, mango trees kill the trees around them. We'll get jackfruit.'" She laughed. "And we'd go on discussing the details of our imaginary house. It was a game, of course, but it was real, too. He wanted to give me things. He knew I was married once, knew my husband drank away our savings in karaoke bars. I could tell that's why he wouldn't let me come to Bangmod. He had to give me something better than that. It was like with our customers, with everyone, it was his nature. He wanted me to win."

She looked down at her empty glass with eyes filmed with tears. "This is why I shouldn't have more than two."

CHAPTER 12

Vijay returned to a dark, deserted Chinatown at four a.m. The metal shutters were down over the shops and a maniac on a motorbike was using the empty road to do wheelies. At the foot of his apartment block the only sign of life was a rat scurrying away from the stairwell. Vijay went up to his room, unrolled his sleeping mat, set the standing fan going and dropped into a dreamless black hole.

He'd left the alarm off, and woke at eight to the sun beating in through the drawn blinds. On the small balcony, where Vijay kept his hot plate and gas cylinder, he had Nescafé for breakfast while looking out over the courtyard's morning life. Mr Anop was moving a couple of empty fish tanks out onto the pavement in front of his shop and sunlight was flashing off the glass. *Pii* Gung was pushing open the doors of the coin laundry. Vijay thought of Bundit waking to similar morning scenes in Bangmod but still dreaming of the Big One.

Gold has fallen into my lap.

He went inside and phoned the old man to tell him he had information about Bundit. "And what do I call you? I don't even know your name."

"How about 'Uncle'? Like that polite young woman in your office." It was *Leung* in Thai.

"And where do you live? I can come and find you."

"I don't want you finding me."

The man promised to visit the office some time mid-morning. Vijay told him to leave the gun at home.

When he got in, Doi looked up from the computer. "A ve-ery late night."

"An early morning, more like." He described both Mae and the casino.

"But she doesn't know *Leung*," Doi said. "That's strange, isn't it?"

"Bundit seems to have had a knack for keeping them all in separate compartments."

"And the woman from Rayong."

"I just wonder what compartment the guy in the Merc fits into."

Vijay settled down to Doi's *Jao Por* translation at the point he'd left off. Which was an early stage. Khun Pleum still in Samut Sakhon, still "working thuggishly" for Sia Heng, in Montri's — Lam's — deathless prose. Vijay found he wasn't sleepy exactly, but had a numb, floating feeling that left him not quite connected to the world around him. By eleven, he'd had his second coffee and found he could edit Montri's work faster by caring about it less. When the office door swung open, Vijay was conscious of mental unreadiness. He steeled himself for the games Leung was bound to arrive with.

Instead, it was Lam who walked in. He looked from Doi to Vijay. "That board outside, why does it say 'detective'?"

He was dressed in de rigueur visual artist fashion: skinny black jeans, black collarless shirt, dark grey Borsalino with a black band.

"Don't worry, that's just a sideline," Vijay said. "This is my associate, Doi, by the way. Doi, this is Lam."

"That doesn't make sense," said Lam. "How can you be a detective as a sideline?"

"I have a friend in the police, and I found myself helping foreigners who'd been scammed. It's just a thing I do now and then. We like to stay agile in terms of market opportunities."

"So that's why I still haven't seen any pages." Lam leaned over the desk and peered at Vijay's face. "Your eyes are bloodshot. What's that about?"

"I was up late last night. Friend of mine has a gambling addiction and I was helping him through it."

Lam paced to the window and peered out through the slats of the venetian blinds as though to check he hadn't been followed. "This isn't what I paid for. You haven't sent me any work, your office doesn't look professional and now you're a detective." He brought out his Gauloises packet and shook a cigarette into his palm.

"I can assure you, Doi and I are highly professional. We take our work very seriously. Have you been to any other translators' offices?"

"How do you know I haven't? I might go to one right now."

"Well if you do, you probably won't find it very different from this place."

Lam stood tamping the unlit cigarette against his closed fist, then brought out the packet and stuck it back inside. Vijay wondered if he even smoked. Imagining him like this — Borsalino on his head — firing a .38 through Montri's calf was almost impossible. The image was bizarre, and yet he'd done it. Which made Vijay think that underneath Lam's painstakingly constructed "creative person" persona, there was something else. A different Lam he hadn't yet engaged with.

"So where are these pages? Or are you too busy investigating something?"

Vijay picked up Doi's sheaf from his desk. "We're doing it in stages, that's our strategy roadmap. This is the first stage right here. As you can see, it's reached an advanced level."

Lam came over. "Show them to me."

Vijay handed the pages over and Lam riffled through it. He looked up. "This is not grammatical. I can read English, you know. I've read Camus' *The Outsider* in the original English."

"Right, but like I said, that's just Stage One. We're now poised to transition into Stage Two."

That was when Leung came in. He smiled around the room. "As you can see, no walking stick."

"Who are you?" Lam said.

"This is *Leung*, er . . . Leung. And this is Lam, who we're doing some translating work for. Leung is someone else we do translations for, don't we, Leung?"

"You do what you can. We all do what we can in this life."

"You're working for him as well? Is that why I've had no pages?" Leung turned to Doi and raised his trouser legs. "And why is he showing her his ankles?"

"Just so you know," said Leung.

"Know what?" asked Lam.

"He's here to discuss a future project, aren't you, Leung?" Vijay said. "I like to get my ducks lined up."

"Know they're safe with me," said Leung. "The fact is, I'm a very safe person."

"You people are all quite slippery, aren't you?" Lam said. "So where's the next stage?"

"It's here, I'm just getting to it."

Lam snatched up the pages on Vijay's desk and squinted at them. "You've got very bad handwriting. And there's a lot of crossing out."

"I've been trying to find the right voice."

"What right voice? Montri had the right voice, you just have to translate what he wrote."

Leung went across and peered over Lam's shoulder. "He *has* got bad handwriting, hasn't he?"

Lam looked at him. "So what does he do for you?"

"Oh, we have long discussions, Vijay and I. We go back years. I used to have a business, you see, helping foreigners get retirement visas. All those documents to put into Thai. Vijay was the best translator I ever hired. Certainly the most reliable."

"He's been very slow as far as I'm concerned."

"I shouldn't worry about slow if I were you. Reliability's the thing to look for. I've had years of experience with these people."

Lam looked him up and down. "You're saying that wearing those clothes? Do you think you're what a successful person looks like?"

Leung's mild expression didn't waver. "I sold my business a long time ago. Nowadays I dress for myself."

Lam handed the pages back to Vijay. "Right. Well . . . reliability is good, but I'm going to have to start seeing some work. I have to okay them first, remember? You can't just send something to a publisher."

Vijay held the papers up. "Absolutely. Got it."

Lam went to the door, then turned and had a final sneery look around the room, just to make sure everyone knew what he thought of them.

After he'd gone, Leung said, "That's a very tightly wound young man. What exactly are you doing for him?"

"Translating a novel, it's a long story. And thanks, by the way."

He took the seat in front of Vijay's desk. "A novel he's written, do you mean? So who's this Montri person?"

"It's complicated. Anyway, look, I asked you here to talk about Bundit."

"That name, Montri . . . it sounds familiar."

"It should do, it's common enough."

Leung looked at Vijay with a degree of amusement. "Wasn't there a Montri someone in the news recently?"

"Could have been, I can't remember. About Bundit. You do know he was working in an underground casino?"

"He mentioned it. Just in passing. It wasn't a project, just something to do until our next one came along."

"You're sure it wasn't more than that?"

"He told me he was a greeter. Which is the kind of thing he was good at. He knew how to get on the right side of people, how to flatter them. He could look at you just once and know all your vanities."

"Do you know where this casino was?"

"Quite far out, he said, in the north of the city, around the Phahonyothin area."

"It's at the boundary between Bangmod and Tungkru. Less than a ten-minute drive from where he lived."

Vijay saw the shock cross Leung's face. Then he put on the "mild old man" expression that was his mask.

"I'm not making this up," Vijay said. "I actually went there and lost some of my client's money. I spoke to people who remembered him."

"Don't think you can try and surprise me with stories like that," Leung said. "It was the way he worked. Bundit needed his space. He always kept a few little details for himself."

"He must have told you it was in Phahonyothin for a reason. Maybe to explain why he'd get back to Bangmod so late?" He couldn't tell if his guess had landed. Now that Leung had had time to gather himself, he was unreadable. "There was a croupier there he was serious about. She was the reason."

That at least got a chuckle out of him. "Vijay, this world is full of women who were serious about Bundit and thought he was serious about them."

"Okay, so what about a guy in a red Merc?"

Leung rolled his eyes. "Oh, *him*."

Colonel Sanserm, Vijay thought, spreading goodwill and cheer wherever he went. "He was in Bangmod a lot, from what I heard. Which means you must have run into him. Bundit must have given you some kind of story."

Leung's poker face remained fixed. "He did."

"But not that he knew him from the casino, I'm guessing."

Leung shook his head.

"So what then?"

"Oh, you know. Nothing special. Just that he was a fellow he knew. A good guy. Bundit thought everyone was a good guy. It wasn't an act, he really cared about people."

"What was Sanserm like?"

Leung pursed his lips. "He thought he was a big shot. We'd go and eat near Bundit's apartment, and Sanserm would head off to the 7-Eleven and come back with a bottle of Black Label. Then he'd make a show of sharing it out, asking people at the next table if they wanted some. This fellow eating his lunch at a twenty-baht food stall. He thought the whiskey made him something special."

"He was a big drinker then?"

Leung nodded. "He'd work his way through the bottle and then want to drive home. Bundit would have to take him up to his room and make coffee."

"You must have asked at some point what Bundit was up to."

"Don't say 'up to' like that. I told you, he really did care about people, it wasn't an act."

"That's a funny thing to say about a conman."

Leung sighed. "People like you never understand about people like us. The world's not black and white. You shouldn't see it that way."

"So how should I see it?"

"He brought fantasies to people who needed them. He let them live bigger. We both did."

"It was a sort of health care, was it, what you were doing? Like a very expensive course of vitamins?"

"You can't run a project on someone who's content. But the world's full of people who long for larger lives. We took them as close to success as they would ever have come. None of them can say they didn't enjoy the ride while it lasted."

"It sounds like Sanserm was ripe for a project. That must have piqued your interest."

Leung's gaze was as indifferent as before.

"I'm guessing you tried to find out what Bundit was up to and couldn't. In fact, I'm starting to think this is not such an 'old pals' act after all. The two of you knew what each other was capable of. I don't suppose you ever trusted each other completely for two consecutive minutes."

He shook his head. "You're still not getting it."

"When Bundit disappeared, in the back of your mind was the suspicion he'd finally pulled the big one and left you behind. That's what's bothering you, isn't it?"

"You don't understand, we *were* real friends. Yes, it's possible this is Bundit's own planned disappearance. And yes, that's why I had someone in Bangmod phone me if anyone came asking. But I'll tell you something, if I find him, he'll be glad to see me."

"Going back to Sanserm. You're a good noticer of people and, given your suspicions, I bet you were busy noticing him. There must be something more about him you can tell me."

He didn't reply.

"The car he drove," Vijay continued. "I bet you took a good look at it. Maybe even wrote down the licence number in a notebook, am I right?"

There was still nothing but Leung's benevolent gaze, and the sense of wheels spinning out of sight.

"Oh come on, I've got a friend who's a cop," Vijay said. "He can trace this plate and maybe Sanserm's still driving it."

"What if he still is?"

"Well, that's something isn't it? If you want to find Bundit, you have to keep pushing doors . . . Look, if I do find him, I'll share the information."

"Why should you? You're not working for me. And your client might not want to share."

"She doesn't have to know. And anyway, what have you got to lose? Just find this notebook, bring it back here—"

"I don't need a notebook. Do you think I'm such an old fool? We never wrote down the important things. *Dor-dek, wor-wan*, two, two five, eight."

Vijay scribbled it at the top of one of Doi's pages.

"Do me a favour," Leung said. "If you find him, before you tell your client, let Bundit know I'm still looking for him. After all these years."

"I promise to do that."

He held Vijay's gaze. "What was the last truthful thing you said?"

"You're one to talk."

He levered himself up from the chair and made his way to the door. He stopped with his hand on the doorknob. "I've just remembered where I heard the name Montri. He's that writer, isn't he? The one who got shot. And you're going to put his book into English? You know, if Khun Pleum decides he doesn't like the idea, he won't send a kindly old man like me after you."

"Kindly old man? You had a gun last time you were here."

"Exactly. That *will* count as kind compared to whomever Khun Pleum sends."

It was his exit line. Vijay waited for him to finish clomping down the stairs and turned to Doi. "The kind of people we get strolling in here."

"I like him, actually. He reminds me of my dad."

"Your dad's not a conman, is he?"

"Of course not. He runs a pet shop, I told you that. I just think, if Leung met my dad, they'd get on really well."

Vijay left that utterly inexplicable thought and phoned Mana to read him the number of the licence plate. Mana replied that it would be tomorrow before he could get on to it. "We're being hassled by idiots higher up. They've got nothing better to do with their time so they go round visiting police stations, asking stupid questions."

With that done, Vijay phoned Petch and told him he was interested in a family called the Phuttaraksas. "Think you could ask your friends in the Business department?"

"Sure, if you tell me what you're looking for."

"Oh, nothing specific. Just any general info on their commercial dealings. Any gossip, current or ancient."

"I know it's something big then. It's always something big when you start getting vague."

"Petch, honestly, right now it sounds vague because it is. I'm working on a missing person case and I think they might be tied into it somewhere. But I don't know how."

"So why do you think they're tied in?"

"Trust me, if anything newsworthy comes out of this, you'll be the first person I talk to."

Going back to Doi's pages, Vijay started on the kind of overripe prose that would pass muster with Lam and then his mind wandered. He found himself thinking of Somsak the publisher. Even Bundit had left behind people who cared about him. Who remembered Somsak with any affection? The woman in his bedroom photos, perhaps?

He took out his phone and scrolled back to the picture of the crime scene. Somsak with his head down on his rosewood desk. From the elevation he'd taken it, Somsak might not have been dead at all, but just resting over his papers. In a room that didn't appear to have been searched. Vijay wondered if there was some important fact about this photo that he was missing.

Connecting to the internet, he brought up the S & K Books website and thumbed between the two pictures, playing spot the difference: the desk, the brass lamp, the bookcase. There wasn't one, as far as he could tell. The crime scene photo even reproduced the black-and-silver fountain pen poking out between Somsak's fingers.

And then Vijay was struck by the chilling thought that the whole point about these pictures wasn't their differences, but their remarkable similarity.

At five, he said to Doi, "Let's get out of here before the rain starts."

At a food stall at the foot of his apartment he had a dinner of fish curry and a bottle of Leo. By seven, he was back in his room. The open windows brought the evening sounds of the *soi* — a revving motorbike, laughter, someone's television — but no breeze to shift the close, wet heat.

Vijay found himself wondering what Malinee was doing. It was a question to which he had all the possible answers. If there was going to be an auction tomorrow then she would still be at River City, making sure of tiny details — enough white cloth covers for the chairs, a coaster for the auctioneer's water glass. If not, then she'd be at one of her favourite restaurants. Places she'd taken him to and insisted on paying, whipping out her credit card with the speed of a Kung Fu master. "You can pay later, when, what do they say in English? When your ship comes in." It never felt like a joke either. She'd believed in his success.

To distract himself, Vijay put the phone on his desk, plugged in his headphones and went scrolling through YouTube. He settled for Alan Partridge failing at life and, because of the headphones, it only gradually came to him that someone was knocking on the door with increasing force.

Vijay opened it to find Kritisak beaming on the other side. "*Vijay*," he said, in the tone of someone greeting a long-lost brother, home from the war. The only thing spoiling the fraternal effect was the fact that Lek was behind him. Lek in his usual jeans and muscle T-shirt, showing off the red-and-blue dragon tattoo that ran from his shoulder to his elbow. No holy image, this. It was purely to let you know he was a bona fide *nak leng*. And reinforcing that idea, he'd positioned himself sideways on. It was as though the whole reason for his visit was so that Vijay could study the tattoo again.

"Come in," he said.

They kicked off their shoes and did so. "You live very simply, don't you?" said Kritisak, looking around Vijay's single room. "That's good, I like that." Meanwhile, Lek went past them to inspect the wardrobe. "And how's Khun Pleum? Have you spoken to him lately?"

"I haven't, as such . . . Why's he got his hammer with him?"

"Has he? So he has. He misses his days of carpentry, don't you Lek?" Kritisak added in a conspiratorial whisper, "It was a simpler time."

"Yeah, I'll bet."

He put an arm around Vijay's shoulder with the jovial cheer that, Vijay had come to realise, represented Kritisak at his most dangerous. "So, how are you doing with the rest of my money?"

"Well, it's coming along. As you know, I'm employed by Khun Pleum and he's paying me twice my normal — he's hitting my wardrobe, Sia Geng."

"That's his instincts, Vijay. Anytime he's around wood, he's like this. He's descended from a long line of carpenters. It's in his genes, a biological memory. But never mind him, let's talk about you. Let's talk about your next payment."

"That wardrobe's chipboard, he's going to dent it if he hits it like that."

"Ah, you think so?" asked Kritisak, deeply interested. He paused to watch Lek. "You're right, you're right. There's a dent." He brought his attention back to Vijay. "So, what are we thinking for your next payment? I'm thinking 30,000 baht would put us on track. How does that sound?"

"It sounds like you're still charging me interest."

"Of course, of course. Now that you're working for Khun Pleum. A man like that, what would he think of me, if he was to find out I wasn't charging you interest?"

"I promise not to tell him if you don't."

Kritisak wagged his finger. "Vijay, you're such a joker."

Lek had now left the wardrobe and had moved over to Vijay's bookshelf, which, not being chipboard, was putting up more resistance.

"I can definitely get the money. I'll just ask him for an advance. The thing is, I'm going to need a few days to do it." A splintering sound came from the bookshelf. Unlike the wardrobe, the wood had torn along the grain. "Obviously, Khun Pleum is like yourself. He's in a results-orientated business."

Kritisak nodded encouragingly. Meanwhile, Lek had stopped hammering.

"That trip to the casino gave me a lead. A person who knows the guy I'm looking for. I've got the licence plate of his car and a policeman friend of mine is going to trace it. Once I've tracked him down and had a chat, I can go and see Khun Pleum with, you know, some concrete information. When I do that, I'll ask for an advance."

"And Khun Pleum knows I helped with this casino? He knows I got you in?"

"Absolutely."

He turned to Lek. "You see, this is what I've been telling you. This business is all about lending money to the right people. Vijay helps me and we help him. That's the way the world works." He went back to the door and Lek followed. He was like a large dog who'd been taken on a long walk and was now sated with exercise. In the doorway, Kritisak said, "I'm so glad I was right about you."

After they'd gone, Vijay looked at the damage. The chipboard wardrobe had crumpled under the hammer's impact, leaving circular dents. The bookcase, however, had splintered and ripped along the grain of the wood, making an ugly and unfixable gash. But on the plus side, at least he knew where to get the money from. He still had 28,900 baht of Ploy's casino cash. Everything he'd said about Khun Pleum applied to her. He just had to find Colonel Sanserm. Once he had some information for Ploy, he could claim to need another casino trip and would probably drop the rest of the money. Obviously, there was the question of what this second visit was supposed to turn up, but then that was the further-away problem.

You had to manage the nearest problem first.

CHAPTER 13

At around three a.m. Vijay woke to a shattering storm. It felt as though the whole city was under siege. Unable to sleep, he lay on his back listening to the unstoppable fury of the rain. He found himself thinking of Somsak's crime scene photo: Somsak surrounded by the paraphernalia of publishing, Somsak as the man of letters he'd pretended to be. By daybreak, the storm had moved on, leaving a cool morning behind. At work, Vijay's mind cleared with the air, and he had a breakthrough on *Jao Por*.

Doi watched him scribble. "You've solved the voice."

"Trial run," he told her, mainly because he knew she would offer to type up what he'd done, and he couldn't risk her seeing it.

Since work was going well, Vijay and Doi took a late lunch, and were still in the noodle place when Mana phoned.

"Bad news. It's not with this colonel of yours anymore. The owner is one Chinnapong Loertanawong and from the date of birth, he's twenty-five." He read out a *soi* off Sathon Road.

Vijay pondered waiting till evening, given the owner would probably still be at work, but then thought, *What the hell.* He could talk to the neighbours if nothing else.

The drive took him by the towering glass blocks of the business district, and then away past a large Chinese cemetery, forlorn in the grey light. Finally, the GPS led him down a narrow *soi* of terrace houses, each with a gated concrete yard. Some of these high metal gates had cars parked behind them, but not Chinnapong's. In his yard, there was a mess of paint tins, rusted at the edges, a bald female mannequin with one arm missing and, in one corner, a spirit house where a bottle of Fanta and two incense sticks were the votive offerings.

Vijay parked as close to the gate as possible. When he rang the bell, a young man came out almost immediately. He had long hair and jeans ripped at both knees. Vijay *wai*ed. "Khun Chinnapong, I wonder if I could talk to you about a car?"

The man gave him a beaming smile and said mystifyingly, "Already? Wow." Rattling the gate back, he peered at Vijay. "You're not Thai, are you?"

"I'm British. Indian parents."

Chinnapong switched from Thai to the American-accented English produced by Bangkok's international schools. "Hey, that's cool, man."

"A red Mercedes, licence number *dor-dek*, *wor-wan*, two, two, five, eight."

"Sure, sure, come in. We can talk about all of them."

Inside were two men sitting on an old blue sofa. Both were of a similar age to Chinnapong. One — reserved, watchful, sitting with his legs crossed — had a buzz cut, single earring and a Slipknot T-shirt. The other, of a stockier build, had a wide unkempt beard edging its way up his cheeks. He was wearing blue-tinted mirrored sunglasses that reflected a room with a student feel to it — a poster of an art exhibition at Silpakorn University on the wall, a guitar leaning in a corner, a long, low bookshelf sagging in the middle. Still speaking in English, Chinnapong said, "This guy's from Britain."

Mirror Shades said in English, "It's good you're taking an interest." His words were given a gnomic quality by his lack of expression and the fact that you couldn't see his eyes.

Chinnapong carried over a couple of rickety-looking wooden chairs spattered with flecks of sky-blue paint. He set them facing the sofa. "Here, sit." And then: "That was quick, wasn't it?"

Vijay took a seat. "So, about the red Mercedes."

Chinnapong took the other chair. "That was our beginning, kind of our inspiration—"

Mirror Shades put his palm up as a stop sign. He said in Thai, "He's not making any notes."

"Do you want me to?" Vijay said.

"We'd prefer voice recording," said Slipknot. "Then we don't get into some argument later about who said what."

The other two had the matter-of-fact expressions that suggested this was a normal request. Vijay took out phone and opened the voice-recorder app. "You mean you want me to record our conversation on this?"

Mirror Shades adopted the tone of someone explaining to a simpleton. "Yes, that would be a recording."

"Are we having to tell you this?" Slipknot said.

Vijay pressed record, held the phone out to Chinnapong and said, "The Mercedes."

"It was my uncle's car. He drove it for years."

"And was your uncle a Colonel Sanserm?"

"What? No, he's called Worawit, he's not a colonel. Anyway, he fixed it up and drove it. That stuff doesn't bother him. You speak Thai, right? You know *kee neow*? Well, that's him. He got it at a cheap price, and that was all that mattered. Two years ago he upgraded and gave it to me. And he was like, 'Thailand's a modern country now, we don't have any more ghosts.'"

"Ghosts?"

"Right, and I'm like, do I really want to drive this? But that's what gave us the idea for the whole installation, basically."

Mirror Shades said, "What do you think of the title?"

"He thinks it's vague," Chinnapong said to Vijay.

"I don't think so, I know," Mirror Shades said. "The Cars That Ate Bangkok. It's vague. Now The Death Car Exhibition is out there. It pops."

"So, who do you actually write for?" asked Chinnapong.

"Khun Chinnapong, I think I need to speak to your uncle," Vijay said.

* * *

It took Vijay the rest of the day. The man was a mechanic, out in Bang Bon, who'd "heard about the Merc from a friend".

"He knew the woman," the mechanic told him. "She was going to fix it up and sell it on, so I got in quick. Offered to buy it as it was. 20,000 baht — you tell me that's not a good deal. She's got to straighten out the bumper, put in a new radiator, put in a new fan. Plus, the fan shaft's cracked, and the windscreen obviously, where the guy's head went through.

"How much do you think all that costs? Add it up. Paying her that much, it's a gift. I'm making merit here. Plus, it's a dead guy's car. Factor that in. This is Thailand, who's going to buy it? Not that I was bothered myself, you understand. See this amulet? *Jatukam*. Cost me more than that piece of crap, but it's an investment, is the point. With this on, I'm protected from anything."

* * *

Vijay found her at home in the early evening. Home being a five-storey apartment block that was only a slight upgrade from his. The walls were cracked red cement, with a common balcony running the length of each floor.

When she opened the door, the first thing Vijay saw was her husband. A head-and-shoulders photo in his uniform above a red Chinese shrine. Perhaps it was the graduation picture from his staff college, as the man in it must have been in his early twenties. He wore a close military-grade haircut, and was clean-shaven and clear-eyed. Sanserm with it all still ahead of him.

Beside the incense tapers, she'd set an open bottle of Leo beer. Next to the shrine, a cheap vinyl sofa faced a television. Above the television was a cabinet with some porcelain knick-knacks and a wedding picture in a plastic frame. An open door in the small room revealed a smaller bedroom. He'd gambled in the Phuttaraksas' casino but this was how he'd lived.

His widow was a plain, wide-hipped woman in her late fifties. Vijay handed over a business card and said he wanted to ask her about Khun Sanserm. She nodded, as though acknowledging a long-overdue interest in her husband's life.

She ushered him to one end of the sofa and sat at the other end, hands in her lap.

"It's *pii* Far, right?" Vijay said. "I got your name and address from the man you sold the car to."

She nodded and looked at the card again. "So. You're a detective. What do you want to know?"

"To start with, when did your husband die?"

"The eleventh of November, 2005." And she looked across at the photo as though for confirmation.

"And where did the crash happen?"

"On the Rama II Road, early in the morning. Two o'clock, they told me." She added defensively, "No one died but him."

"I'm thinking maybe they found some alcohol in his blood."

That got a small, reluctant nod out of her.

"Where was he coming home from?"

"A pub, that big Holland Beer place."

"Did he go out often?"

"No," she said quickly, and then: "I wouldn't say often. Lots of men go drinking sometimes."

"Was it only Holland Beer or were there other pubs?"

"Why are you asking? What is all of this to you?" And she turned her palms up as though to indicate the futility of questions: her husband was gone.

194

"He was a friend of someone I'm trying to find," said Vijay. "A man named Bundit. Did he ever mention that name?"

She shook her head.

"Apart from Holland Beer, were there any other places he liked?"

"It was usually other places. He went to the houses of friends. They'd drink beer, play some cards."

"Did you ever meet any of these friends?"

She gave him a look of reproach. "What does that mean? It wasn't women, if that's what you're going to say. My husband loved me." She put her hands together and rotated her wedding band. "It was himself he didn't love."

"Did he ever tell you about visiting a casino?" Vijay asked. "I have reason to believe that's where many of his evenings were spent."

"He always liked to play a bit of cards, ever since his army days. It was something to pass the time in the barracks. They weren't really supposed to, but as long as it was only for cigarettes or spare change the NCOs let them."

Vijay looked around the modest flat she'd maintained so scrupulously. The picture of King Rama IX that obviously received regular dusting, the Buddha on a shelf over the door, the hydrangeas in a vase on a foldable wooden table. "These would have been high-stakes games," he said. "I've been to the casino in question. You need money and contacts to get in."

"I don't understand."

"Did you have any savings he could dip into? Maybe he sold a piece of land at some point? I mean, *pii* Far, where did he get the money from?"

"You're making a mistake. It wasn't a casino, he played cards with friends. From his regiment."

"But you never met any of them?"

"I'm his wife, I looked after our money. I know what he spent. It was a couple of thousand baht at the end of the week."

"What about the Mercedes? Where did the funds for that come from?"

"He inherited money not long after we were married. He brought it brand new and then he kept fixing it up, just wouldn't sell it." She looked over at the young man in the picture. "And that was the car he died in." She added, "I tried. I tried to make him stop. Drinking didn't even make him happy, not really. He'd drink and come home with all his disappointments."

"Which were?"

"Just . . . that he hadn't done better in life. He'd lie there in bed, staring at the ceiling and say, 'I had too many again. I'm no good for you, Far.'"

"When you say 'hadn't done better in life', what do you mean by that? Okay, so he didn't make general, but then, even in Thailand, not every officer does."

"He didn't only spend the inheritance on the car. Most of it went on a book-binding business. Lots of officers do that," she added, guarding his reputation from Vijay's opinions. "Have their little commercial thing on the side. We were stationed in Ayutthaya then, and he was sure there were opportunities. He bought all the equipment, rented a workshop and told me in five years, we'd be making the textbooks for every school in the province."

"But that didn't happen?"

She clasped her hands again. "My husband was never a businessman. When he came back from cards, he used to lie there in the dark and I knew from his breathing he was still awake. But too ashamed to speak to me. He'd suck mints on the way home because he knew I didn't like the beer smell. And we'd lie there, shoulder to shoulder until he slept. And I'd know the next morning he would make me *khao tom* and coffee for breakfast. And I'd know I was married to someone who loved me but didn't love himself."

She looked across at the picture where Sanserm's future hadn't yet happened, and Vijay had the sense of her talking more for the picture than for him. "Failing in business bothered him too much. There was always this level of success he couldn't reach. But he never failed me, until he left me too soon. In this life you don't have to do brilliant things . . . eat in foreign restaurants, shop in air-conditioned malls, wear expensive clothes. I don't know why he couldn't see that. Holding on to one person is a brilliant thing."

* * *

On the way back to Chinatown, the sky took a half-hearted attempt at rain. Putting the wipers on slow, Vijay drove thinking about Colonel Sanserm's hungering life. Then his mobile went with Supaporn's number.

"Well?" she said.

"I'm pleased to say, I've secured a global view of Khun Pleum's movements. Now I'm looking to drill down to a granular level."

"Words, you're just dribbling words."

"Why don't we meet and table the next stage of my investigation? We can fix up a mutually beneficial timeline."

"This is just a lot of nonsense to cover up the fact that you haven't done anything."

"Khun Supaporn, as I told you before, I've activated one of my best people—"

"Rubbish, you don't have people. My husband has people. You're just some conman sitting in an office, taking my money while pretending to do something. How do I know you've investigated anything at all? And don't start with that whole 'lion at the watering hole' speech."

"Look at it the other way," Vijay said. "How do you know he has a *mia noi*? You must have read the book in full, right? You can see how it's written. The author wants to make him look as bad as possible."

"So why use this detail?"

"Because he wanted something credible. It's no good saying Khun Pleum is an alcoholic, or has a *yaa baa* addiction, because the people who know him know he's too disciplined for those things. But this is Thailand. Say a rich man has a *mia noi* and everyone nods their head."

There was a pause. "It's not just that — his behaviour's changed. He doesn't want to be around me anymore. He buys me these jewellery trinkets, these spa retreats, all just as an excuse for spending less time with me."

Christ, the trials of the one per cent, Vijay thought. "Did he give you a necklace recently, by any chance?"

"He did."

"My guy saw him buying it. That's the only jewellery he's told me about."

"There you are then. If it's not jewellery, think what he *is* doing for her."

Vijay was about to point out the flaw in that reasoning when she said, "I'm giving you an ultimatum. If you don't bring me a name and address in the next three days, I'm going to tell my husband you've been working for me."

"If you do that, you'll never know for sure if he was having an affair or not. And by the way, how is this going to make you look?"

"Not as bad as you, I can assure you of that. In fact, do you want to know something? I'm going to tell him it was your idea all along. I'll say you weaselled my phone number out of one of his staff, and then you called me up and told me about the *mia noi* in the novel. You said you'd already had someone following Pleum and you suspected she was real. You told me you were in a position to find out who she was, since you were close to Pleum now. And then you demanded twice your regular fee."

"Look, let's not get carried away here."

"I've known Pleum since he was fourteen. Which of us do you think he's going to believe?"

Vijay swung the pickup over to the kerb. Behind him, a car horn blared. He yanked the handbrake up. "Look, Khun Supaporn, myself and my associate — who does actually exist — are doing the very best we can to find the *mia noi*. But you've got to understand, this isn't exactly low-hanging fruit.

In fact, it's really *high*-hanging fruit. From the ground, you can't even see it at all. You have to get halfway up the tree, which is about where my associate is at the moment . . ."

"I have no idea what it is you're saying."

That, thought Vijay, *makes two of us*. He tried a different tack. "What I'm getting at here is that you've got to help me."

"By doing what?"

"There's a saying in English, 'Might as well be hung for a sheep as a lamb'. If I give you her name and he finds out it's me you got it from, then I'm finished anyway. So I might as well not tell him and wait for your deadline to expire. I want a real assurance from you that—"

"Fine, fine, you're my little secret."

"I'm going to need something a lot more genuine than that, *meung*," said Vijay, unable to check his temper.

There was a frosty silence.

"Right, you grubby little man, I absolutely promise my husband won't know I got the information from you. And you've got three days to get me that information."

She rang off and Vijay dropped the phone onto the passenger seat. It was starting to feel radioactive with bad news. He pulled back out into the traffic and drove the rest of the way thinking about Khun Pleum. It was all very well Supaporn saying he wasn't going to discover the source, but the fact was, once she had the woman's identity, there would be no further need to keep him out of the picture. And even if she tried, who was to say Khun Pleum couldn't figure it out anyway? Especially as Somchai already seemed to suspect he was working for her. And the funny thing was, Vijay thought, that his original nearest worry, Kritisak, would tomorrow successfully become his further-away worry when he had the money okayed by Ploy.

* * *

For once Vijay slept late — until ten in the morning — due in the most part to his staying awake till half past four. He'd lain on his sleeping mat in the dark, listening to rain tapping on the windows, as the faces of Kritisak, Supaporn and Khun Pleum approached and receded in turn, while behind them, Somchai sat watching with his pitiless sniper's gaze.

After showering, Vijay read through a couple of text messages from Tong. Khun Pleum was on the move. He phoned Doi to let her know he'd be in soon. It was ten forty-five by the time he reached the office, some *pa tong go* in a bag for breakfast.

"You must have had a good night," said Doi, watching him spooning coffee into a mug.

"A better evening," Vijay said and told her about his trip to see Colonel Sanserm's widow.

"So she really didn't know the way he was gambling?"

"It was an honest reaction, as far as I could tell."

"Then where did he get the funds?"

"Money laundering would have fit the bill, if only casinos were legal here. But as they're not, I've got no idea."

"And none of this money ever went back to her?"

"Even though she was loved by him." Vijay could see Doi giving that a look. "You weren't there," he said. "She couldn't have talked like that if it wasn't true."

"So then what?"

He thought of young Sanserm above the shrine, his crew cut and steady gaze and the world yet to disappoint him. "It feels like . . . I don't know, the money was something shameful, so he had to get rid of it this way. In secret."

"And then Bundit—" Doi counted the name off on her finger — "there's what he was doing in all this."

"As far as I can tell, Sanserm's slow slide off the rails coincided with Bundit becoming a greeter at the casino. And that seems to be partly because Bundit was extending his credit."

"But we don't know why."

"Other than that, he was a conman and had a conman's antennae. And something told him Sanserm was both vulnerable and worth preying on." Vijay finished his coffee and offered Doi some *pa tong go*. "You know what?" he said. "I think I should tell Ploy about all this. It's good to keep our clients in the loop."

He phoned and told her he was on the way to Sukhumvit with news. She replied by saying she wouldn't be there, but that they could meet at Asiatique in the early afternoon. It was a wooden promenade on the Chao Phraya River. Once the site of warehouses, it had been redeveloped into an upmarket area of restaurants, bars, market stalls and a large Ferris wheel. Having put the phone down, Vijay found Doi looking at him with amusement.

"You're going to see her?"

"Sure. I've got to keep her abreast of developments."

"Vijay, everything you've just told me, you could say over the phone."

"Right, but it's important to give our clients the personal touch. We don't want them thinking I'm some conman, sitting in my office taking their money and not doing anything."

Doi grinned at him. "*That's* why?"

"Obviously."

Vijay went back to his idea for the *Jao Por* translation and in between surreptitiously checked his phone. He'd switched off the notification ping for text messages, so now just the white LED in the front corner lit. Which happened frequently, and announced texts written at an increasing level of abstraction:

going car
open door
lobby

So Tong was obviously on to something. Or at least, he thought he was.

Doi asked Vijay if he wanted her to type up any pages, and he successfully fobbed her off by claiming there was too much scribble and rewriting on them. At noon, they went to *pii* Nuch's noodle shop and Doi paid for lunch. "Better save your money for your client — I'm sure you'll want to buy her a drink."

Vijay left for Asiatique at two p.m. He texted Ploy he was on the way as he went down the stairs. In the pickup, he scrolled through some more messages from Tong.

yes!!

maybe

her behind

Vijay sent him an encouraging reply, just to show he was appreciating the thrill of the chase. Then sent a second message telling him that if he found the *mia noi*, he should leave Khun Pleum and stay with her.

On the drive to the river, Vijay mulled over Supaporn. He needed to get securely into Khun Pleum's good books before her deadline expired, and could think of only one way of doing so.

* * *

Asiatique on a weekday afternoon was fairly empty. Most of the art and craft stalls hadn't yet opened and the wooden deck over the Chao Phraya was free of its weekend crowd. A few scattered tourists took selfies against the sun-struck river skyline.

Ploy had said they'd meet at a place called Aubade, which turned out to be a high-end bar of chairs upholstered in plush red velvet, and marble tabletops. She was already there when Vijay arrived, sitting with her back to the door, dressed to an even higher level of elegance than the first time they'd met: a calf-length grey skirt and a dark blue long-sleeved blouse cut to leave her shoulders bare; her hair piled up on her head and held in place with a diamond-studded clip that matched the sparkle of her diamond earrings. When she saw Vijay, she gave an eager smile that made his pulse jump. He slid into the booth.

"You said you had good news." She was leaning into the table when she said it and the expectation in her face made her even more beautiful.

At that moment, Vijay wanted so very much to find Bundit. "It's encouraging," he said. "I mean, I think that visit to the casino definitely turned up something."

She nodded at that. A tiny, hopeful nod that sent her long earrings swaying. When a waiter appeared at Vijay's elbow, she said, "Order what you like, I'm paying."

Vijay asked for a bottle of water and then gave her a rundown of his casino trip, followed by the visit to Sanserm's widow. Just for good measure, he said it was Mae at the casino who'd given him the licence number of the Merc.

"Really? She what . . . wrote it down?"

"Just remembered it, I think." Vijay added, "He was there till they closed, from what I can tell. And then they'd go out to the car and Bundit would pour Sanserm into it."

The waiter arrived with the bottle and, with a level of ceremony bordering on satire, poured it into a tall frosted glass.

"I feel he's hinting I should have had a beer," Vijay said.

"D'you want a beer? Order one if you like."

"That's okay, I've got to drive back." He took his phone out and set it next to the glass. Sure enough, the white light was flashing. He swiped and read: *right*.

Ploy looked at him quizzically.

"I've got this guy following someone," Vijay explained. "I told him to keep me informed and now he texts me with everything." He showed her the screen.

She giggled. "So what's 'right'?"

"No idea. He's probably on his motorbike, texting with one hand to let me know he's turning right."

"You should tell him to be careful."

"The other thing is, this woman, Mae — she seemed very close to Bundit. To hear her tell it, they were going to settle down, buy a house in the suburbs and fall into domestic bliss."

Ploy looked away. "I don't think Bundit was ever going to settle down with anyone."

"Right, but I don't know how much you want to tell your friend about this." The light on the phone blinked and Vijay swiped to find Tong had sent: *?*

He sighed and showed it to Ploy. *What does that mean?* he texted back. "Actually, how much have you told her so far?" he asked.

"Not a great deal. I want to find Bundit or find out what happened to him and then give her the news."

"It's connected to Sanserm, I'm sure of that. He comes into Bundit's life, Bundit extends him credit and then disappears."

"But you don't know why."

The phone blinked. Tong had written: *I'm done mia noi*

He followed that with another message containing a single question mark.

"I think, it might be a good idea to go to the casino again to find out. Hang on a minute." He typed: *What does that mean? Can you reply in whole sentences?* "I've still got about 30,000 baht of your friend's money," he continued. "I know I said I wouldn't spend it all—"

The phone blinked again.

Because you're talking to her.

Ploy smiled and craned across the table. "Now what's he written?"

Vijay's hand jerked as he switched the screen off. "Oh nothing. He just — he went right too late and lost her. It happens." He looked away from Ploy's rosebud lips to the scene beyond the window. The promenade and the muddy river, and by the railing, a figure in an orange motorbike taxi vest, who put up his hand and waved.

"Look, sorry, can you hang on for one second, I just want to give him some instructions."

Get back out of sight and follow her when she leaves, he typed.

"So what is this other case you're working on?" Ploy said.

"Oh, it's just a domestic thing. That's what most of my work tends to be."

There was a pause, then her perfect complexion dimpled into a smile. "You were telling me. About the casino."

"Right." He found he had lost his train of thought completely. "Actually, what was I saying?"

She giggled. "*Vijay*. You were saying you needed to go back there."

He nodded. "Right. That's it. Mae's not the only one who remembers Bundit, and I think I can get a bit more out of them. But obviously, I don't want it to look like I went there just to ask questions. So I'll need to drop some more cash."

"Fine, I'll tell her. It's not a problem."

"Can I just ask, how did you actually find me? We're trying to drum up more work and it's useful to know how people come to us."

"From a friend. She lives in Chinatown and she saw your sign."

"Great. So. Bigger sign goes on the list."

"This man Sanserm," Ploy said. "It doesn't make much sense, does it?"

"You mean, why Bundit extended him credit?"

"I mean why m—, why knowing him brought Bundit into danger."

Vijay frowned. "Your friend. If I could just know something more about her . . ."

"I can't tell you anything else. I thought I'd made that clear?"

Vijay thought about Ploy and Khun Pleum and Supaporn's lethal deadline. Suddenly everything had the perfect fit of a tightly locking handcuff. "Right. I'll go back to the casino this evening."

"But you haven't told me about the guy in the red Mercedes. You said on the phone you talked to his widow."

"Yeah. Okay. Well, she was living very simply. And didn't have a clue Sanserm was gambling for high stakes. So."

Ploy put her chin on her hand. "Are you all right? You seem very preoccupied all of a sudden."

"Sure, I'm fine. Just thinking out my strategy for this evening. I mean, strategy for talking to people. And the cards as well, obviously. I'm thinking out my strategy for everything."

CHAPTER 14

On the drive home from Asiatique, Vijay was so deep in thought he tangled himself up in a minotaur's labyrinth of one-way streets. As a result, it was almost five by the time he made it back to the office. Doi was packing up to leave.

She took the purse out of her drawer and locked it. "I've finished *Jao Por* so I thought I'd go." She looked up at him. "What?"

"Why don't you take a seat for a minute? I've got something to tell you."

She did so and placed the purse on her desk.

"I learned today that Ploy, our client, is Khun Pleum's *mia noi*."

Doi's mouth opened soundlessly. "You're joking. She told you that?"

"Not her, Tong. He's been following Khun Pleum."

"What would he do that for?"

"The usual. 1,000 baht a day and I'll pay for his lunch, but it's got to be somewhere reasonable, like at a food stall."

Doi clenched her hands into fists and said with an air of infinite forbearance, "Vijay, I mean *why* is Tong following him?"

"The thing is, I may or may not have accepted a job from Khun Pleum's wife to find out if he has a mistress."

"*May or may not*? What does *that* mean?"

"Well okay, may, if we're going to be pedantic about it."

Doi's eyes widened, and her mouth dropped open again. "Vijay, are you crazy? Why would you take a case like that?"

"There's no reason I can't do two things at once."

"Two things? This is like putting a noose around your head, then kicking away the chair while shooting yourself in the face and calling it multitasking."

"Technically speaking, that would actually be multi—"

"What do you think Khun Pleum's going to do when he finds out you've been investigating him?"

"There's no reason he should find out, provided Supaporn can be discreet about the whole thing. Which should be within her abilities. The thing is, I wasn't expecting the *mia noi* to be one of my other clients. So there's this whole ethical kind of dimension . . ."

In a manner of slow collapse, Doi slumped her shoulders and thumped her forehead on the desk.

"Yeah, so. Great you're not overreacting or anything."

She jerked back upright. "Overreacting? What's the correct response to news like this? Updating my Facebook status?"

"I was hoping you could help me think this through. I mean, it's beyond coincidence."

"Vijay, of course it is. So what? They were talking and he mentioned he'd hired you because you did work for that guy—"

"Adisorn."

"And her friend wants Bundit found, and if you're good enough for Khun Pleum . . ."

"Right, but it was never a question of only being good enough. He wanted to hire someone so cheap people would never guess the connection. Plus, I don't think this friend even exists. The descriptions of her are so vague and changeable. I think it's Ploy who wants Bundit found, but for reasons she doesn't want to reveal."

Doi ran her fingers through her hair. "You know, I left school when I was fifteen. I didn't do that because I thought one day I was going to be a CEO driving a Mercedes. I never expected to become amazingly rich." She gestured to the office around them. "This is okay, isn't it? What's so bad here that you have to be so desperate for money?"

"Hey, I'm not desperate, just . . . you know, looking to keep us agile. I'm extending our build capacity. Anyway, don't worry. I'll fix this."

"How?"

"We don't have to tell Supaporn about Ploy. We just wait for a decent interval and then say we couldn't find anything. What?"

"She might not believe us."

"Not a problem, what's she going to do? Tell Khun Pleum, 'I hired your detective to investigate you, but I don't think he's all that reliable.'"

That, at least, got a smile out of her. "You can take it easy tomorrow, now that the book's done. In fact, stay at home if you like."

"You don't want me here? I thought you said it was important for the office to look busy when clients arrive?"

"I don't think we need to go overboard with that. I'll phone you if some translation work comes up. And let's face it, we're not taking any more clients on the detective side."

After she'd gone, Vijay moved over to her desk and began typing the new version of *Jao Por* into the computer. He decided the first two chapters would probably be enough to establish the voice and style he wanted. He then phoned Somchai and had a chat about the book. The man was largely sceptical about everything Vijay told him, but his loyalty to Khun Pleum's needs won out in the end, as Vijay had suspected it would. After that, he called Leung for a chat he was much less sure about. They had a short preamble about what he was doing, and no, he wasn't going to tell Vijay where he was.

Vijay then said, "This woman who's looking for Bundit. I'm pretty sure you know who she is."

"Now why would you imagine that?"

"Something's been bothering me all this time about that evening in the empty house. And now I know what it is. That coughing fit you had. 'She's looking for him' is what I think you were about to say. And I don't think it was a question."

"Your memory's playing tricks on you. Maybe it's because you're getting desperate."

"What would I be desperate about? I'm on a regular salary here, paid a week in advance. The coughing thing was to try and distract me."

"I'm an old man, I cough sometimes. Really, Vijay, I don't think you're cut out for this kind of work."

"Look, if you help me now and I find him, I'll give you his address. But if you won't help, then I don't see why I should."

"Once you've found him, you'll be under no obligation to tell me anything anyway. I won't even know it's happened."

"True, but what have you got to lose?"

There was silence at the other end.

"Was the person you were picturing in her mid-twenties, around five foot five?" Vijay continued.

Leung sighed. "She was fourteen the last time I saw her. But yes. Ploy would be in her mid-twenties by now. I'm sure she grew into quite a beautiful young woman."

"And she is?"

"Bundit's daughter."

"I wonder why she didn't tell me that to begin with."

"Who knows? Perhaps she's got her father's guarded ways. Bundit never gave you the whole story either."

"So what, you think? After all this time she just wants her dad back in her life?"

"She adored him, Vijay. But from a distance, that was the problem. He farmed her out to different women over the years. I sometimes think he chose his women purely for their ability to look after Ploy. And then when things were going well, he'd come roaring back into her life. She'd be in some tiny apartment over a shop and he'd turn up with his entourage and take her out for a grand adventure. The zoo, or an amusement arcade, or ice cream in Lumpini Park, or all of those things. And then he'd finish the day in some hotel restaurant fifty floors up. The sun would be setting over the city, turning the skyscrapers into gold, and I'd watch while Bundit presented the view as though he owned everything she was looking at."

"I wonder why she didn't know he was living in Bangmod," Vijay said.

"He never saw her during the bad times. He had his pride that way. I'm not sure she ever knew about his prison sentences."

"Well she knows now, I told her. It didn't get much of a reaction though. In fact, the way I've been talking to her about him, it hasn't exactly been complimentary and she hasn't reacted at all."

He gave a sad chuckle. "She's her father's daughter."

"Fine, but . . . do you think she has other reasons for wanting him found now? Reasons other than just having her dad back?"

"I remember one time, she must have been about ten. Bundit was calling himself Na Nakhon then and bringing all kinds of people together. It wasn't even a con, for a while. So many people thought of him as a man of influence that he really *had* influence. Anyway, he owned — or had borrowed, I'm not sure — this huge silver Bentley. And he decided it was time to see Ploy again. So we went to her school and he gave the headmaster a story about her mother having had a stroke and wanting Ploy to come to the hospital. Then we all drove down to Hua Hin and checked into a five-star hotel. And this is the thing I still remember. Her walking down the beach with Bundit, holding one of his hands in both of hers, and looking up at him as though she would stop him from ever leaving again. And I thought, she loves him too much.

He wasn't a man to love, Vijay. And I may not always have been either."

He paused. "If you tell her what you know, maybe you could ask if she still remembers me? And if she does, maybe you could give her my number?"

By the time he rang off, the quick tropical night had fallen and the day's humidity had lifted. Vijay wondered if the rainy season was finally over. No more flooded *soi*, no more cockroaches being driven out from the drains to go scuttling down the corridors of his building.

The phone went, with Petch's number.

"Hi, Vijay, that family you wanted to know about, the Phuttaraksas? I've been asking around — my friend here, a guy at *Khaosod*, plus a guy I know who used to work for *Matichon*."

"And?"

"Well . . . nothing, really. They've been hotel owners for generations now — Phuket, Krabi, those kinds of places. There doesn't seem to be much else to them. Politically speaking, they've kept their heads down. Never really sided with Thaksin, and never joined the Yellow Shirts and opposed him. Though I suppose most of their staff must be Yellow Shirts, what with being in the south. It doesn't seem like the Junta either favours or suspects them."

"Nothing in their past? No rumours about . . . anything?"

"Not that I've heard. Their places are mostly three star, so not the destinations of the rich and famous. These days, they're probably full of Chinese tour groups."

"Okay, well, thanks all the same."

"Still not going to tell me what you were looking for?"

"I can't tell you now, Petch. I'll feel like an idiot, given it didn't come to anything."

With that, Petch asked when they were going to have their next card session and Vijay had a manic urge to describe his casino adventure. But he knew Petch. There was no way the man wouldn't go down there and try to talk his way in. So he promised he'd clear some time after his current case was over.

He locked up the office and drove home thinking about how the Phuttaraksas had flown under the radar for so many decades. And what that meant for him, and for Bundit.

* * *

The next day, Vijay paid Kritisak his 30,000 baht. He waited till three p.m. to do it, purely to find out what the man did with himself between meals. The answer turned out to be enthroning himself at the same table with a plate of spring rolls on the go. Vijay wondered why he didn't weigh more.

Back in the office, Vijay emailed the first two chapters of *Jao Por* to Lam as a single Word file. It didn't take long. At just past four, his phone went with a number he didn't recognise.

"Vijay, I've read your pages."

"That was quick."

Lam's voice was tight, controlled. "I don't know if you've completely got the idea. I don't know if you understand what I wanted."

"Oh, I understand all right," Vijay said. "I just think this version's better. I mean, we're trying to sell books. That is the point of the exercise. The way I've done it, you've got a tale of rags to riches. Everyone likes those. It's heart-warming."

"He's a gangster, Vijay."

"Sure, he *was*, but these days, he's pretty much respectable. He has a construction firm, takes meetings with government ministers. I don't know if the reading public care about his past all that much."

A nasal bark came down the line and Vijay realised Lam was trying to cough up laughter. "Look, maybe you need me to explain the concept. I don't want you to waste time going in the wrong direction."

"No need, it's already done."

"What?"

"The translation's finished. I just sent you two chapters for you to get the idea."

"It's not *finished*, Vijay. It's not finished until I've okayed it. I have to sign off."

"Lam, trust me. This novel is going to sell. I've already got a meeting with Silkworm Books lined up. I can see this on shelves. It's going to go over big time."

Vijay ended the call and the phone rang before he had time to put it down.

"You don't understand, Vijay. I'm the one. I make the decisions."

"Right, but there's nothing left to decide on. Tell you what," Vijay said, starting to enjoy himself, "why don't I send you the whole thing? It's a great read. A real page-turner."

"Vijay, I'll come and see you," said Lam with better control than Vijay would have credited. "Wouldn't that be easier? Wouldn't it be easier to talk about this face to face?"

"If you really think you need to."

"I've got a lot of work to do right now. An installation. I won't be free till the evening. Why don't I come to your home?"

"You can see me at the office," Vijay said. "I'm actually going to be here quite late. Probably till nine or ten. We've had a new job come in. This guy, he wants a whole textbook put into Thai, but on a tight deadline. So I'm going to have to move on to that. You know how it is. I can take the meeting tomorrow with Silkworm, but that will have to be my last involvement on this project."

"Okay, no problem. I'll see you there."

Vijay pushed his chair back, put his feet up on the desk and had another chat with Somchai. He reminded the man of how heavy the traffic was on Yaowarat Road and told him to leave early. After a pause, Somchai said, "You think you're quite clever, don't you? Setting all this up. We used to come across people like you, every so often. The Clever Boys. And it would always turn out Pleum had something they didn't. A different quality."

"But now I'm looking after Pleum's interests. This is what he hired me for."

"Right." Somchai ended the call.

Vijay plugged his phone into the charger and then had another internet search for the Phuttaraksas. The family head was a dignified looking man in probably his early sixties, with side-parted hair and greying sideburns. In the only two pictures Vijay could find, he was wearing dark suits and sensible ties. The wife was one of those women of a certain age in jacket-skirt combinations of thick Thai silk. You just knew she was on the board of some royal charity or other and regularly paid for the renovation of needy temples.

Eventually Vijay got bored, night came on, and all the things happened that were supposed to happen. By the time Lam turned up (just after nine thirty) Vijay had gone back to watching *Alan Partridge* clips.

Lam was wearing a black waistcoat over a collarless white shirt, tight black jeans and the inevitable Borsalino. Vijay took his feet off the desk and moved his chair up. "Take a seat." And then, when Lam went to close the door: "Leave it open. There's no through breeze with it shut. I've been sweating like a pig all day."

Lam remained standing. "You don't even look as though you're doing any work. Why's your desk clear?" He tilted his head to look at Vijay's phone. "YouTube? You're sitting here watching YouTube?"

"Just taking a break. I've been going at the textbook all day. It got to the point where I couldn't bear to look at it anymore." Vijay tapped the bottom drawer of his desk. "It's all in here. The whole novel in English. Doi and I always deliver."

Lam stood tapping a nail on the desk, then abruptly sat down. "You haven't got the idea. You weren't supposed to go and talk to a publisher."

"Silkworm are good, you can find their books at Kinokuniya."

"I *know*, Vijay." He jerked forwards. "But the story has to be told in a certain way. It's not just a book. It's an artwork, a happening."

"Right, but no one's going to read the happening when it's written in such crappy, overblown prose." Seeing him flinch, Vijay continued, "Montri didn't do you any favours, you know. I suppose it's because he's a friend that you didn't want to tell him how bad his writing was? Not a good idea. Sometimes, Lam, you've got to be cruel to be kind."

"You didn't like the style then?" He swivelled round to look at the water stain above the filing cabinet. "Didn't meet the standards of your precious little office, I suppose? You and that Thai woman who can't even put English into grammatical sentences."

"That's it!" Vijay said, putting his hands behind his head. "You've got it in one. So are we done then?"

"No, we're not done." At which point, Vijay started wondering whether Somchai had moved from the empty room next to the office and into the corridor. The door to Lam's anger seemed likely to swing open all at once. Hopefully Somchai understood that.

"If we're not done," Vijay said, "then frankly I don't see what's left. I've delivered on the project, and in a really short space of time. I've also hugely improved the material I was given, even if I do say so myself." He opened his hands. "But I'm going to be fair about this. I didn't mention an editing charge when I first talked to Montri, and so there isn't going to be one. I'm giving you my original rate."

"You're going to email Silkworm and tell them you're withdrawing the manuscript," Lam said.

"You must be joking, I'm meeting one of their editors next week."

"No, you're not, Vijay. No, you're not. Why can't you understand the words coming out of my mouth? You weren't hired to fix up meetings with editors. You can't just come in and ruin my project."

Lam's rising voice had surely brought Somchai into the corridor by now.

"It's hardly ruined. Improved beyond all recognition, surely?"

"This isn't an act, is it? You are actually some kind of moron." He reached into what Vijay realised was a shoulder holster under the waistcoat. "If this doesn't help you understand what I'm saying, then I'm going to use it."

It was a slim, snub-nosed little thing that fitted into his palm. Surely not the .38 that shot Montri, and not likely to be accurate over a long distance. But it would be accurate across the width of the desk.

"Woah, Lam! There's no need to point a gun at me," Vijay cried, hoping Somchai could hear him.

"So now you're listening. This is what it takes. You people think you're so clever, but when I have a gun, everything changes."

"*People*. The other person being Somsak the publisher, I suppose? He told you he had the copyright for all translations and wouldn't give it up."

"I didn't go there to negotiate."

"Just to take him back to his study and make him pose like his website photo. Did you ask him to smile as well?"

Lam giggled. "He couldn't, not properly. Just sat there blubbering about how he hadn't wanted his life. And you know what? I might have killed him anyway, even if he'd given me the copyright that first time. He thought he could cheat me. He thought I was just some kid. Like you. That's what you thought, isn't it? But you're not so brave now."

And that, Vijay thought, just had to be the perfect cue for Somchai's entrance.

He waited.

Nothing happened.

Lam raised the gun and sighted down the barrel.

"That's not a .38, is it?" Vijay said. "You used a different gun to kill Somsak and a different gun to shoot Montri."

"So?"

"Well . . . you must have a lot of guns," he finished lamely. Still no Somchai. "My guess is that shooting Montri set you off on a certain path. It's no fun just owning guns, is it, Lam? Keeping them oiled just to fire at cardboard targets.

Did you get a thrill seeing what a handgun could do to actual human flesh? What was it, by the way?"

Lam lowered the automatic. "It was a Glock. Thinned for concealed carry." He brought the automatic back up. "This one's a Beretta."

Vijay said, in the loudest voice he could credibly use, "Lam, killing me's not going to solve anything."

Lam lowered the gun a second time while looking genuinely puzzled. "How does that make any sense? Of course it solves everything. You can't talk to Silkworm, can you? Honestly, Vijay, you're really not the sharpest tool in the box." He brought the gun back up.

"You'll get caught eventually." The nerves were evident in his voice now.

And then from the doorway, Somchai spoke. "Put the gun down, *luk*. You don't need to do that." He was holding a handgun of his own and pointing it at Lam. His had a silencer fitted to the barrel.

"Jesus Christ, at last." Vijay slumped back in his chair.

"Leung Ton, what are you doing here?"

"I'm looking after you."

"I don't understand."

"Translations — Detective, remember?" Vijay said. "Your father hired me." He added to Somchai, "You did hear all that?"

Somchai ignored him. "Just hand over the gun, *luk*."

Lam kept the Beretta aimed at Vijay. "You don't know what he's like. He's an idiot."

"I know he is, I was listening. You've shown great control not shooting him."

Lam nodded. "I have, haven't I?"

Somchai reached across with his left hand and took the automatic from Lam's semi-resistant fingers. All the while, he was talking. "Your father doesn't want his son to do these kinds of things. He worked so hard growing up — we both did — so that our children would have a different kind of life. He doesn't want you to shoot people, Lam."

He turned so that the single black eye of his silencer was pointing at Vijay. "That's what I'm here for."

* * *

"Oh, come on. Come on." Looking back later, Vijay found he couldn't even remember what had come out of his mouth after the words "come on". It was probably, he thought, a certain amount of basic level gibbering. He had a feeling that at one point, he'd pleaded with Somchai to not throw the shark out with the bathwater. Either that or implored him not to jump the baby. Vijay did remember though, that he'd felt his balls shrinking up into his body. It was an actual physical sensation.

Somchai didn't react to anything he said, and under his dead stare, Leung and the empty house in Chinatown seemed like a nostalgic, less threatening time in his life.

"I could have gone to the police, you know," Vijay said. "I could have had my cop friend standing there."

"But you didn't, did you? You Clever Boys always miss the obvious."

Lam was looking from Somchai to Vijay with an expression of growing delight. "Shoot him! Shoot him, Leung Ton."

"He's not a dog, Lam," Vijay said. "You can't just set him on me." To Somchai he added, "I'm working for your boss, remember? And I've delivered. I've found out what he wanted to know."

"That doesn't stop me from looking after Pleum's interests."

"You're going to shoot one of his employees? Do you think he'd like that?"

"When Pleum hired you, he didn't know his son was involved. Now it's different."

Lam giggled. "Shoot him in the leg first, then shoot him in the head."

"We don't do it like that, Lam. This is a job, not a game."

Inspired by terror, Vijay said, "Everything's a game to Lam though, isn't it? The rest of the world doesn't have an outside reality. He's been brought up to see us all as replaceable servants."

"Stop that. Don't insult the boy."

Vijay noticed that Somchai didn't look at Lam when he said it. In fact, since he'd entered the room, he'd tried to look at him as little as possible. Vijay imagined Somchai's village eyes taking in Lam's "creative person" persona: the skinny jeans, the waistcoat, the Borsalino. "Why not? Why shouldn't he hear a few home truths? He was happy enough insulting Khun Pleum. Your wife read what he wrote, she must have told you. He wanted it written that way. He demanded the changes from Montri."

Lam shrugged. "So what if I did?"

"It's a pity you can't read English, Khun Somchai," Vijay said. "You should see my version. I made Khun Pleum sound like a hero and Lam wants to kill me for it."

Somchai turned his head slightly. Lam was standing with his hands curled into tight, angry fists. Somchai brought his gaze back to Vijay.

"A sixteen-year-old boy walks into the lion's den unarmed, about to be taught a lesson in pain, and comes out with a job offer. Who has ever pulled that off?" Vijay continued.

"I'm so *bored* of that story," Lam said. "Do you know how many times I've had to listen to it? And I bet you it wasn't even that dangerous."

Somchai kept his eyes on Vijay. "It was, Lam. Sia Heng was a very dangerous man. He'd killed people for lesser crimes than your father's."

"What's it got to do with me? I didn't ask him to do any of that."

And now Somchai could finally bring himself to look Lam in the face. "If your father hadn't done those things, taken those risks, you wouldn't have the life you have today."

"You think the life I have is so great? They don't let me do anything. Just want me to be some robot-like Gai."

Somchai spoke almost through gritted teeth. "Your father grew up in a one-room wooden shack the size of your ensuite bathroom. His own bathroom was a clay barrel of rainwater and a scoop. Our roofs were sheets of corrugated metal. They trapped the heat and you had to keep the windows open. Every night, the mosquitoes came in."

"So we have to suffer just because he did?"

Vijay could hear Somchai's voice crack. "Suffer?"

"There's Gai, he didn't even want to marry that Achira woman. It's just Dad, he wants to connect us to this old-money family." Lam laughed. "We get the respectability and if someone gives them problems, Dad has them whacked."

Somchai said with deadly quiet, "Lam. Don't speak. About your father. Like that."

"Whose bidding are you going to do?" Vijay asked, "Khun Pleum's or his?"

"Pleum has always wanted me to protect his children." Somchai winced. "If he was here, he would want Lam protected."

"Yeah, he would," said Lam. "You don't know what Dad's like." He took a big slab of a phone out of his waistcoat pocket and swiped the screen on. "See this? I could phone him right now and tell him what's happening and I'd bet he'd decide to have you whacked." He laughed and said to Somchai, "Look at his face. Look how shocked he is. What's the matter? You don't think I'll phone him?"

"We're not phoning anyone, Lam."

Once Vijay could trust his voice to work normally, he said, "Aim told me you had a girlfriend at Silpakorn. That wouldn't be her by any chance, would it?"

"Why? You don't think I could have a girlfriend who looks like this?"

"Oh, I can believe it all right," Vijay said, looking at Ploy's picture. "It's getting more believable by the minute." She was in a cream off-the-shoulder blouse, looking up at the camera with her chin lowered. Ploy at her sexiest.

Vijay turned to Somchai. "For one thing, I don't have any proof he killed Somsak. For another, I know the way this country works and I know he'll never do jail time unless he kills someone with more influence than Khun Pleum. Plus—" Vijay put his palm up before Somchai could get a word in — "I get that you don't want Khun Pleum to know his son wrote the book. You don't have to kill me for that. I'm willing to go and tell him I couldn't come up with anything. He won't be happy, but I don't suppose he whacks people as readily as Lam seems to think. I'll need your help though. I need you to talk me up. Tell him I consulted with you about the case. Tell him I impressed the hell out of you. I was clever, hardworking, the whole deal." Before he could interrupt, Vijay said, "This is in your interests, Somchai. If he thinks I was a lousy private detective, then he's just going to hire a better one. You're not protecting Khun Pleum from *me*, you're protecting him from knowledge. And you have a better chance of doing that by keeping me alive."

Somchai lowered the gun so that it pointed at the table. Lam looked from Vijay to him. "What about protecting me? That's what you're supposed to be doing, Leung Ton."

"You're not in any danger from him, Lam."

"There's my book. He messed my book up, and now he's going to meet Silkworm."

"There's no meeting," Vijay said. "I said that just to get a rise out of you. If you don't believe me, you can phone them and ask. I haven't even translated the whole thing, just those two chapters." He added, "I'll pay you back the money you sent me."

Somchai put a hand on Lam's shoulder. "We're leaving now." As Lam's mouth opened, Somchai dug his fingers in and slowly but firmly turned him around. He walked him to the door, said something Vijay didn't catch and ushered him out. He then came back to stand in front of Vijay's desk.

"I'm going to have a talk with the boy. I didn't want to do it here. I didn't want him to lose face in front of you. But when I've finished, there is going to be no chance of his tell-ing Pleum who wrote the book. Do you understand what I'm saying, Vijay? If Pleum finds out, then I'll know it came from you. And I'll come back." He looked around the office. "In spite of appearances, you're not actually stupid, are you? That day on the tower, for example. You forced yourself to laugh and then tried to convince me you believed it was a man-nequin." He gestured with his gun hand. It was somewhere between a threat and the illustration of a point. "That took quick thinking and control. You're smart enough. Smart enough to know what happens if I return."

After he'd gone, Vijay sat back in his chair. *Believed* it was a mannequin? But that could have been just another layer of bluff. Couldn't it?

He then swiped the YouTube page off his phone to reveal the voice-recorder app underneath. He pressed stop, saved the file, emailed it to himself and then deleted it from the device's memory. Not that he was optimistic enough to think he'd have any chance in court against one of Khun Pleum's progeny. At least not while their father was alive and well. But Vijay didn't like the idea of Somsak's murder being written off the books. Even if he couldn't think what he was going to do about it.

CHAPTER 15

General Padet sipped his lemon soda under the table's broad awning. "I still hit fifty balls twice a week."

They were at the outdoor café beside his driving range. The nets were behind him in the sunlight, and Vijay could hear the *thwack* of golf balls being struck in the muggy late afternoon. He'd come to talk about Colonel Sanserm.

The morning had been uneventful. Vijay had fixed up his meeting with Padet and then chatted on the phone with Tong, who'd called to say he'd tracked Ploy back to a highly prestigious condo on Sathon Road. That turned out to mean the condo was called "The Highly Prestigious", upscale condo names in Bangkok being the Land That Irony Forgot.

Vijay had told Tong to keep watch and let him know if she went anywhere. By noon she still hadn't. He had thought about paying her a visit, but didn't know what he'd be able to get out of her. Plus, who could she be waiting for other than Khun Pleum? So he had stayed in Chinatown, had lunch alone and missed having Doi to talk to. She had phoned when he got back to the office and asked about coming back in. ("And why do I think you're up to something, Vijay?") He had told Doi she deserved a holiday, just in case Lam returned.

In the afternoon, he had driven east, to General Padet's suburban golf spot. The man looked in good shape for what Vijay assumed was his early sixties. A full head of dark hair (dyed?) and a white polo shirt not quite loose enough to hide his paunch. He was now retired, he said. He lived for his golf and his grandchildren. "But not in that order!" he added, with the fluency of a well-used line. General Padet liked discussing his satisfactions.

Vijay watched him sip his soda. "You're like a negative image of Sanserm. Not that I ever met him."

"Am I?" The man swirled the ice in his drink. "We weren't so different when we were cadets. Though I suppose our lives went in very different directions after that." He sighed. "He wasn't a bad man, you know."

"From what his wife said, he seemed to have become bitter about not making general. She said it was because he didn't know the right people."

"That's not the *only* reason for becoming a general." Padet chuckled. "Though we do have more generals than most countries, I have to admit."

"So why do you think it didn't happen for Sanserm?"

"I would say . . . he was someone looking for shortcuts in the wrong places. In his life, in his work. I remember once, as a cadet, he spray-painted an entrenching tool because he couldn't be bothered to clean the mud off. He thought, give it a new coat and no one will know the difference." Padet chuckled again. "You could see all these bumps under the green paint, even at a distance. Our drill sergeant almost killed him, and I mean that literally. The man gave him a forty-pound pack, took him out in the midday sun and ran him into the ground."

"But that didn't change him?"

"There aren't shortcuts to managing people, to passing staff exams. At least, not if you don't come from the right family. And neither of us did." He added, "The only thing that changed, I would say, is where he looked. For instance, he inherited a big chunk of money and his first thought was to find a shortcut to increasing it."

"I thought he started a business?"

Padet shook his head. "We were stationed in Ayutthaya at the time. He hooked up with some official who told him tall tales about getting local government contracts. The whole thing was a con. This man had no influence at all. The fact was, Sanserm was someone who could be played very easily."

"When you knew him, did he gamble much?"

"Not a great deal. We played cards a bit in the barracks to pass the time, but only for drinking money."

"He seems to have developed a gambling problem later in his life."

"I wouldn't know," said Padet. "We fell out of touch. Not because I didn't want it, you understand. It was him. I used to phone sometimes, just to chat or suggest a meal, and you could sense a . . . a resistance. He would always have other plans." He leaned forwards. "Do you expect to see his wife again?"

"I might do."

"If so, could you make this clear? When I spoke to her at the cremation, I felt . . . I felt she thought I'd dropped Sanserm. I gave her my card, asked her to phone if she needed anything, and she said, 'I don't want to disturb you. You must be so busy now that you're a general.' Why would she have said that? She must know I'm retired."

"She still has the card, General Padet. That's how I got your phone number."

"Ah, that's good."

"What do you think it was that bothered Sanserm so much? About you."

"I never looked down on him, if that's what you mean. But he became bitter, I would say, over the years. They moved us about a lot, in the early days, when we were lieutenants. Lopburi, then Korat, then Samut Sakhon, then Ayutthaya, then down south at Patani — which was getting to be a hot zone, what with the Muslim insurgents taking pot shots at us. Then back to Lopburi. He was always talking about the army's centre of influence being Bangkok. Which it is, by the way. He always said if he'd got Bangkok earlier, he would have risen quicker.

"But you still managed it."

"Quite." Padet stirred his ice cubes with his straw. He was so relaxed, Vijay couldn't see him cheating his way to the top. He was either what he appeared to be, a retired family man with nothing to hide, or a spectacularly clever sociopath.

"Was he a big drinker when you were friends?"

"We both were in the early days. Mekhong whiskey with ice and soda. It was that sort of environment. Part of being a man was drinking with your comrades."

"But you slowed down later?"

"It's not the drink when you get older, it's the recovery the next day. You come to realise you can't survive a young man's pace." He drained his glass. "They didn't have children, did they?"

Vijay shook his head. "Not as far as I could tell."

"I suppose that was the thing with Sanserm. He wanted to carry on living like someone younger. Someone with his best days and his promotions still ahead of him."

EPILOGUE

Now

Vijay made it back to Chinatown in the day's last light. Needing to think, he let himself back into the office and poured out the last of the iced tea. He pushed his chair back, stuck his feet on the desk, and then, instead of pondering the case, thought about how empty the office felt without Doi around. The place was a preview of the safe, lonely road he could have taken by letting her go instead of borrowing money from Kritisak. And it made Vijay think he'd done the right thing. Whatever else you could say about his time in Thailand, his working life wasn't just him anymore. He had employed someone. He had amounted to something.

He went back to thinking about the brief, unhappy life of Colonel Sanserm, the hungering easy mark, and that was when his phone went. Supaporn. He answered with his excuses prepared, but didn't have the chance to get a word in.

"Useless, do you know that? Do you realise . . . how utterly *useless* you have been to me?" There was a catch in her voice, and Vijay realised she was on the verge of tears. "You completely foul, worthless—" With the sob that followed, she cut the line. He tried calling her back but she'd switched her phone off.

Vijay placed his mobile down in the centre of the desk and wondered what this presaged. Deciding to wait things out in the office, he took the headphones out of his drawer and connected to YouTube, but found *Alan Partridge* clips weren't doing it. He tried phoning Supaporn again but the phone was still off. He used his phone to play chess, but couldn't concentrate and lost quickly at a low level. Outside the windows, night fell and the air's prickling humidity seemed to increase. Or was that just his imagination?

The phone rang with an unknown number. It was just over an hour after Supaporn's call.

"You'd like to come and see me, wouldn't you?" came Khun Pleum's voice. "You'd like to come and see me right now."

"Um . . . Sure, I could . . . I mean, I'm always available for my clients. Where are you, Khun Pleum?"

"I'm at our family home. It's off Rama III." He gave Vijay the *soi* number and said he'd know the place when he saw it. "You're not going to take long, are you? You're going to leave immediately."

"Sure . . . I'm not engaged in — in things . . . right now."

"Because I've had a long day. I've had a long talk with my sons about changes I'm going to make to my life. And to theirs. And I don't want to waste time waiting for you to turn up."

"I understand, Khun Pleum."

"You'll come here under your own steam, won't you? I'm not going to have to send someone to come and get you. You're not going to be that sort of person."

"Of course not, Khun Pleum."

Vijay ended the call, and then had his brief fantasy of driving south until he hit the Malaysian border. But it was a ridiculous idea. He wasn't going to leave Doi to Khun Pleum's tender mercies. Looking around the room, Vijay wondered what he should take. There was nothing he could think of, other than the phone in his hand and his car keys. No lucky rabbit's foot, no revolver. He considered phoning Mana to let him know where he was going. But what could Mana do about it? Khun Pleum owned policemen far above Mana's pay grade.

In the pickup, edging his way out of Chinatown, Vijay's thoughts skittered. He pictured himself facing a long sofa with Khun Pleum at one end and Supaporn at the other.

"I understand you convinced my wife to have me investigated?"

The best counter argument was surely that Vijay wasn't that crazy. He could describe how Supaporn had her suspicions, bring up Khun Pleum's lack of attention to her. Perhaps the whole evening would devolve into an insane couple's therapy session.

Though that still left the reference to his sons. Surely Khun Pleum hadn't found out Lam wrote the book? Or he suspected one of them had written it — hence the use of "sons" plural? In which case, Vijay would just have to stonewall, and hope the man believed him.

It was going on half past eight by the time Vijay made it out to Rama III. The GPS on his phone guided him down a dark *soi*, the thick, clotted shadows of a banana plantation on one side of the road, and on the other, comfortably large houses set back behind spacious front gardens. For a brief moment he considered delaying things by going to the wrong place. And then Vijay saw what Khun Pleum had meant by not being able to miss it.

The road curved around to reveal high white walls, interrupted at one point by wrought iron gates. Through these lay well-lit grounds, the thin sliver of the moon resting on a flat expanse of dark water, high trees with lights set below them. He pulled up to the grass verge in front of the gates and rang the bell. A man in a white collarless shirt eventually arrived, saw him and spoke into a walkie-talkie. Vijay began explaining who he was and before he'd finished, the man had already pressed a button to slide the gates back.

Vijay stepped into the grounds. "If you did this by hand, it would be great exercise, wouldn't it?" This got him a non-plussed look. "There's shoulder muscles, thigh muscles, you could call it the iron-gate workout—" He realised he was babbling and stopped.

The man gestured for Vijay to follow him. Up ahead, ridiculously far ahead, was Khun Pleum's neoclassical mansion, blazing light from its very many windows.

Your father grew up in a one-room wooden shack the size of your ensuite bathroom. It was a heart-warming rags-to-riches tale, if you ignored where the riches had come from.

The servant took him along a winding gravel path towards the house. They passed huge trees, lit in a way that made them pale and ghostlike. Vijay couldn't see anything artistic in Supaporn's arrangement of the flora, but then he wasn't really in the mood to appreciate such things.

They went up wide stone steps to a huge patio, unlit and empty, and through to the house. From the humid night, the shock of the air conditioning was immediate. Everything was brightly lit, but had a film-set quality. The large rooms of Louis XIV furniture, the overstuffed silk sofas, the high-backed gilt-edged chairs around polished tables, the dripping gold leaf and the gleaming marble floor. Following the servant was like taking a tour around a French stately home. Everything looked so unused, Vijay expected the rooms to be roped off. But then, he thought, who actually lived here? Surely not Lam anymore. And what about his brothers? Vijay wondered if it was just Khun Pleum and his wife now, out-numbered by their noiseless staff.

They went down a long corridor illuminated by spotlit alcoves. In each one was a different treasure, a gold Buddha of the slim Lopburi style, a Chinese vase, a long curved dagger in a jewel-encrusted scabbard. The spoils of a pirate who'd come home from the sea. At the corridor's end the servant knocked on a door and waited for the reply in an "at attention" pose, thumbs by the seams of his trousers. When he had it, he opened the door for Vijay to enter.

Inside was a dark, leathery study carrying the aroma of Khun Pleum's cigars, and Khun Pleum at the far end, seated behind a wide mahogany desk. He had a cigar on the go, resting in the cylindrical indent in the lip of a copper ashtray. Apart from that, a blotter with leather edges and an iPad, the desk was bare. The only light in the room was from a standard lamp set to one side. It was strong enough to show Vijay the single chair facing the desk.

"Vijay," said Khun Pleum and nothing else.

Putting on his most innocent, eager-to-please expression, Vijay strode to the chair and sat down. He leaned forwards with his elbows on his knees. "So, what would you like to see me about?"

Khun Pleum met that with a stony stare. "What do you think? What do you think would have made me call you out here at this time of night?"

It was a good question, Vijay thought. And since Supaporn wasn't present, he wasn't sure how to answer it. Unless she was turning up later? "I suppose you'd like an update on how the case is going?"

"An 'update'?" Khun Pleum took the cigar off the copper ashtray and sat back with it. "I seem to remember one of my assistants asked you what was happening and the answer was nothing at all." He fumed out smoke and said, "So yes, Vijay, why don't you give me an update?"

"Well . . . Have you spoken to Somchai, by any chance?"

Khun Pleum frowned. "*Pii* Ton? What does he have to do with this?"

Brilliant. Just bleeding brilliant. "As it happens, I have been working very closely with Somchai on your case. You see, I had the feeling this was something that came out of your past, and so I've investigated that past with his help." He took his phone out. "In fact, why don't we call him right now and he can tell you just what I've been doing."

"I don't want to disturb Ton at this time of night." Khun Pleum pulled on the cigar again. "Why don't you tell me yourself what you've come up with?"

Vijay gave him a lightly edited version of his efforts with Montri, leaving out the dog not barking and Somsak being a crook. He didn't want Montri dragged in for questioning.

"So, from your 'getting close' to this writer, what have you discovered? Where did he get his details?"

"From the internet, pretty much. Websites, mirror sites, forums — this guy, he's a demon for research. He's the kind of person Google was built for. It fills a hole in his life, I would say."

"What about the descriptions of my house?"

"Google Earth combined with Google Street View. He showed me the screenshots."

"And the detail of my wife installing gold-plated taps in her ensuite bathroom? How did that come about? Did he show you a screenshot of the plumber?"

"I would say that was . . . a lucky guess."

Khun Pleum tapped off his cigar ash. "Are you under the impression that insulting my intelligence is a good idea?"

"Obviously not, Khun Pleum. The fact is, I haven't yet ascertained the precise origin of that exact detail. The thing you've got to remember is that private detective work is not like building a wall. Or rather, it is, but the bricks are hidden around the country, and then when you find them, they try to convince you they're not bricks at all, but rocks of a suspiciously uniform nature." Vijay stopped to have a look at how this was being taken. It was impossible to tell. Khun Pleum was holding the cigar up at ear height and watching him with close, unsmiling concentration. Vijay took out his phone again. "I know Khun Somchai is someone you trust and I think if you could just have a talk with him about what I've been doing, he would confirm that I've actually been doing a lot."

"Oh, I know you've been doing a lot, Vijay. I don't need Ton to tell me that. My impression is that you are both very hardworking and extremely devious." He put the cigar back in the ashtray lip and clasped his hands together, fingers intertwined. A "chairman of the board" pose. "If I were my younger self, you might not still be alive. However—" he lifted the iPad off the desk — "there have been some changes in my life, which we don't need to go into. And I'm not the man I was." He began swiping. Angled away from him, Vijay couldn't see the screen.

"Some parts of my work have needed more attention than others," Khun Pleum went on. "We had contracts lined up with the last government and since the coup, things need to be renegotiated. A different set of people need to be shown the fruits of my appreciation." He looked up from the iPad. "You understand?"

"Absolutely, Khun Pleum. You have to line up your deliverables and look at how to deliver your achievables."

"So other things get pushed back. When a greeter at one of my casinos tells me about a rather suspicious customer, I don't immediately pay any attention. This man gains entry by using the name of one of our most frequent gamblers. But he doesn't behave like a gambler himself. He needs the roulette betting explained to him. And then in his cheap suit, he loses 13,000 baht without seeming bothered. Instead, he seems more interested in talking to my staff. And when my greeter phones the man whose name he used, it turns out they've never even met. This man was just doing a favour for a friend who, it turns out, is a loan shark in Chinatown."

Khun Pleum turned the iPad round to display an image from a security camera of good enough definition to be a really bad magazine advert: *You're Never Out of Luck with Primark*. "That is you, isn't it?"

After a pause, Vijay said, "Your casino? I thought it belonged to the Phuttaraksas?"

Khun Pleum made a shooing gesture with his right hand. "Don't pretend to be dense, Vijay."

"No, really. I thought it was. Everyone round there thinks it's theirs. Come on, you must know that's the impression. You sited the thing in their compound." *And how many other compounds over the years?* Vijay wondered. He thought of Khun Pleum's surprising entry into the city's business elite.

How many gamblers in that community had seen their credit extended, not knowing they were slowly falling in debt to an upstart *jao por* from Samut Sakhon?

"You're going to tell me you've been investigating the Phuttaraksas on the side? Investigating them for what?"

"No, not exactly, though it's true I did take another case." Vijay suddenly found his mouth was very dry. "Would it be possible for me to get a glass of water?"

"No."

His thoughts spun on. Fragments of an awful, dark jigsaw pieced themselves together. "I was hired by Ploy. Your *mia noi*, I mean. To find someone."

Khun Pleum's mouth tightened. "I would be very careful about the next thing you invent."

"I'm not making anything up. But let me ask you a question. When you hired me, you did mention it to her, right? Maybe showed her my card?" There was no assent in the man's face, just a look of anger, barely held in check. "I'm going to take that as a yes. So that's how she found me."

"And how did you find out about the two of us?" He dropped his hands below the table. "I would advise you not to claim she told you herself."

"Right. She didn't. But in an attempt to productise information on this case, to get a competitive advantage, we were following you. And when I say 'we', I mean myself . . . and my phone. I followed you with my phone." Vijay waved it at him. "Great battery this thing's got."

"So it turns out I've been paying you all this money to discover my own movements." Vijay had the impression of Khun Pleum's hands shifting under the desk.

"That's not the only thing I was doing. There's the writer, don't forget." Vijay tried to swallow but his mouth was still too dry. "Ploy hired me for a missing person case. At least, that's what she said, but now I realise it was something else. She asked me once if I thought people could change. I thought she was talking about someone else, but she meant you. At the end of a very long project, she found herself

234

hoping she was wrong. And around then, you must have mentioned hiring me."

"The project is?"

"To kill you, Khun Pleum."

His hands shifted again. "You really are a case study, Vijay. The limited but devious mind. Backed into a corner, you attempt an even bigger lie."

"Okay, let me ask you another question. Why does your son Lam have a picture of Ploy as the screensaver on his phone? Don't take my word for it, call him here on some pretext and get the phone off him."

"Buying you enough time to come up with your next invention?"

"She was his girlfriend. She used him to reach you. I'm guessing you met Ploy shortly after saying goodbye to Lam. Dinner, a coffee, something like that."

For the first time, Vijay thought he saw doubt crossing Khun Pleum's face. "How much farther does your ridiculous story go? Why would she want to kill me?"

"Her father went missing after working for you. In that same casino in Bangmod. You know who I'm talking about. Bundit. I don't know how she figured out it was your casino. The regular gamblers don't even know. Though they have their suspicions. At least, the loan shark's friend does. Anyway, that's why." He paused, but Khun Pleum didn't say anything. "I'm glad you're taking time to consider what I've told you," Vijay said.

"I'm not considering anything. I've been pressing this button under my desk and no one's come." He sighed and pushed his chair back. "You can't get the staff." As he went past Vijay, he said, "Don't bother going anywhere. I'm not someone you can run from." And then when he opened the door, he said, more to himself than Vijay, "And why are the lights off? *Lek!*"

Coming up behind him, Vijay could see the spotlights had gone. Lacking windows, the corridor was now pitch black. "She's here," he said, and had the sense of Khun Pleum's body turning towards him.

"Your lies aren't getting you anywhere," Khun Pleum said.

He started down the corridor, his heels clicking on the marble, and Vijay followed. In spite of everything, he couldn't stop himself from wanting to protect the man. Or perhaps it wasn't Khun Pleum as he was now who Vijay was protecting — it was that twelve-year-old boy squatting on the pavement in Samut Sakhon, pressing down patches on bicycle tires and promising his mother he'd see them to a better life. Vijay don't know if Khun Pleum deserved a more decent ending, but that boy did. He called out, "She knew about the casino but she didn't tell me."

Up ahead, Khun Pleum seemed to stop moving.

"That was the test. She wanted to find out if I'd take her money and then not do anything for it. But the thing is, we had different parts of the same puzzle."

Khun Pleum's steps went on. "Look, the rest of the house is dark as well. And where are the servants?"

Vijay caught up with him. "Let's get some lights on."

Khun Pleum snorted. "What's the matter? Are you scared of the dark?"

He continued around the black shapes of his stately home furniture. Vijay ran a palm over the wall, came to the light switch and clicked it. Nothing happened. "Look, someone's been selectively tripping the circuit breakers."

"This is ridiculous," Khun Pleum said. "*Lek*!"

Through gaps in the curtains, Vijay could see the garden, which was now better lit than the house. He half-expected men in black to come swarming up the patio steps, but everything was empty and silent. In its unlit state, the house felt abandoned, its treasures left unguarded as the occupants fled an approaching army. Khun Pleum went on, bumping into a sofa and then moving around it.

"At some point, Bundit must have boasted that he was working in a casino owned by you. That's what I think. I don't see how she could have found out otherwise. He was a conman, did I mention that?"

Vijay's eyes were now becoming accustomed to the dark. He could make out Khun Pleum moving through the archway to the next room. He still owed something to the man's pitiless childhood. "Because she didn't tell me," he called out, "we had different parts of the same jigsaw. The part I had was Colonel Sanserm."

That made him stop.

"Somchai told me about how you went after the man who killed Sia Heng. How you shot him without really interrogating him first. You never tried to get the name of the soldier who set up the Claymore." Now Vijay had his attention. A deeper stillness descended in the room's quiet.

"Somchai said there wasn't any point taking on the Thai army, but that doesn't make sense. This wasn't an executive order from the commander-in-chief, it was just one sapper moonlighting. Sanserm." He waited, but nothing came from Khun Pleum. Silence in his vast house. "And meanwhile, this man Neung, who had supposedly ordered the hit, was drinking in an out-of-the-way bar, ideal for being hit in turn. But then Sia Heng was right about him all along. He *was* content with his little money laundering thing from Chonburi and running his cockfights and feeling like a big shot. The person with unbounded ambitions was you."

Vijay waited. Still nothing. He said into the silence, "No doubt over the years it occurred to Sanserm he didn't even get paid all that much, at least not in comparison to your stunning rise. Just enough for a Merc and a business plan that failed. Oh, and he got to gamble in your casinos. And then Bundit arrived and Sanserm's unhappiness made his antennae twitch, and he started extending Sanserm's credit. And when it got back to you, I'm guessing that fact alone was enough to get rid of him. But Bundit's daughter is here now, in this house, and she's going to make you pay."

"Ploy loves me," Khun Pleum said, and walked on through a long, marble-floored drawing room. Vijay could now make out the rectangles of pictures on the wall, but couldn't see clearly what they were.

"She invented a client when she came to see me," Vijay called. "And then said if she can't have Bundit back in her life, then there's going to be a price to pay."

At the far end, Khun Pleum went through a doorway and Vijay was close enough behind to hear a single muffled word. "You."

The muzzle flash and the noise came at the same time. The noise was deafening. It was so loud, Vijay didn't even hear the body drop. He went into the room and saw the man stretched out on the floor. "Ploy," he said to the figure hunched over on the sofa, now rocking backwards and forwards, but it was just a word that fell out of his mouth at that moment. It obviously wasn't her. The figure reached over to click on a lamp on a small table. Vijay hadn't thought to check if the lights in this section worked.

In the soft yellow glow, Supaporn was terrifying. Her eyeliner had run in dark streaks down her cheeks, but her crying was long over. She now looked dry-eyed and slightly mad. "Vijay," she said harshly. She was still holding the gun with both hands, the barrel pointing at the floor. She now looked down at it, as though surprised to find it there. "He told me after he told the boys. He thought he could leave and just cancel our whole past. Everything we'd done, everything we'd meant to each other."

"Why don't I take that for you?" Vijay said.

She looked up with her slightly mad eyes. "I found *him*, not the other way round."

"I understand." He reached his hand out. She was looking at him rather than at the gun and he managed to get his hand on the still warm barrel. She looked down again and seemed confused by the revolver's presence, puzzled at the death that had come out of it. He gave a gentle tug of the barrel and she said, enunciating the words clearly, "No, this one's mine."

Vijay said, "I'll look after it now."

She stared at Khun Pleum's body, draped in the sofa's shadow. "It's not love if you're willing to let go."

He gave another gentle tug on the gun. "Here we are. Here we are."

There was a slight resistance, then she let go. As she did, she looked up. "I never stopped loving him and I'm proud of that."

And as though in response to her statement, the sound of applause rose from the garden. Rain on thick leaves.

It always happens like that, Vijay thought. Dry days of sunlight go by and you think, that's it now, the rainy season is finished. But then it turns out that, no, it's not over.

It's not over at all.

THE END

Thank you for reading this book.

If you enjoyed it please leave feedback on Amazon or Goodreads, and if there is anything we missed or you have a question about, then please get in touch. We appreciate you choosing our book.

Founded in 2014 in Shoreditch, London, we at Joffe Books pride ourselves on our history of innovative publishing. We were thrilled to be shortlisted for Independent Publisher of the Year at the British Book Awards.

www.joffebooks.com

We're very grateful to eagle-eyed readers who take the time to contact us. Please send any errors you find to corrections@joffebooks.com. We'll get them fixed ASAP.